The Dino Diaries

RHETT DAWN

www.mascotbooks.com

For more information, please contact:

Mascot Books
620 Herndon Parkway, Suite 320
Herndon, VA 20170
info@mascotbooks.com
Library of Congress Control Number: 2020909557
CPSIA Code: PRV0421A
ISBN-13: 978-1-64543-461-0

Printed in the United States

THE DINO DIARIES

This book is dedicated to all those who cherish the lost art
of the written word.

READ THIS FIRST...

I'm still not one hundred percent sure what love is, but I was close enough to know it is most certainly a double-edged sword. Not to be a cynic, but I have witnessed so many relationships fall apart in my fifty-two years on this Earth, that I don't think I regret staying a bachelor. Don't get me wrong. I love women. A world without women in it wouldn't be worth living for me. There are a few women in my past, I am sure, who might beg to differ with that declaration, but the ones I have talked to about it usually end up admitting that although I can't commit, I was always a loving partner. My guy friends think I am just a scoundrel who is "living the life." Sometimes, I feel that way. Other times, I wonder what I have missed. I decided to chronicle my bachelor life to help me understand myself and to let the world know I am not a scoundrel. After reading this, you can judge for yourself.

Humble Beginnings

I was born in 1966 to a mother who gave me up for adoption when I was one. I was told I was two-thirds American mutt and one-third Greek. I was named Dino after my mother's Italian crush Dino Danelli, the drummer from the rock-and-roll group, The Rascals. My father was her high school sweetheart who went to Vietnam and didn't know I existed. He died there. I don't really remember much before elementary school, except the smell. Whenever I walk into a hospital or older government building while they are cleaning, it always triggers memories of being shuttled from one place to another and of the people talking in hushed tones about my fate. I don't know if it is the smell of fake clean, ammonia, or disinfectant, but I wouldn't be upset if I never smelled it again.

By the time I was ten, I had been to a half-dozen homes and would eventually go to another four before I left at eighteen. Almost all of those homes formed both my love and my wariness of women. All but two homes had female siblings who loved me, hated me, resented me, competed with me, sabotaged me, fussed over me, mothered me, teased me, or tortured me—all for their own personal gain. By the time I went out on my own, I was sure women were like cats and men were like dogs. When I read the popular politics that states we are all the same, I laugh. I have lived the experiment that proves those assertions false.

I had settled in the Alexandria, Virginia area by the time I was a teenager and stayed close even after I graduated high school and went out on my own. I still live nearby, just across the Potomac River in Maryland.

Despite the revolving door, I had a pretty normal childhood. I think we all just adapt to our circumstance, and unless someone names you a victim, you don't know it; you just seek happiness within your own existence. I was never really mistreated or abused, and on the flip side there was a lot less pity than most people imagine. Thanks, however, to the numerous siblings, I did manage to learn an awful lot about the female mind. It has at times turned out to be a double-edged sword.

I now live in a small house in a great nice neighborhood in a place called Glen Echo that I was fortunate enough to acquire before property values went crazy.

My first sexual "experience" occurred when I had a paper route delivering the *Alexandria Gazette*. It didn't involve any physical contact, or even any eye contact, but it triggered something in my mind and body that let me know sex and women were my manifest destiny.

I was fourteen, and although I had discovered my body and got aroused when the wind blew, I hadn't really put it all together.

It was summertime, around seven a.m. on a Sunday. I was delivering papers house-to-house, dropping them on front porches or putting them in the racks on the houses in middle-class Alexandria, right off of Pickett Street, where I lived. When I came to the house of a fortyish woman whose name I can't remember, she met me at the door and asked me if I would help her for a minute in the backyard. She said the iron staircase was falling away from the house, and she needed to get a brick or two under it until she could find someone to fix it. I went around the house, where she met me, gingerly walking down the steps as if she thought they might fall. She asked me to lift and push the heavy staircase back towards the house so she could place bricks underneath to make it stay up.

She wore a cotton bathrobe and, as I soon discovered, no shirt or bra underneath.

Every time I pushed the staircase up, she would bend over with the brick, her bathrobe would fall open, and I would see one very full breast, and half of the other. It was mesmerizing. I leaned back to get a better view and the resulting movement made the staircase fall away from the house so she couldn't get the bricks into place. We repeated this scenario three or four times until her bathrobe had opened fully in the frustration, so that I could look and push at the same time. After the bricks were in place she just stood up and closed the bathrobe, never realizing that I had seen anything. I spent the next month dreaming about her breasts, pleasuring myself late into the night. I also started looking at all women obsessively, looking for an errant button, a tight blouse, or the gods' willing, a pair of panties from a woman who wasn't quite careful enough with her valuables when she was getting in or out of a car or sitting on a park bench. I didn't feel guilty, and I still don't. I wasn't obvious. I was discreet, probably to a fault. When I was in foster homes, the girls were very private because I was not really family, and they, I am sure, were instructed to close their doors and retain their privacy when it came to me. I knew no other way, and just assumed that people were private with their bodies, family or not.

I guess because I had dealt with so many step siblings over the years, I wasn't really interested in girls from a relationship standpoint. I would lust after them, and had a rotating stable of girls I liked to fantasize about to a point of orgasm. I even liked the flirting and attention I would get sometimes, but I never really felt like I needed a girlfriend. I was a bit of a jock and hung out with my guy friends, talking all day every day about girls, and how we would fuck them if we got the chance. It was ninety percent talk, as I am sure it was in every high school. I "made out" with a few girls and even felt a few breasts in a heated moment in a back room at a party, but it was all superficial. I felt no impending doom if I didn't get laid; I just assumed the opportunity would present itself at some point. Since I didn't lose my virginity until I was almost nineteen, perhaps I should have worked a little harder to make the opportunity present itself sooner. That, however, doesn't mean I didn't have sex.

Trisha

When I was fifteen-years-and-eight-months old (I know this because I got my learners permit the same month) I was living in a foster home with a fifty-two-year-old woman named Ellen who worked as an operating room nurse at Georgetown University hospital in Washington DC. She had two sons, both at Quantico marine base about fifty miles south of Alexandria. They were cool guys, and would occasionally come home for the weekend and take me sailing on the Potomac. We got along well, and I was just rolling along with what I considered to be a normal life of playing some sports, listening to Journey and Led Zeppelin, and drinking a few beers when we could score them. I of course was still obsessed with women's bodies and I spent a lot of time hanging out at the local malls just taking in the sights.

Ellen, as she allowed me to call her, was ordered to work a six-day, twelve-hour shift from eight p.m. to eight a.m. as they were doing some special training for overseas doctors. She had a friend, Trisha, who was thirty-four with brown, shoulder-length hair, reasonably attractive, and who also was a nurse who came to stay the six nights, and sleepover, using Ellen's room. I had met her before, but she was not really on my radar. I have often wondered why that was the case but concluded that at the time I either had my routine and was seeing enough cleavage and legs at the mall to keep me sane or was showing some sort of respect for Ellen by keeping my mind out of the gutter when it came to her friends. Once I was alone in the house with Trisha, all bets were off as far as the latter went.

Ellen left for work around seven the first night and said Trisha would be there around eight-thirty or nine. She said to not give her "any grief," to be in bed by eleven, and not to be late for school.

Trisha arrived around nine. I was laying on the couch watching TV when she came in. In a typical teenager fashion, I didn't even get up. I lifted my head and said "Hi." She asked me if I had eaten, and I said yes. She asked if my school work was done, and I said it was. She said she was "exhausted" from working a double and was going to take a bath and go to bed. She went into the kitchen and pulled a bottle of wine out of the refrigerator and poured it into a glass. She was talking about work, and I was half paying attention to her and whatever lame sitcom was on TV. She came out and stood in front of me and asked what time I woke up for school. I said seven, and she then asked if she needed to wake me, or if I was good on my own. I said I was good.

She was wearing a nursing uniform, which consisted of a white blouse, white skirt, and white stockings. She had kicked off her shoes at the front door. She went back into the kitchen, and I heard the ice maker clink some cubes into her glass. She stood in front of the breakfast counter that separated the TV room from the kitchen and spoke about how work was killing her with the nonstop patients. I looked up to say something polite in response. I saw her hiking down her white pantyhose past her knees and stepping out of them from the opening below the counter, where two bar stools sat. She was only exposing her legs from just above the knees down, but it was free, and it was exciting. I realized that, other than in movies, I had never actually seen a woman disrobe beyond pulling off a sweater with a shirt underneath. My senses were on red alert, and I was looking at Trisha in a whole new light.

She came into the TV room and motioned for me to scoot over so she could sit down too. I sat up.

"You can still lay down, there's plenty of room," she said innocently, grabbing the throw pillow I was using, and placing the pillow over her left leg and kind of guiding me back down like a dog on a couch you don't

6

want to kick off.

"Besides, I'm only going to sit for a few minutes. I am going to have some wine, take a long hot bath, and then get some sleep."

I lay down. My face was pointed at the TV, but my eyes were focused on the inside of her right thigh about two inches above the knee. I was within a foot of a live woman's flesh, and it was having its effects on me. Her saying she was going to take a "long hot bath" didn't help. I was wearing gym shorts and a T-shirt, and had an erection that could have cut glass. I was afraid to even move for fear that it would protrude me into some explaining I had no answer for.

She smelled a little musky, I presumed from the long workday. It wasn't an odor; it was a scent, and it was wonderful. She rested her left arm across my back, and her right arm rested on the end of the couch holding the wine. She asked what we were watching and I told her.

She sipped her wine and when a commercial came on she tugged on my hair.

"Wow, your hair is really thick," she said as she ran her hands through it.

It was an electrifying feeling, and I still remember that at the time, all I could think of was, "don't come." I didn't want her to stop, but I couldn't bear for it to go on. She must have sensed something was going on because she stopped and asked me if I would go and refill her wine while the commercial was on. I remember her apologizing and saying she just didn't want to get up because she was so tired.

I was frozen. I couldn't say no, but I was in no position to get up with a tent pole sticking out of my gym shorts either. I decided something had to happen, so I sat up and twisted to my left away from her and walked the long way behind the couch so she hopefully wouldn't turn her head and see my predicament. She held her glass up in the air in kind of a "hand-off" fashion.

"One glass of wine coming right up," I said and went to the refrigerator and refilled her glass. The whole time I was trying to "will" my erection down, and it was working enough that it wouldn't be a dead giveaway as much as a probable cause for a search.

I went back into the TV room the same way I came out, behind the couch, stopping behind her with the glass, and holding it over her head. She took it, and then twisted her whole body until she was sitting sideways on the couch with her left leg now bent and her calf on the couch, which exposed another couple of inches of her other leg, which had its domino effect all the way down to my cock, which was trying to evidently pop out of my pants to get a look too. She started to say something, but I interrupted her.

"I need to go to the bathroom," I said and turned away just as she looked at my crotch.

"Are you alright?" she asked.

"I just have to pee," I responded. "I've been holding it for a commercial and forgot."

I went into the bathroom and took myself out and orgasmed in about twenty seconds. I took a washcloth and cleaned myself up. I flushed the toilet to make noise and then came out. When I came back into the TV room, Trisha was standing in the kitchen. I was worried that she was going to say something about what had just happened, although I had no idea what she would have said, but she just held up the bottle of wine, saying "I'm off for a hot soak and a good night's sleep. I guess I will see you tomorrow night, okay?"

She walked past me, carrying her glass of wine and the bottle in one hand, and her overnight bag with the pantyhose draped over it in the other. She gave me a hip bump as she passed.

"Don't stay up too late. Promise?" she said.

I nodded and went and sat on the couch to think about what had just happened. As I sat there trying to figure out how I went from zero to a hundred in two seconds flat, I started getting hard again. All I could think of was her in the bathtub, *naked*. I tried to watch TV, but couldn't concentrate. After about ten minutes I decided to go to bed and think. There I could at least do something to relieve the stress that was building up.

As I walked down the hallway, I saw that Ellen's door was ajar and the light was on. I kept the hallway light off, walked past my room, and peered in. There was Trisha's overnight bag opened on the bed, and next to it were her clothes. I eased the door ajar a little more and saw that the door to the attached bathroom was all the way open. I listened but didn't hear anything. I wanted to go in and have a look but was afraid of getting caught. I just stood there with my erection for a couple of minutes, trying to talk myself into going in. The desire was overwhelming.

I was on the verge of a decision when I heard the bathwater turn on for about twenty seconds. I convinced myself she was adding hot water and, therefore, was going to stay awhile. I did the math of my escape time, and decided to go in. I crept in slowly, watching the bathroom. I couldn't see her, but could see the bottle of wine on the floor, and knew she was still in the tub. I went to the overnight bag and looked inside. I saw panties and a bra and it was like finding gold. I picked up her stockings and felt them gently, as if they were made of the finest silk. I put them to my face and breathed them in. They were the same musky scent that made me crazy on the couch.

My erection was back in full force, and my heart was pounding from the excitement and the risk. I slowly made my way along the wall to see if I could see into the tub. Suddenly, her arm appeared and grabbed the bottle of wine off the floor, and she poured another glass. I could tell by the angle that her back was to the door, which gave me the courage to go closer. She would have to turn all the way around and half-climb out of the tub to see me. I crossed the doorway and peered in. She was lying back with her right arm on the tub ledge, holding the wine glass and leaning back against the back of the tub and wall. I could see both of her breasts fully. I was almost hyperventilating now and was sure she would hear me breathing. I stayed there and watched her relax and sip her wine. Every time she sipped, her arm would move her breasts. It was mesmerizing watching them resettle into place. After a few minutes she downed the rest of the glass and set the wine glass next to the bottle. I got scared and headed for the door. I heard the water fall off her as she stood up. I went to my room and closed the door.

After a few seconds, I realized that she would have to walk to her suitcase to get her clothes, and I'd probably be able to see everything. I slowly opened my door and looked down the hall. Everything was the same. I crept down the hallway again and looked in. She was still in the bathroom. I slowly moved the door open a little further, making sure I could get a good look, and waited. About thirty seconds later, she came out in a towel and went to the dresser, where she started brushing her hair in the mirror. After about ten seconds, she let the towel fall away and hung it over the chair. She brushed her hair for another minute or so, then went to the overnight bag and pulled out a cotton pullover nightgown, and put it on. When she lifted the nightgown over her head with her arms raised, I stuck my head in a little farther, just enough to get a good look at her triangle of pubic hair that was golden brown and way prettier than the few pictures I had seen in magazines.

Once she had the nightgown on, she seemed to notice the door ajar and started walking towards the door. I ran to my room and went in, closing the door behind me as I saw her open her door to look out. I didn't think she could have possibly seen me.

I climbed into bed and lay there in silence for a while, listening to see if she had maybe seen me and was going to come in and confront me. After a couple of minutes, I was convinced I had committed the perfect crime. I pulled my tube of hand creme out of the drawer, pulled down my shorts and underwear, and pleasured myself to the thoughts of Trisha, thinking about every inch of her flesh that I had just seen. I came quickly. I did a half sit-up and pulled my T-shirt off to clean up the mess. I tossed the T-shirt on the floor and lay there in bliss with my shorts and underwear to my knees along with the top sheet.

I was coming out of a nice recovery period, when all of a sudden, I saw the hallway light come on under the door. I awoke instantly and froze. Trisha knocked on my door.

"Dino?" she said, and opened the door a millisecond after I pulled the sheet to my chest. My shorts and underwear were still around my knees. She leaned against the partially opened the door and said, "Can we talk for a second?"

I pretended to be asleep and acted groggy. She opened the door all the way, and the hallway light lit up the room. I was caught dead to rights. It was obvious that my pants were down, there was a tube of hand creme on the dresser, and my shirt covered in semen was on the floor. She ignored it all.

"First off," she said, "I'm not mad, and you're not in trouble, and I was just going to talk to you about this tomorrow night, but I can't have you running off to school tomorrow, telling all of your friends that you saw your step-mother's friend naked."

I just lay there. I didn't know whether to deny it or apologize.

"If you promise not to tell anyone what happened," she continued, "I promise not to tell Ellen. Does that sound fair?"

I just said, "Yes."

"Okay." she said, "Don't worry. We'll talk, and everything will be fine." She bent down, picked up my semen-soaked shirt and tossed it on the chair. She left closing the door behind her. I was wide awake for about ten minutes and then collapsed from all the adrenaline and slept all night.

I got up to go to school and noticed her bedroom door was all the way shut. I worried all day.

I kept my promise and didn't say a thing to anyone. I'm not sure why. I guess I knew what I did was wrong, and I sure didn't want Ellen to find out somehow. I had moved enough times already, and only had a couple of years left to go before I was out on my own.

I stayed out until around seven thirty. I wasn't looking forward to "the talk" that I was sure was coming. I assumed she was just nice to me so I wouldn't run and brag to the world that I had seen her naked. When I walked through the door, she was sitting there in the kitchen, eating a pizza and drinking wine.

"Want some?" she said.

"Sure."

I got a glass from the cabinet, filled it with ice cubes and water, sat down, took a slice of pizza, and began eating.

"How was school today?"

"Fine."

"Do you have homework?"

"Nah."

There was kind of an awkward silence, and then she said, "Can we talk about last night for a minute?"

"I guess."

She began speaking in a tone that was a lot gentler than I expected.

"Like I said last night, I'm not mad. I should have shut the door. I just didn't think about it. I'm not excusing you for invading my privacy, but I get it, you're almost sixteen and curious."

I looked at my pizza and said, "I *am* sorry."

"I know. That's another reason why I'm not upset. But I do need to explain something. It's awkward for me, because now I feel like whenever you look at me, it's as if you have X-ray vision. I *feel* naked."

"But I don't . . ."

You don't have to lie." She interrupted me with a laugh. "We just have to both accept it. You saw me naked, and not just for a second but for a while."

"But I didn't . . . I . . ."

"Don't start lying now. I know you were there a while," she said. "I'm just going to tell you. My clothes were moved around on the bed, which means you were in the room while I was in the tub, and unless you went out and only came back as I saw you back away from the door you got quite an eyeful."

"I'm sorry."

"I know, that's why I'm not mad."

"So, what happens now?" I said.

"Nothing," she said.

"Are you going to tell Ellen?"

"Maybe in ten or fifteen years when you are married with a couple of kids."

I smiled. I was happy she was letting me off the hook. I realized how stressed out I had been all day as it washed away. I grabbed another slice of pizza and asked her if she wanted more wine. She said she did, so I got the bottle from the refrigerator, and she held up her glass for me to pour. I sat back down. I wasn't swollen like the night before, but was glad that I was wearing a long basketball jersey, just in case the wind blew.

We ate pizza and chit chatted about nothing for a few minutes.

When things became quiet she asked, "So, do you have a girlfriend?"

"I'm playing the field," which we both knew was slang for no.

"How many girlfriends have you had?"

"Like girlfriend-girlfriends?"

"Yeah, girlfriend -girlfriends."

"That would be zero."

"Haven't found any you like, huh?"

"I guess."

There was another awkward silence, like she wanted me to expound on the matter, but I didn't really have anything to say. I was in fact pretty inexperienced at that point. I hadn't done much more than paw a couple of girls through their clothes as we kissed at parties.

"So, does that mean you're a virgin?"

"No."

"So, you're not a virgin?"

"No."

"It's okay if you are."

"I don't want to talk about it."

She laughed. She said, "So, let me get this straight: you get to see me parading around naked, but I can't ask you a simple question and get an honest answer?"

"So, what if I am?"

She picked up the bottle of wine and refilled her glass. I realized that she had been drinking before I came home, and this had to be at least her third full glass. She was smaller than me, and I knew what three glasses would have done to me from what little drinking I had experimented with.

"I was just curious," she said.

"Why?" I was the one curious now, and could feel tingling in my pants that wasn't as much sexual arousal, as it was a titillation of general excitement.

"Well, if you were innocently looking because you are inexperienced, then I don't have anything to worry about. But if you were looking because you think you're going to have sex with me, then we have an issue we need to straighten out."

"I was just looking."

"So how many women have you ever seen naked like that?"

"One."

"Me?"

"Yeah."

She took a sip from her wine and said, "I'm sorry, I'm not trying to embarrass you. "I'm glad you're still chaste."

"Chased?"

"Chaste, it means pure, innocent, inexperienced."

"Why is that a good thing?"

"It's not good or bad. It just is what it is. Sometimes if you have sex before you're ready, it messes things up later."

"How?"

"I don't know. I guess you just don't get the full benefit. There is more to it than just sex."

"Like what?"

She laughed again. "You'll figure it out. Just remember: sex is mostly in the mind, and right now your body is pushing your mind around. You'll figure it out."

"Why don't you just tell me?"

She smiled as if she was thinking and was quiet for a minute. Then she said "Okay, what do you want to know?"

"I don't know. I just don't want to screw up."

"Okay, well if you don't want to screw up, then the first thing you have to do is realize you are having sex to please the girl, not yourself."

I started to say something and she interrupted me and said, "You will always be able to have a good time. For girls, it isn't as physical as much as it is the entire package."

She was refilling her glass again, and I was now sure she was at least somewhat drunk. I thought I might get her to spill all the secrets to pleasing a woman to me, so I got a lot more confident and asked, "Well, what's the best way to touch a woman?"

"It depends on the woman. It also depends on the circumstances."

"Circumstances?"

"Sure. Sometimes a woman needs to be caressed, and sometimes she needs to be, how do I say this… rubbed vigorously."

I was hard as stone now. I was glad I was sitting at the table, and doubly glad I was wearing the jersey in case I had to stand.

She looked at me and said, "How old are you again?"

"Fifteen years, eight months."

"Fifteen years, eight months?"

"And you didn't say a word to anyone about last night?"

"Nobody."

"Do you swear?"

"I swear."

I didn't know what she was thinking, but I was about to explode from all of the possibilities. She hesitated for another long moment then said, "So, I have a question for you."

"Okay."

"If we were to go into that front bathroom there, turn off all the lights, and take a shower together—no sex—would you promise to never ever under any circumstances tell anyone?"

"I swear."

"Do you swear to let me control everything that goes on and be the decider for where you touch and where you don't?"

"I swear."

She downed the rest of that glass of wine and said, "Well, let's go before I change my mind."

She pushed her chair back and stood up. I could tell she was pretty tipsy, which gave me more confidence. I didn't know what was going to happen, but being graded on a curve because of her situation surely couldn't hurt. She was wearing the same style nursing outfit as last night with the white blouse, skirt, and pantyhose. She stepped out of the white leather nursing shoes and half-tiptoed across the carpet and into the bathroom. I remember thinking that she was the same size as the girls from my school, and that I was maybe about to enter the adult world for the first time.

She walked into the bathroom and I followed. She pulled the shower curtain back and turned on the water. She set the temperature and then faced me. She said, "Hit the light switch."

I reached over, turned the light off, and we were in pitch black. There was no window, and the fan shut off with the switch, so it also began getting a little steamy. She put her hands on my chest and said, "Give me your hands." I put my hands in hers and she said, "Unbutton my blouse," as she put my hands to the top button. I fumbled with the first button for three seconds that felt like an hour. I moved to the second, and when I slid down to the third, my fingers touched the front center of her bra, and an electric shock went through me. I didn't know where we were going, but I knew it was going to be good. I continued unbuttoning until I hit her waist line. She pulled her shirt out of the top of her skirt, and I undid the last button. It fell open.

I remember thinking at that moment that I didn't have x-ray vision, but what I had seen less than twenty-four hours ago had given me the ability to see in the dark. She took my hands and put them on her stomach for a few seconds and then lifted them up to her shoulders. She was using a very sensual voice now and said, "Slide my blouse off."

I did as instructed. I slid it back over her shoulders and down her back, getting imaginary electric shocks from her bra straps as my wrists slid over them. I pulled the blouse down her back and pushed it off her arms. Our bodies were close now, and her face was in the nape of my neck. Her bra was pushing into my chest. I could feel the stiffness of it through the thin basketball jersey. Once the blouse fell away, she stepped back and put her hands on my chest again and said, "Hands." I found her hands. She took my fingertips and brought them to the front of her bra and said, "Okay, unclasp this." I unclasped it and it fell away.

I resisted the urge to feel her breasts with all of my might. I wanted to touch her so bad. I still had my fingers against her chest, where I had let it fall away. She took my hands. I was sure she was going to place them over her breasts, but she didn't. She, instead, put them on her shoulders onto the bra straps and said, "Lift up." I lifted the straps and felt her arms lift up, and I pulled the bra off and let it drop to the floor. She caught my arms on the way down, and I was still sure I was going to be able to feel her breasts. She had other plans.

She took my hands and lifted my arms up. She then slid her hands down and grabbed my jersey. She lifted it as high as she could, and I helped pull it off the rest of the way and sent it to the floor to join the other clothes. She took my arms and found my hands. I was getting lightheaded from the steam, the anticipation, and the raw excitement.

"Get on your knees," she said, holding my hands with one hand while she gently pushed my shoulder, guiding me to the floor. She put my hands on her waist band and said, "Now my skirt." I fumbled around and found a clasp and a zipper and undid them both. She helped, and the skirt slid to the floor. I still had my hands against her stomach and felt her knees both rise and fall as she stepped out of it. She reached down and put my fingers inside the waistband of her pantyhose and said, "Slow and gentle." She rested her hands on my shoulders.

I really needed to adjust myself, as I was poking the inside of my sweatpants at an awkward angle that was almost painful. I wriggled my hips and that moved things enough that I was okay. I had one hand on each side of her waist. I slowly pulled the waistband down over her small hips. I pulled down with two fingers, and I remember feeling the softness of her butt on my other fingers as they grazed smooth skin. Once they were pulled down below her waist, I was unsure what to do. I wanted to move my hands to the front but was afraid she would think I was trying to feel between her legs.

She took her hands from my shoulders and said, "Back and forth, one leg at a time, slowly," as she took my hands and put them around one of her thighs. I slid the panty hose down a couple of inches until I felt the tension from them become uneven, and then moved to the other side. As I wrapped my hands around her left leg, the back of my right hand grazed her pubic hair and I shivered. If my erection wasn't at such an awkward angle, I am sure I would have come right then and there. I caught my breath and continued my task until I helped her step out of them as she placed her hands on my head for balance. She slid her hands from my head down to my shoulders and grabbed my arms and stood me up. She put her hands on my stomach and said, "My turn." She moved her hands to my waist, and then down the side of my legs to my ankles and back up, letting me know she was now on her knees.

Trisha grabbed my sweatpants from the side and pulled them down in one fell swoop, pulling them half painfully over my swollen cock. She was much more careful with the underwear. She put her hands on the waistband at my sides and slid around until she was near the front. I could feel the pressure of my erection pushing against the cotton of my underwear. She pulled my underwear forward hard, assuming I was aroused, and pulled them down without touching me. She lifted my feet up one at a time and had me step out of both my sweatpants and underwear at the same time. I couldn't help but imagine myself only inches from her face, and it made me almost come. I was afraid to touch myself in any way because I was ready to explode.

The room was now filled with steam, sweat, and musk, and we hadn't even gotten into the shower yet. She stood up and said, "Here we go," and put her hands on my torso and guided me toward the sound of the water. I felt the shower curtain on my arms and climbed in. She climbed in right behind me and stood between me and the shower head. The water felt good. Even when it wasn't hitting me, the overall warmth and steam was really nice. She found my hands and placed a bar of soap in them and said, "Build up a lather." I rubbed the soap into a lather and she took back the soap.

"Do my back," she said, and turned around and put my hands onto the small of her back.

I began soaping up her body from the bottom of her back to the top of her shoulders, being very careful not to go to the front without permission, which I was hoping for but not fully convinced would be forthcoming. When I went back down to the bottom of her back she reached around and grabbed my hands and soaped them up again. She then put them back where they were and pushed them down to her butt. I was in total bliss at this point.

That moment was the highlight of my life up until then. I couldn't imagine any better feeling. I was about to be proven wrong.

I washed her butt cheeks, but was careful not to venture too far as I was still nervous about where the boundaries were. She must have sensed my hesitation and said, "Do my legs." I gladly obeyed and squatted down and washed the back of her legs down to her ankles and back up again. As I got near the top of her legs she reached through and grabbed my hands and helped me wash the inside of both of her thighs almost all the way. She stopped just short of her crotch. She pushed my hands back through and said, "Stand up."

She took my hands and soaped them up again, and then with her back to me, pulled them under her arms and placed my soapy hands over her breasts with her hands over mine. At the same moment I felt the firmness of her breasts, my erection rubbed against her butt cheeks, which were still soapy. I came. I groaned uncontrollably, and was trying to not poke her, but the natural thrusts kept making me bump into her which just made the orgasm longer. She said, "It's okay, let it happen."

I had no say in the matter at that point, but was glad she wasn't freaking out. I was on the verge of fainting for a few seconds, and when I did catch my breath, I realized that my hands were still on her breasts with her hands over mine. She said, "Are you alright?"

I said, "Yes."

A second later she said, "Let's see, where were we? Oh yeah," and began rubbing her breasts with my hands while I floated in recovery, trying to catch up.

She massaged her breasts slowly with my hands and then took one hand away and found more soap. She moved my hands slowly to her stomach, and we soaped up everything thoroughly as we moved downward. She took both my hands again and moved them down between her legs. I felt my hands touch her pubic hair, and it was an indescribable pleasure. I imagined the color from the night before and could feel my hands gliding through the soft brown hair that was a few shades darker than her head. It was a perfect triangle, and soft. She opened her legs and washed herself with my hands. I just let her do whatever she wanted. I don't know if I was afraid, turned on, or thinking that by letting her control things I was gaining even more secrets than she had already shared.

After we rubbed the soap around for a minute or so, she turned us directly towards the water. Keeping my hands between her legs, she turned them upright, holding them like cups, catching handfuls of water and rinsing herself off by splashing the water all the way up where the shower stream couldn't go. We did this for a minute and then she said, "Now you," and positioned herself behind me. I wasn't expecting that at all. I just assumed that this was about me touching her.

She began by soaping up my back the same way I did hers, she then moved to my shoulders and lifted my arms one at a time washing them, going to my armpits and down my side to my waist. I was stiff again and worried that at some point she would bump into it, and although I hoped she would be glad, I was worried that she would be upset. I was stupid.

After my arms and sides, she soaped up her hands and washed my butt. She was way more aggressive than I had been, and it made me worry that I had been too gentle for her. The anxiety of that was trumped by the pleasure, and I quickly let it go. She bent down and washed my thighs, moving quickly to my ankles and then back up. She did both sides and then stood up and said, "Okay, turn around."

I turned around to face her with the water now pounding on my back. It felt good. I had rinsed myself off when I was facing forward. I was still assuming she would stop at washing me all the way. She soaped up her hands and washed my face. I closed my eyes, and before she moved on, she pulled my face into the water and rinsed it to get the soap off. She moved to my chest and spent long enough on my nipples that we both knew she was there on purpose. She moved to my stomach and then down the sides of my hips to the front of my legs. She washed the front of my thighs for a very long time as if deciding whether she should cross a line or not.

After about thirty seconds she slid her hands up and found my hands and soaped them up and washed me using my own hands the same way we washed her breasts. I was hard, and she was definitely in control of what my hands were doing. Her fingers were grazing me and I could tell her hands from mine. She moved us sideways and let the water hit our hands as she continued her motions, now rinsing instead of soaping. I was in no danger of any accidents at this point because I was empty from the tremendous orgasm I'd already had.

After about thirty seconds, she stood up and turned us around in a circle to rinse me off. She then climbed back in front of me, presumably to rinse herself. It was still pitch black. She turned the water off and pulled the curtain back, saying, "Step out. I stepped onto the floor and immediately felt a towel drying me off from the top down. She dried everything, except where I wanted her to. She grabbed my hand and put the towel in it and wiped me off with my hand on the towel. It felt great, so I had no complaints.

She then took the towel from my hand and handed me another. This one was much larger and fluffier.

She said, "Now me," and backed into the towel, so I started drying her backside. I went down her back and skipped her butt, and then went down to her feet and worked my way back up. When I got to her butt, I had drawn some courage and dried her aggressively with the thick towel. I couldn't really feel anything through the thick towel, but it felt right to be strong at that moment. She didn't flinch.

After I was done there, she turned herself around and pushed me down to the floor. I started drying her ankles and knees and was working my way up to paradise. When I got to the top of her thighs, she put her hands over mine and dried herself with my hands over the towel. When we were done drying between her legs she moved up to her breasts and I rose with her. She spent a long time with the towel and my hands on her breasts, as if perhaps she didn't want this to end any more than I did. She slowly stopped and stepped back pulling my hands away and letting them go. She then said, "You go to your bedroom and close the door. This never happened, right?"

I said, "Right."

She guided me to the door, opened it, and gently pushed me out into the hallway. I went straight to my room and closed the door loudly and listened. I heard the bathroom door open, her run down the hallway, and the door to Ellen's bedroom close. I put on a T-shirt and underwear and laid in bed for a while, but it was only nine thirty and I was full of adrenaline. I put on some shorts and went and cleaned up the kitchen, and then went to bed and laid back down. I had calmed down now and spent the next hour reliving every moment in the dark as I would do many more times in the upcoming months.

The next night and the night after that, Trisha was just friendly but acted as if nothing had ever transpired between us. At first, I thought I did something wrong, but she was too friendly for that, so I just assumed that she was just trying to help me gain a little experience, and that I shouldn't look a gift horse in the mouth.

The third night she went to bed first but came out about half an hour later in a bath robe, and asked me if I would come back to her room so she could show me something. I wasn't worried and didn't really think anything was going to happen, but there was always that wishful thinking that occurs in situations like this. When we got to the room she sat on the bed and patted it next to her and said, "Sit."

I sat down and said, "What's up?"

At this point, I was half expecting a lecture or her making me promise to keep my mouth shut. She only had one more night after this before Ellen's duty was over and she would be gone.

She said, "You've been really good about our secrets, right?"

"Yes. I haven't said a word to anyone. I swear."

"I believe you."

She was quiet for a few seconds and then said, "We can't have sex, you're too young, I'm too old, and it wouldn't be right, but I do want to help you so you will be a good lover for whatever girl you end up with."

"Okay…"

"Well, if I were to let you look at me, like up close, and show you some things, will you promise to keep your hands to yourself?"

"Yes."

"I'm serious. If you can't control yourself, then we need to not do this."

"I promise."

"Okay. I need you to go to the end of the bed and get on your knees."

I did as she asked. She moved to the end of the bed and sat with her hands on her lap, as if getting her nerve up. She slowly opened the bathrobe and was naked underneath. I was inches away from the place I had seen from ten feet and touched in the dark. She said, "Okay, are you ready to learn something new?"

I nodded. She leaned back a little, opened her legs, and pulled herself apart and said, "I assume you've seen pictures?"

I nodded again.

She said, "Okay, well, here is what we have. This is what most guys think is the only part that matters." She exposed herself a little more and said, "But it's only half of the equation." She then pulled a little sheath back and said, "This is where all the real magic happens." She leaned back on her elbows and slid back on the bed, lifting her feet onto it. She was now spread wide and I could see everything. I was in heaven again for the second time in a week. She was wet. It was obvious. She must have seen that I was noticing because she said, "When a woman gets aroused, her body lubricates so she will be ready for sex."

I said, "Are you aroused now?"

"Sort of, but its more nervousness than anything else. We shouldn't really be doing this."

I nodded again and kept looking.

She took one of her hands, and put two fingers between the lips of her vagina and used the lubrication to wipe on to the sheath she had pulled back and asked, "Have you ever heard of the clitoris?"

"Yes."

"Well, that's what this is right here." And she exposed it fully with three fingers, wiping the lubrication on it with her middle finger.

She asked, "Do you know about oral sex?"

"I know what it is."

She smiled and said, "Well, I'm going to tell you anyway, just to be sure. If you want to please a woman, you need to understand how things work. This is the clit, and it is just like the head of your penis. It's where all the nerve endings are. When you perform oral sex on a woman, you start here." She slid her hand back down to the opening. "But after about thirty seconds you need to work your way up here so you can really please her. Do you wanna know the secret to making a woman orgasm?"

"Yes," I said in a near-hypnotized state. I could smell her sex, and it was driving me crazy. I was also stone hard and could feel myself inching closer. I wasn't going to cross any lines, but I was ready for anything at that point.

"Buttered popcorn."

I looked at her and said, "What?"

"Buttered popcorn. If you want to really drive a woman crazy, you start here and work your way up to here, but once you get here, you take your mouth and you pretend you are sucking the butter off a piece of popcorn. You do it very gently so you don't break the popcorn in half. You do that for a while and then you want to know what you do next?"

"What?"

"You switch to a tootsie pop."

"I don't get it."

"Don't worry, most men don't. Here's the situation: at first, you need to be gentle because it is so sensitive, but after a while it becomes a little less, so you will need to use more pressure; so you start out like you are sucking butter off of popcorn, and then when she's ready, you switch, and pretend you are sucking on a Tootsie Pop trying to get to the center… but no biting!" She smiled.

"How will I know?"

"You'll know."

"But how?"

"Okay, when you first start, she will be lying still, and then as she starts to get into it, she will begin moaning and moving her hips. Remember, you are doing it to please her, so you need to always give her what she wants. When it's your turn, she will do the same for you."

"But, how will I know when I'm finished?" I felt like a complete idiot because it all fell into place at that moment. A woman comes like a man, but doesn't shoot out semen. I would know the same way a girl could tell, just like when it happens to me. It's obvious. She didn't know about my revelation, so she answered anyway.

"The girl will let you know. You won't have any worries there, but you need to know that sometimes girls don't always orgasm. It doesn't mean we don't like what you're doing; it just doesn't always happen, so don't feel bad."

"I want to try it."

"Not with me. I have already crossed too many lines. Besides, you need to practice on popcorn first so you can be good at it."

She sat there on her elbows holding herself open for me to have one last long gaze to burn into my brain before she slowly sat up and closed her robe.

"Okay, off to bed."

It took me less than thirty seconds to orgasm, and I was asleep three minutes after that.

The following night was her last night, and I was hoping for another lesson or shower or whatever, but she just played it cool all night. We watched TV until it was time for bed. I said goodnight and she smiled and said, "Sleep well."

I went in and took a quick shower, still hoping something might happen. I dried myself off, dressed in shorts and T-shirt, and went and got in bed. Nothing.

A few minutes later as I was lying there, wondering whether I should take care of myself, there was a knock on my door and Trisha opened it a crack and said, "I have some presents for you. Can I come in?" She was dressed in her cotton nightgown, and was carrying a plastic bag.

I said, "Sure," and she came the rest of the way in, pulled my desk chair over as I sat up halfway in bed, and she sat down next to the edge.

She said, "Crazy week huh?"

I replied, "I'll say."

"I have some things for you."

"Okay."

I wasn't expecting gifts. She opened the bag and pulled out two magazines: one was *Penthouse* and the other was *Hustler,* both of which were cherished more for their pictures than their articles.

She said, "These are so you will forget about me."

"I'm never gonna forget about you."

"That's what I'm afraid of. We've been bad, and we need to get it behind us sooner rather than later."

I could tell she was having mixed feelings about what had transpired, and I didn't want her to think I would spill the beans, so I said, "I swore to not say anything, and I won't. I promise."

"I know you won't. I just don't want you to obsess about me. There are plenty of girls out there for you, but it might be a little while before you meet one, so I thought these might carry you over."

"Thanks."

"I also got you these." She pulled out a bottle of baby oil and a bag of Tootsie Pops. "This will feel a lot more natural than that hand cream you have been using, and these will help you practice so you can be ready when the time comes."

I must have turned beet red as I realized she *had* seen it lying there open the first night she came in after catching me spying on her.

"Don't worry," she went on. "I know what guys do. It's normal and nothing to be ashamed of."

"It's embarrassing."

"No, its fine. In fact, I think it's kind of cool."

"What?"

"Sure, I've watched guys do it before. I had a boyfriend who did it when I couldn't have sex."

"Why couldn't you have sex?"

"My period, silly."

"Oh."

She was quiet for a second and then picked up the baby oil and said, "Could I watch ?"

I was flabbergasted, embarrassed, excited, confused, and a lot of other adjectives that slip the mind.

I said, "I'm embarrassed."

"So, I don't excite you then?"

"No, it's not that!"

"And you're gonna do it as soon as I leave, right?" She looked down towards my crotch, which was swelling the top sheets. "You can keep your eyes closed, if it will help," she added.

"Do you really want to watch?"

"Sure. Why not?"

"I don't know. It's just embarrassing."

She stood up, went into the hallway, and turned on the hall light, then came back in and turned the light off in my room, but left the door ajar so we were in only the dim light from the hall.

"There. Now, just close your eyes and pretend I'm not here."

I closed my eyes and lay there for a minute. I was fully erect and didn't know whether to be happy or worried that the entire event might only take thirty seconds. I slid the sheet down, exposing my swollen shorts. I lay there trying to get my nerve up enough to continue when I felt her hand grab the bottom of my T-shirt and slide it up, exposing my stomach. I shivered. I put my hands on my shorts, lifted my hips and slowly slid them down to my knees, and lowered myself back down. I adjusted myself and confirmed that I was fully aroused. I laid my hands on my stomach and paused wondering if I could go through with it or not. Trisha gently put her hands on mine and rubbed baby oil all over them. There was no going back now. She lifted my hands and set them on my erection and left them there. I made a fist around myself with my left hand and put my right hand on my thigh. I slowly stroked myself from top to bottom, imagining her watching.

She said, "Can you make it last?"

"I don't know."

"Girls like a guy who can last. Can you do it twice?"

"Sometimes."

I came. It was involuntary. Just like in the shower.

"Wow, that's cool!" She was smiling, which made me feel less flustered. "Stay there, don't move." She went to the bathroom and grabbed a hand towel and put it over me. I wiped myself off. She said, "Close your eyes again."

"Why?"

"Because I'm not finished watching, and I want you to do it some more."

"But I think I'm empty."

"That's okay, I just like watching you rub it."

"Really?"

"Really."

"But I'm not sure…"

At that moment, I felt a huge amount of baby oil get poured right over the head of my penis, and I put my hand down there to catch it. That was all it took. I started stroking myself with my eyes closed, wanting to open them to see if she was really watching. After a few seconds, I opened them into a squint to see her intently staring at my hand as it moved up and down.

She quietly said, "What do you think about when you do this?"

"You."

"No, I mean before me."

"I don't know. Girls from school and stuff."

"What do you imagine?"

"That I'm like touching them, or having sex with them."

"Do you imagine your hands on their bodies?"

"Yes."

"Can you stop moving your hand for a second?"

I stopped and said, "Why?"

"I want you to do something for me."

"What?"

"I want you to keep your hand still and thrust your hips like you are actually having sex with a girl. That's how you should practice for when the time comes."

I held my wrist still and pumped myself into my hand, simulating sex just as she described. I opened my eyes a little and saw her much closer now. She was watching me move. It gave me confidence, and I began thrusting with more purpose. I was too spent to orgasm, but it felt great all the same. I was done with the embarrassment and felt like I was turning her on, which excited me greatly. I wondered why she would want to watch, but then realized if given the chance I would watch her all night.

After a couple of minutes, I was worn out. I lay back down and transitioned from thrusting my hand to my hand thrusting my shaft in a medium to slow speed.

She said, "You're spent, aren't you?"

"I'm frustrated."

"Don't worry! You'll be ready for action again in a few hours. I promise."

She put the towel over my hand and said, "You know the rules, right?"

"This never happened?"

"This never happened."

She stood up, put the chair back, walked over to the edge of the bed and said, "And neither did this," as she lifted her nightgown in the front, exposing her beautiful triangle of hair to me one last time.

She let it drop, kissed two fingers and put them to my lips, and said, "Sleep well." She left, closing the door behind her.

I drifted off to sleep with my hand on my half-hard cock and thoughts of her in my head.

About three-thirty a.m. I awoke to Trisha coming into my room. All the lights were off, and she was being very quiet. I pretended to stay asleep and thought this might be a good thing. She went over and pulled down the blinds, making the room almost completely dark, except for shadows. She slowly came to the bed and slid the sheet down very gently, taking care not to wake me. I was swelling from the excitement, and worried that she would know I was awake. It didn't matter.

She slid the sheet all the way down past my crotch, lifted the waistband of my shorts, and pulled them down as much as she could. She put her mouth over my rapidly swelling cock. I had always imagined it would feel like a vacuum cleaner or something, but the only way I can describe it is her mouth was gliding up and down on me as if it were tailor-made for me personally. There was no suction; just a perfect fit. It was warm, wet, and exciting.

She put her hand inside my shorts and was holding the base with her fingers, holding my shorts at bay with her wrist. She continued her magic, and I just lay there taking it all in. I had had a few hours of sleep and was fully recovered. There was no question as to whether I was going to come, only when.

She was slow and steady and in full control of what was happening with my body. I could feel it building and the intensity was causing my hips to gyrate slowly with her plunges on me. We were one, and if I could have locked in one feeling of euphoria to have for life, then that would have been it. We passed that feeling, and I was approaching an intense orgasm. I put my hand on her head to pull her away, so she wouldn't get any in her mouth. She slid out, and said "It's okay let it go," and then put her mouth back on me and continued for another thirty seconds or so until I came in hard thrusts into her mouth. She slowed down with me, and then opened her mouth, allowing my semen to leak out onto my stomach, with her hand still on my shaft.

I lay there with my fingers in her hair in a daze. She climbed up and whispered, "Don't move." She left and returned about a minute later with a wet washcloth and a towel. She wiped me down with the warm wet cloth, saving my semen-covered stomach for last. When she was done, she dried me off completely, and then right before she put me away, she put her mouth on my still semi-hard cock, and went all the way down, and this time she sucked as if to make sure she didn't miss a drop. She pulled away, tucked me back into my shorts, pulled my shirt back down, kissed me on the forehead, and left.

When I got up the next morning, she was gone. I noticed a note on the table. that said:

Ellen, Dino was great all week. He's a good kid. Get some rest, and call me later.
Trisha

I didn't see Trisha for almost two months but thought about her constantly. I wanted to learn more and was addicted to the memories of her nakedness, her smells, and her touch. I understood why she bought me the magazines, but they didn't work. I would lay in bed for hours late into the night, just imagining what I could do with my newfound knowledge, if only she would come stay again. Eventually, I brought others into my fantasies, but I always came back to her in the end.

When I did see Trisha again, it was when Ellen and I were at a restaurant. Trisha came in with a man who was about thirty-five or forty with his arm around her. I thought I should feel jealous, but in reality I felt superior. Our love was a secret that she and I would always have, and even if she married him, he would never have that. After I saw her, she faded from my fantasies, as I suppose she had become unobtainable, and I naturally moved on. I still think of Trisha from time to time, and am grateful for the experience.

Holly

I spent the next year and a half trying to lose my virginity, but it wasn't going particularly well. I was popular enough but had no serious interest in an actual girlfriend. I guess it was just my experiences at the foster homes with the stepsiblings, but girls never seemed genuine to me, and it made me leery. I made out with a few girls at parties and got a girl's top off once, but her pants were a vault. Another girl let me slide my hand under her skirt and put two fingers inside her while we kissed for about thirty seconds before she got nervous, and that didn't pan out. I was just rolling with it, but was looking forward to sex, and it was on my mind constantly.

I did have a chance to lose my virginity when I was almost eighteen. I had been working that summer at the boat ramp in Alexandria when a man with a fifty-foot yacht docked out in the Potomac River motored up in his dinghy, and asked me if I could shuttle his friends over to his boat in my skiff when they arrived. He gave me ten bucks in advance and called them on his suitcase cellphone and told them who to look for. He restarted the dinghy and went over to the yacht to wait for them.

Half an hour later, four girls in their early twenties showed up in a BMW and came over to me and asked if I was Dino. They said they were there for the ride to the boat. It surprised me a little because the guy was older. I learned a lot about the equation between women and money while working there, and that was just the first lesson of many. They told me he owned a flooring company that "paved" the White House and Supreme Court and he was loaded. I could have guessed it was something like that. When we got to the yacht, it turned out to be an old 1940s Egg Harbor, all-wooden boat with custom woodwork everywhere. It was beautiful.

As I was helping the girls climb onto the boat in their summer dresses with bathing suits underneath (which was a thoroughly enjoyable task) the owner, Tony, leaned over the side of the yacht and asked me if I knew anything about boat engines. I said, "Just a little."

"Do you want to make a few bucks fixing a hose?"

"Sure."

I was more interested in seeing the bathing suits under the dresses than the leak, but money was good too. He took me to the bottom level of the boat, where he had moved a table and carpet and opened a trap door. Inside were two big diesel engines, one of which was leaking fuel out of a hose. He asked if I thought I could fix it and pointed to a big box next to the engines with tools, hoses, clamps, and other emergency spare parts. I looked at it and said, "If I cut the hose back a couple of inches and put it back on, you should be fine."

"Do it."

I climbed into the engine bay and crouched down and repaired the hose. When I was done, I threw everything in the box and said, "Can you start the engine so I can make sure it's okay?" He nodded, went up the steps, and about thirty seconds later, he fired up the engines. They were incredibly loud with the trap doors open, but they weren't leaking. I went to the steps and hollered, "We're all good." He shut the engines down, came back down and said, "All fixed?"

"All fixed."

"You're a lifesaver! What's your name again?"

"Dino."

"Well, Dino, you saved the day." He pulled out a wad of cash, peeled off a fifty like it was nothing, and said, "Is this enough?"

I looked at him and said "That's too much. It only took five minutes."

He said, "It's not the time. It's the value, my boy. It's the value. A brain surgeon only operates for an hour, but it's twenty grand. Get it? You saved the day."

I didn't argue.

I went up to the deck and was embarrassed as I realized I was covered in diesel fuel and grease. Tony came out with a bottle of dish detergent and said, "Take off your shirt." I pulled the shirt off and he squirted the detergent all over my arms and said, "Rub him up, girls. He got us going."

The girls were all in bikinis now. A dark-haired girl grabbed one of my arms started rubbing the soap in. One of the other girls said, "I'll get some water and a rag." I stood there, leaning over the side of the boat as best I could. The second girl came back with a soaking wet rag and washed my arms and my right leg which had grease stains on the skin.

When I was lathered up, I said, "Hang on," and jumped into the water, rinsed myself off and climbed back up the ladder. I picked up my shirt to put it back on, but it was done. I as discreetly as possible took in all the girls, and was amazed at the what later Tony told me was "quality trim" that was standing before me.

Tony said "We're headed to ego alley in Georgetown, you wanna go? We're meeting some of my buddies, but we have to bring the girls back here anyway"

I hesitated, not because I didn't want to go, but I was underage and surely out of my league. Besides, I was now shirtless.

I said, "I don't have a clean shirt, maybe another time."

The dark-haired girl said, "Aw, c'mon, it'll be fun. You have a shirt somewhere, don't you Tony?"

He said, "It's settled then. "Tie the skiff to the pole, and let's get going. We're already late."

I climbed into the skiff and transferred my rope from his boat to the pole and then unhooked his boat from the pole. He had already fired up the motors. I climbed aboard and gave him the thumbs up. He took off. I was on my first yacht ride with four very attractive girls who were surely not virgins. It was going to be a good day.

One of the other girls came out with a T-shirt and put it on me. We went upstream past DC, looking at the monuments as we passed. We went past the famous Watergate Hotel that brought down Richard Nixon, past the Kennedy center, and pulled up at the dock on the Georgetown Waterfront, otherwise known as Ego Alley, because it's where the elite came to be seen with their boats, including, I supposed, Tony.

His friends were there waiting. They came aboard with a bunch of crabs they had gotten from the seafood market, and a cooler of beer. They set up tables on the deck and we feasted. The girls ate, drank, and paraded around in their bikinis for the many passersby. Tony's friends were all businessmen, the youngest of whom was surely over forty. The girls were more or less off to themselves on the front deck. One of the guys referred to them as "boat beavers." I figured that maybe I had as much a chance of getting laid as they did, which in my mind was close to zero.

As the afternoon went on and everybody got a little more intoxicated, I wandered over and started talking to the girls. They were from Potomac, where Tony lived. I had gotten the impression that they all lived off their parents and the kindness of rich acquaintances. They made a little fun of Tony and his buddies, and let it be known that they were there for the fun and nothing else. A little while afterward, Tony came up and said we were headed for a ride down to see Mount Vernon, George Washington's home, about five miles downstream, then back to Alexandria, where he would drop off the girls and me and head back to St. Michaels with his buddies to play cards at the boathouse. I had downed a couple of beers, and it was all okay with me.

I was a little concerned about leaving the skiff, but Larry, the guy who owned it, did let me use it on weekends since I worked for him part-time during the week, cleaning boats and repairing sails. As we drove past Alexandria, I looked over and it was still where I left it. No worries.

We were all on the forward deck, watching the shoreline for Mt. Vernon, when the dark-haired girl, whose name was Holly, tugged at my new borrowed T-shirt and pulled me downstairs to where the cabins were. I followed. When we were alone, she kissed me, and I kissed her back. She was pleasantly drunk, but well aware of what was going on. I guided her over to the couch and kicked the door shut with my foot.

"What if we get caught?" I said.

She looked at me and said, "Caught?"

"Never mind," I said and reached over and locked the door.

I remember thinking that I had blown it. I told them I was twenty and they didn't question it. I popped her top off and started caressing her. Holly had medium breasts with small dark nipples and very slight tan lines, where she obviously sunbathed topless and probably often. I suckled the nipples as I gently caressed the sides of her breasts. She tossed her head back and moaned and I took that as a yes to slide my hand down her bathing suit. I put my fingers inside of her and she was already wet. I slid her bottoms off and she had just a little tuft of hair, the rest had been shaved clean. I pulled my T-shirt off with one hand and tossed it aside. She reached down and grabbed my cock through my shorts and started undoing the buttons as I rubbed between her legs.

She said, "Do you have a condom?"

I said, "No," and prayed she had an alternative.

I started thinking that I could go ask one of the men or Tony and dismissed that as too embarrassing. Holly stopped unbuttoning my pants and said, "Then these stay on… for now"

She lay back on the couch. I took that as my cue to give her oral sex and dropped to my knees on the floor. I leaned over her body, kissing her stomach. I moved my hands to her breasts as my mouth went the other direction. She had distinct tan lines from her bikini, and I imagined her as some rich girl, sunbathing topless by the pool every day.

As I got closer, I remembered Trisha's lesson and went down and licked the opening for a little while. The taste and smell were overwhelming. I was reaching that state of euphoria again and knew this was, by far, the happiest place on earth. I slid my hands down to her waist and moved my mouth up towards her clit. I pulled back the hood and slowly started to suck the "butter off the popcorn." Holly loved it. She was afraid to move while I did that for a while.

After a couple of minutes, she started pushing herself to my mouth and gyrating with some audible moaning. I knew then it was time to switch to a "Tootsie Pop." I became more aggressive, sucking, licking, and trying to balance out the pressure with her pushing herself to me. After about ten minutes, she reached down and put her fingers in my thick hair and held on tight. She pulled me gently at first, then harder and harder towards her, which I took as a sign to go faster with more suction. The intensity climbed and then exploded. She bucked against my mouth, and I held on for dear life, wanting it to go on forever.

I had never felt so powerful in my entire life. I knew what she was feeling because I had felt it myself, and the thought of being able to make her feel that way was a milestone, a defining moment of my life and one of the greatest joys that can never be taken away. She pulled my head back and caught her breath as I kissed her thighs. I was ready to go right back to what I was doing, but she was exhausted. She pulled me up on the couch with her and kissed me deeply. I thought it was funny that she didn't care where I had just been. I didn't care. I just remember noticing it. We kissed for a while, then she said, "I need my bottoms." I found them and gave them to her, and she quickly scooted them on. She said, "Now, we're all safe again," and lay back down beside me and put her hand on my crotch.

She finished unbuttoning my shorts and slid them down as we kissed. She pulled her hand back and wet it with her mouth, put it on me, and started stroking me as we kissed. She was skilled, and it felt good. The unfamiliarity of it was exciting. I was leaking precum now, and she was using it to lubricate the shaft. It only took about two minutes to make me come. We kissed the whole time, and it felt great.

When it was over, she held her hand there for a minute, then she sort of rolled toward me, signaling to let her up. She went into the boat's miniature bathroom and tossed me a towel that was way too big, and then closed the door. I put my T-shirt back on and buttoned up. She came out and I handed her her top.

She put a breast in my mouth and said, "That was fun." She put the top on as I got one last look at her, and then as she opened the door she said, "We better get back up top before we get caught," and laughed and ran up the steps with me right behind.

When we got topside, nobody even cared. They had already passed Mt. Vernon and turned around, and were halfway back to the skiff. A few minutes later we arrived, and I helped the girls in the skiff and offered Tony back his shirt.

"Keep it," he said, giving me a smile, like the shirt was part of the deal along with the fifty, the beer, and Holly.

When we got to shore, Holly pulled a business card out of her pocket that one of the guys on the boat had given her and said, "Do you have a pen?" I went to my boss's tool box on the dock pulled a pen out. She wrote down her number.

"Call me," she said. "That was fun."

I said, "Thanks," and off they went. I tied up the skiff, locked up everything else, and headed down through Alexandria to home. As I was driving my old beat-up Volkswagen beetle down King street, I said to myself, "How appropriate! Someone must have known I was coming," because that is exactly how I felt.

Rebecca

I didn't lose my virginity until a year later. It was early fall. I was eighteen and had just graduated from high school a few months before. I was hanging out in downtown Washington, DC when I met a girl at a party held by American University undergrads. In the preceding year, I had managed to make out with less than a half a dozen girls, go down on two, but awkwardly due to the situations, and I got exactly three hand jobs. I was not a ladies' man by any stretch. It wasn't that I didn't meet girls; I just didn't have the aggressiveness it took to make things happen. I think I wanted to know more about what was in the girls head first, and I always seemed to run out the clock. I considered getting a girlfriend so I could have sex, but I knew that as soon as I lost my virginity, I would lose interest in her in favor of all the other possibilities.

Rebecca was a second-year student from Great Falls, Virginia, a wealthy enclave just outside of DC on the Potomac River. She was very pretty with medium-length, slightly curly brown hair. She was average height, had medium breasts, and flawless skin. I couldn't tell the rest because she was dressed in a plaid skirt with leggings and a sweater. It was a cool, fall evening, and her chest looked great in the sweater. She approached me and we began talking. She found out I didn't go to AU, which seemed to please her. I got the feeling she might be looking for a one-night stand but perhaps didn't want to encourage any stalkers.

An hour later, we were back in her dorm room. We went in and she hung beads on the doorknob and shut and locked the door. She took the gum out of her mouth, tossed it in the trash can and said, "I have roommates," leaving me to conclude the obvious reason for the beads. She came up to me and we kissed. I went right for her chest, and she raised her arms, letting me pull the sweater right off. She undid her own bra from the front and let it fall to the sides, exposing her very luscious and full breasts. I cupped them. She reached over and grabbed the beer she had carried in with her, sipped it and said, "You like?"

I said "Oh yeah," and put my mouth on them and suckled and caressed them aggressively. She took another sip of her beer, set it down, and then removed her bra the rest of the way, and tossed it to the floor. She backed up and sat on the end of the bed. We were both a little drunk at this point. I walked over to her, leaned down, and kissed her while fondling her breasts. She pulled me onto the bed. We kissed for a short while, with her kissing me as hard as I kissed her. It was very exciting to have a girl in that state of passion. She slowly pushed me backwards and I climbed off of her, waiting to see what was going to happen next.

Once I was up, she lay back down, put her hands under her skirt, pulled her leggings down to her knees, and kicked off her shoes, and I began helping getting them off the rest of the way. She was wearing very generic, white cotton bikini underwear. I slid my hand under her skirt as I climbed back on and began to kiss her. I was rubbing the outside of her underwear. I could tell she was excited, and could feel the wetness through the cotton. She pushed me up again, and I took the cue to pull off her underwear. She let me, lifting her hips to assist and smiling at my reaction and excitement. She had short pubic hair that looked like she had at one point shaved, but was now letting it grow back. I put my hand between her legs and found her wetness, inserted my fingers, and began finger-fucking her in a slow, deliberate motion. She moaned happily.

I was getting ready to slide her skirt up and go down on her when she sat up and reached for my pants. She undid my belt buckle as I pulled off my sweatshirt and tossed it aside. I helped with the buckle and the zipper. She pulled my jeans down and pushed them hard to the floor and helped as I stepped out of them. I kicked off my shoes in the process, but my socks stayed on. I was wearing a pair of boxers, and once my pants were off, she pulled them down and within a second had my cock in her mouth. She was completely different than Trisha. Rebecca was sucking, and sucking hard. She was also stroking, I presumed, to make sure I was as hard as possible. She then pushed my boxers the rest of the way to the floor, and as soon as I stepped out of them, she let go of me and lay back, lifting her hips and pulling her skirt up with her hands. I was still standing at the edge of the bed, and she scrunched herself to the edge, lifted her legs, folding her knees towards her chest, and exposed herself to me.

Before I even had time to look at her, she grabbed my cock and started rubbing it on the outside of her pussy, lubricating me for what I was sure was going to come next. I leaned forward a little bit and she slid me in. She said, "Push," and I did. It felt as good as I imagined it would, but I felt foolish for her having to tell me to push. I didn't know if it was normal, or if my lack of experience was showing. My mind quickly went back to the matter at hand, and I started thrusting in and out and looking for clues from her as to what she wanted. She put her hands on my waist and started thrusting at me. It was obvious she wanted to be fucked, and I did my best to give her what she wanted. I put my hands on the bed and leaned forward thrusting as deep as I could in the rhythm she established. I could feel the coarseness of her pubic hair and it actually turned me on a little bit because it made me feel like this girl needed sex and wanted it hard. She wasn't giving me something; she was taking something from me that she wanted as badly as I wanted her. I got into it, and just kept thrusting hard. She was getting turned on and groaning almost like a man as she pumped harder at me.

I soon realized that she didn't want me to keep going; she was trying to make me come.

"I'm going to come," I said. She growled, "Yeah," and thrust harder, her fingers digging into my waist. I came hard and thrust through the orgasm. I felt the come shoot inside of her. She was happy and started almost laughing, and grit her teeth and said, "That was good."

I was still leaning over with my feet on the floor and my hands on her bed. She took her hands off my hips, and I got the message that she wanted me to get up so I did. She sat up and kissed my chest.

"Would you get me a towel?" she asked, pointing to a shelf of folded laundry on the other side of the room. I grabbed two, handing her one and using the other for me. I wiped myself down and then put it around my waist. I asked if I could stay the night, and she smiled and said "Sadly, no."

I said, "Why not?"

"Because my boyfriend's coming tomorrow from Duke to see me." She was very nonchalant about it.

"If your boyfriend's coming, why did you just have sex with me?"

"Because he thinks I'm a virgin."

"I don't get it. Why does he think you're a virgin?"

"Because that's what I tell him."

I was totally confused.

I repeated, "I still don't get it? You don't have sex with your boyfriend, but you'll have sex with me?"

"That's right."

"But why?" I was almost laughing.

"Because I don't want you to marry me."

She saw the look on my face and went further.

"I love my boyfriend, and one day I want to marry him, but if we have sex than I have nothing left to bargain with, so I keep him hanging on."

"By withholding sex?"

"I don't *withhold* sex. We fool around, I just keep my underwear on."

"And he's okay with that?"

"Well, he's not leaving, and we are talking marriage, so you tell me?"

"Does he know about . . . uh, me?" I didn't want to presume, but she did just do something with me she had obviously done before.

"Of course not, I told you, I'm a virgin. Which is why you can't stay, and you can't have my number, and you can't approach me in public if you see me with another guy or anyone who might look like my parents."

"Wow!"

"You didn't have a good time?"

"Of course, that's why I wanted to stay."

Rebecca looked down between her legs and used the towel to wipe up what she had missed while we were talking.

"You came a lot."

"Sorry."

"No, that means you liked it."

"That I did."

I looked at the girl that unknowingly took my virginity and wondered if this is the way I would have wanted it or not if I had a choice. I decided it was. She was beautiful, and it was all about sex and nothing more.

I had a thought and asked, "What about birth control?"

"I'm on the pill."

"But you're a virgin."

She looked up at me with a feigned pout and either sarcastically or sinisterly said, "I get cramps really bad, and the doctor says I *have* to be on them."

Either way I was relieved.

She reached out and pulled on my towel. I was still semi-hard and she took the towel and wiped off the leakage that had oozed out while we were talking. Then she put me in her mouth and sucked me more like Trisha did for a good thirty seconds. She stopped and said, "Okay get dressed. I have to get some sleep."

She pulled my towel over her and lay down on her back and watched me get dressed. I did it at a moderate speed, so it didn't look like I wanted to leave or stay. When I was almost done, I asked her, "Do you give your boyfriend blowjobs?"

"Nope, I just let him play with my boobs and use my hands."

"And he's okay with that?"

"Do you want an invitation to the wedding?"

"Okay, I have just never heard of that before."

"Yeah, well half the girls at AU are like that. Successful men want women who are as close to virgins as possible, and girls who want to marry successful men know it. It's stupid, but it's the way the world goes around."

I walked over to the edge of the bed where she was laying there, covered by my towel and asked, "One last look?"

"If you must."

"I must."

I lifted the towel, and she just tossed it aside and opened her legs wide. I pulled the other towel that had been pushed into her crotch, and let it fall to the floor.

I said, "You're really beautiful."

I slid two fingers inside her and she sucked in air and moaned.

"Ughhhh . . . you have to go. I need some sleep."

I just kept fingering her for about thirty more seconds until she put her hands on my wrist and said, "Go." I bent over to kiss her goodbye and she sideswiped me and kissed me on the cheek.

"I have a boyfriend who's going to be here in like eight hours. Go."

I left. What a night!

Lisa, Part 1

After high school graduation, I had gone to work full time for Larry at the Alexandria boat ramp. Ellen said I could stay with her another year rent free, as long as I was working to save money to start my life. When things slowed down for winter, I found a job as a handyman at a DC high-rise about ten blocks from the White House on 12ᵗʰ St. It was called the Willbury, and catered to mostly people thirty and up.

My job was pretty easy, as the place had been updated less than ten years before. I mostly fixed loose railings, changed light bulbs, and maintained the small grounds. They had a pool man and crews to shovel snow and such. I was on call a lot, but rarely got called, and it was an extra 250 bucks a month to carry a pager. After Rebecca took my virginity, I had managed to sleep with a few girls, learning as I went.

DC had a lot of new girls coming in from out-of-town for work, and they hung around the bars afterwards. It seemed that they were in the big city for the first time and really wanted to let their hair down. They may have been looking for that big fish, but I am sure some of them chose me because they knew I wasn't him and they wouldn't feel bad about having a one-night stand with me. It wasn't like I was in their inner circle of friends or one of their business associates, so for them it was a victimless crime. For me, it was fun. Plus, I was gaining much wanted experience.

With that experience, I found out that I was really turned on by woman's minds, especially if they were a little twisted. I wasn't into anything kinky. I just found myself doing my best to get women to confess their most sinful thoughts to me. I would ask them questions about their fantasies and their pasts. I realized that if I could get an opening and get a girl started, I could get her to tell me almost anything or let me say whatever I wanted. I spent a lot of time at work, talking dirty to girls on the phone who were at their desk in a roomful of coworkers. A couple of times I even convinced girls to leave work and have sex with me in my office (aka the tool room). I still hadn't found love, but wasn't even really looking. It was a good time to be me.

By the time summer came around, I had moved into an efficiency suite at the Willbury and had been promoted to head maintenance man, which meant I was now on call for free but got free rent and paid-training classes for HVAC and electrical. I was saving money and having a decent time. The few single people who lived in my building were quite old, but the neighborhood was the DC city scene, so I would cruise the various places at lunchtime and watch women as part of my routine. I would watch them walk by and imagine what they were wearing underneath their clothes, what their nipples looked like, whether they shaved or were trimmed between their legs, and what was the craziest thing they ever did in bed. The thoughts were endless, and it was quite entertaining. If I would see a girl that I saw regularly all of a sudden wearing a lot of makeup but dressed down, that told me she probably had a rough night the night before and was maybe hungover or at least a party girl.

I talked with a lot of girls and would sometimes just sit down and talk with them in the local park as they ate lunch. It was easy to tell when a woman had no interest, and I always gave them their space. I figured the tie went to the runner, and never wanted to be "that guy" that everyone talked about behind his back. Most of the girls I ended up going out with, and sometimes to bed with, liked me well enough. They knew I wasn't really boyfriend material and wasn't ever going to stick around if I were put into the friend zone, as one of the girls once informed me. I wanted to be the guy they could be dirty as hell with without worrying about being analyzed for it.

I only had one tryst with a resident at the Willbury the entire two-and-a-half years I was there. It started with me eavesdropping on two women, sitting at the pool. It wasn't nefarious. They were on the other side of a chain-link fence that had green strips through it to provide privacy to the pool guests. I was on the outside weeding a small flower ledge along the sidewalk. I was on the ground and out of sight to them. I was only about three feet away as they lay in their lounge chairs with their backs almost touching the fence, and me sitting on the sidewalk on the other side. I didn't miss a word.

Lisa was thirty, very pretty, and six months pregnant. She was telling her friend and guest that her husband hadn't touched her since she told him she was pregnant. She said that they fought about it all the time, but he wasn't budging. He was afraid of hurting the baby, and no amount of talk could convince him otherwise.

She went into details about how she was sure it wasn't the pregnancy because he wouldn't even let her "play with his dick." She said it used to pop up if she even bumped into him as they rode the elevator. She also confessed that she was sure that it was just all the extra blood coursing around "down there" but that she had never been hornier in her entire life, and was ready to kidnap a pizza guy. She also said that she felt ugly, and she didn't change in front of him anymore because he would turn away and not look at her. She added that otherwise he was perfect, and she still loved him but didn't understand why he was being like this.

They had a conversation about how he also refused to talk about it with the doctor or a therapist. I didn't know Lisa, other than to smile as we saw each other around the building. I couldn't remember her last name, but knew which floor she was on and figured it out soon enough. The conversation made me hard. She was so open and honest, and it was real. I had never imagined that pregnant women would want sex, but it made sense. I asked a girl I knew who was a nurse about it a couple of days later, and she said that that was in fact "a thing."

About a week after my eavesdropping, I surmised a plan and visited Lisa. The building had been updating smoke detectors as we did service calls so as not to disrupt the clients with intrusions. I saw Lisa leaving the pool one day, apparently going back to her apartment alone. I pulled out my tool bag, my short step ladder, and two smoke detectors. I went up to her apartment on the sixth floor and knocked. When she answered she was still in her bathing suit and pool robe.

"I'm sorry to bother you," I said. "I can come back, but we are updating the smoke detectors, and your neighbor wasn't home, so I figured I would try and see if anyone else on this floor wanted it done while I was here." She paused for a second and I said, "It takes less than ten minutes. They just pop in and out; they are direct replacements."

She pulled the door back and said, "Sure, why not?"

I stepped in and said, "I'll start in the kitchen."

I set up the three-step ladder at the kitchen entrance and climbed up to get to the smoke detector.

I asked her nonchalantly, "Do you know whether you are having a girl or a boy?"

She looked at me, and at first, I thought I might have crossed a line from her expression, but she said, "A boy. We are naming him David after my husband's father."

I took that as a direct defense that she wanted me to know that she was married and not to get any ideas. I wasn't ready to give up yet though, since I was privy to inside information that I had heard right from her own mouth.

I said, "Well, that should make your husband proud," and went back to work.

She said, "He is," and relaxed.

"Well, he's lucky, you look very beautiful that way."

She looked at me, but I looked up, like I was having trouble with the plug.

She said, "Thank you. I don't feel beautiful though, I just feel fat."

I kept working, snapped the detector in place, and then looked her right in the eye.

"You're beautiful all right. Almost all women look beautiful when they're pregnant."

She said, "Do you have kids?"

I said, "No, I'm only twenty, I don't even have a girlfriend, but I was raised by a foster mother who was a nurse, and she used to have these coffee table books of nothing but pregnant women posing. You should be in one."

The truth was that I had seen one the day before when I was browsing in the Upton book store two blocks away, but I did like it.

"There is a book of pregnant models?"

"No. Pregnant women. They aren't models. They are just women who posed as they were growing. It's very beautiful. You should go to the library and check it out."

"Are they clothed?"

"Some are, some aren't, but it's art, not like *Playboy* or anything."

"And you used to look at it."

"All the time."

"All the time?"

"I was fifteen. They were women. You know."

"So, it was pornographic."

I responded, "No more than a Victoria's secret catalog."

I could tell she was intrigued now. She had walked closer to me and was watching my body language to try and figure me out. I played innocent.

She inquired further, "Fifteen-year-old boys like to look at naked pictures of pregnant women?"

"Sure, why not? I told you that you look beautiful, like you're literally full of life. I'll bet your husband loves it."

"Yeah. Uh, no. I guess he missed that class."

"Well, then he's crazy." I said, just looking at her.

I folded up the stepladder and walked towards the hallway to change the other detector.

As I climbed the ladder, I said, "You should find out who makes those books and send them copies of your pregnant pictures. They would probably print them."

"I don't have any."

I stopped what I was doing on the ladder, let my hands drop to my sides and said, "What do you mean you don't have any? You should have like a hundred by now."

I went back to work while she pondered that, and then I continued. "No wonder you don't think you're beautiful; you haven't seen any pictures of yourself."

She was quiet and I went to work installing the smoke detector. As I stepped down, she said, "If I get the camera, would you take a picture of me?"

"Sure, of course."

She went back into the bedroom and came back with a Polaroid camera. She said, "I hope there is film in it."

I took it from her and said, "It says two right here. I don't know if that means there are two left or if it's two out of however many it can take."

She shrugged and said, "I don't know either."

"Well, we will find out soon enough. Let's go by the window." I left my ladder in the hall and walked into the living room. Her window overlooked the street. I stood where the length of the street would be in the background, since we were on the sixth floor.

I said, "Okay, off with the pool robe."

"I don't think so."

"Why not? People see you at the pool every day. I've seen you at the pool."

"Well, that's different. I wasn't posing in front of a man who's not my husband."

I smiled. That let me know she knew I was interested in more that helping her with her pictures.

"You forgot to add who used to look at picture books of semi-naked pregnant women."

"That too."

I paused a second and then said, "Okay, the first one with the robe, then we'll talk."

She went to the window and gave me a profile. I tried to make it artistic, so I told her to look at the flower vase, like she was adjusting the flowers. She did as instructed, and I took the picture. We waited anxiously for it to develop, and it came out great.

"See?" I said. "Beautiful!"

She looked at it and said, "I look fat."

"You look beautiful. Let's take another."

"I'm not taking the robe off."

"That's okay. Let's get one with you looking out the window."

She went to the window, and I told her where to move. I was not about to touch her and scare her way. I waited until she rotated to where I wanted her, and I moved around with the camera to get the angle I thought was most flattering. I snapped the picture and we were a little closer this time, watching it develop together.

When it came into focus, I said, "See? Another winner."

She looked at it and said, "You can barely tell I'm pregnant; it's too close."

I said, "It's called artistic, you can tell. Let's take another." I looked down at the camera, and it read zero. I said, "Uh-oh, we are all out of film. Do you have more?"

She said, "No."

I said, "That's all right, you show these to your husband and he'll come back with five rolls the next day."

She looked half away and said, "Yeah, well that's not happening."

"Well, it should. You have to take pictures. You're only going to be like this for a few more months."

"You're serious, aren't you?"

"Yeah. Trust me, you will regret it big time if you don't get pictures."

"I'll think about it."

"Promise?" I said, picking up my ladder and working bag.

"I promise."

"Good."

"Well, thanks for the smoke detectors. Better now than when the baby is here and everything is a mess."

"Sure! No problem. Listen, if you need anything, just page me on the emergency number. I mean, as you get closer and can't lift something or need to move furniture or whatever. I'd be happy to help."

"Thanks, that's very nice of you."

I smiled, said goodbye, and felt devious as hell. In the elevator, I wondered to myself which of us was hornier.

I laid low the next day when she was at the pool. I didn't know if she wanted to see me or not, but I figured I would give her a couple of days to think about things. It was really exciting knowing how frustrated she was. I imagined how much fun it would be satisfying her. The fact that she was married would have upset me if I wanted to date her, but all I really wanted to do was give her what her husband had no interest in giving her. It was fun to think about.

The second day, Lisa was at the pool with her friend whose name I found out later was Tammy, a girl she went to college with and who worked nights. I saw them at the pool in the same spot and thought of going back to work on the flowers to eavesdrop but decided to give them something to talk about first.

I took my tall stepladder and went to the other side of the pool about fifty feet away and changed a floodlight bulb that wasn't burned out, but since it was daylight and not on, it was my secret. I just put the good bulb back in the new box and put it back on the shelf. While I was up on the ladder, I waved and she waved back. That was it. I took the ladder and disappeared as quickly as I had arrived. I grabbed my spade and a bag of potting soil and came around the back way. I sat on the ledge right behind them. They couldn't see me, but I was only a couple of feet from them and could hear everything. The only thing I needed to do was to make sure I looked busy if someone walked by so they wouldn't talk to me.

When I situated myself and started listening, they were already in full discussion.

Lisa was speaking.

"He's just a kid, he's only twenty."

"Twenty is no kid."

"Uh, when you're thirty it is. Besides, I think he was just being nice."

"Yeah, I'd be nice too if I wanted to take naked pictures of you."

Lisa said, "He just wanted me to take off my pool robe. I was wearing this. That's not naked."

"He used to look at porno books of naked pregnant women."

"Not porno. Art books."

"Were the women naked?"

"Some of them probably were."

"Porno."

"I don't want to talk about it."

Tammy laughed and said, "That's because he looks at porno pregnant women and now wants to take pictures of you."

"We are not talking about this."

"Porno."

I heard one of the aluminum chairs loudly creak. I assumed at least one of them was getting up. I quickly picked up my stuff and disappeared into the back way to the maintenance office. I had heard enough to be confident that I had a good chance of having a fling with her. I would be patient, but it was definitely enticing to think about. I went up a floor and looked out the hall window and saw them still sitting at the same place.

I had an idea. I went back to the office and pulled out one of the disposable cameras we kept around in case there was an accident or vandalism and we needed pictures for evidence. I took it out of the box and discreetly took pictures of her at the pool. I tried to get a few angles. Over the course of an hour, I managed to take all twelve pictures with her sitting, standing, climbing out of the water, drying off with the towel, and reading. There were plenty of corners and bushes for me to take them without getting caught. I figured if someone asked questions I would point to a cracked tile in the pool. The only one who could be upset would be her, but I had a plan.

I knew that Tammy usually went home and didn't go upstairs with her, so when they had said their goodbyes and Lisa came back to gather her stuff, I met her at the pool gate. I said, "Did your husband like the pictures?"

"I didn't show them to him."

"Why not? I told you they're beautiful."

She rolled her eyes. "To you. You're different."

"Did you buy more film?"

"No."

"I knew you wouldn't."

"Good guess."

I hesitated, lowered my voice, and said, "Listen, I don't want you mad at me, so you can just throw this away if you want." I held out the camera.

"Throw it away?"

"Yeah, I took some pictures of you at the pool today, and if you want to see them you can get them developed. If you don't, you can just throw it away. We buy them by the box in case there's an accident or something we need a picture of."

"That's kind of creepy." She wasn't flattered.

"No, that's why I gave you the camera. I knew you weren't going to buy film, and I really think it's a mistake to not have pictures of your own pregnancy."

"This isn't just some trick to get me to pose for you like in the book?"

"I think you're beautiful, and you should have pictures . . . I mean, if you wanted to give me one, that would be cool, but I really do think you should have them or you're gonna regret it."

She looked at me closely. I could tell she was in fact at least a little flattered, but she was also wondering if I was just trying to get laid. I didn't know if that would offend her or not, but I decided to play it cool. I said, "Look, I'm only twenty. You probably think of me as a stupid kid, but I'm not. I have no pictures from my childhood because I was in foster homes, and they always kept them all. I just think you're too beautiful to not have pictures while you look like this. Maybe it's stupid but maybe it's not."

She said, "That word, 'beautiful,' do you think if you keep saying it, I'll change my mind?"

"Would that work?"

She laughed and relaxed. "I'll think about it, okay?"

"That's all I ask."

I smiled and walked backwards towards my workshop. I said it again as I was backing up. "That's all I ask." I turned and disappeared before she could respond.

I didn't see her until the following Monday. I was off weekends and had been playing baseball with some buddies I had met around town both days. I was on call, but the pager was silent.

I saw her at the pool. She was alone, and I was too curious to wait for a better opportunity, so I went out with the test kit to check the PH of the pool water. We had a pool company, but I had a kit just in case someone complained. There were about five or six other people there but no one close enough to hear quiet conversation. I said hello. She smiled broadly and said hi. I took that as a sign that she had probably developed the pictures. I knelt down near her and opened my kit.

"How did the pictures come out?" I took the test tubes out of the bag.

She responded, "How do you know I had them developed?"

"Just wishful thinking. Can I see them?"

"I haven't told you whether I even had them developed or not."

"I have faith."

She shook her head. I said, "Well?"

"Well, what?"

"When do I get to see them?"

She said, "You saw them when you took them."

"So, you did get them developed."

"Okay," she laughed, "you can see them but not here. I'll page you."

I tested the water to make things official and then waited for my pager to go off.

Finally, three hours later at three thirty, it beeped and it was her. I called her number back and said, "Lisa, this is Dino. You paged me?"

"Hi. Do you really want to look at these? They are not flattering at all."

"Yes." I left a vacuum, so that she couldn't change her mind.

"Well, we may as well get it over with. Can you come up now?"

"I'll be there in ten minutes."

I brushed my teeth just in case, put the two packs of Polaroid film I had bought over the weekend in my tool bag, and rode the elevator to the sixth floor. I walked to apartment 604 and knocked on the door. Lisa opened the door wearing a maternity dress that was a pretty yellow. I couldn't decide if she had put it on for me or not. It wasn't revealing or particularly flattering, but it was thin and bright.

She looked nervous as a cat, but was happy to see me. She said "I don't think you're going to like them."

"There's only one way to find out. Where are they?"

"In the kitchen."

I walked to the kitchen, and the packet from the photo store was sitting there, closed. I sat down and put my tool bag on the floor.

I put my hand over the packet. "Can I see?" I said.

She leaned against the doorway and put her hair behind her ear and said, "You're gonna hate them."

I just smiled. I pulled them out and started slowly going through them.

"Told ya," she said.

I looked at her and said, "The photographer sucks, but the subject matter looks great."

"I'm fat."

"You're hot."

"I thought I was beautiful."

"You're beautifully hot."

"Yeah."

I was ecstatic that she took the hot remark without even batting an eyelash. I wanted her to know I wanted more. I just didn't want to chase her away. She stayed leaning against the doorway as I looked at them one by one.

I said, "We should take more."

"No, we should throw those away and not take any more."

"You want to throw them away?"

"Yeah."

I pushed them into a pile and said, "Well, if you don't want them, I guess I'll just take them with me," and looked at her smiling.

"And what are you going to do with them?"

"Look at them."

Yeah, I don't think so. You need to go get one of those books and look at it."

I laughed. I said, "You need to keep these, and you need to take more. You can't not do this."

"And I suppose you want to be the one that takes them?"

"Well, sure, but I would settle for just being able to see them."

"You're nuts."

I started looking through the pictures again. She watched for a minute.

"Haven't you been tortured enough?" she said.

I didn't answer and kept looking. After another few seconds I said, "Can I, at least, have one to take with me?"

"Why?"

"To look at."

"That's weird."

"Please?"

"One, and if you show anybody, I'll kill you. Understand?"

"I promise."

I went through the pictures and picked the one with the most cleavage, so she would know exactly why I wanted it.

As I put the others back in the packet she said, "Which one did you pick? I showed it to her and she said, "Figures," and took the packet from me and hid it in the back of a kitchen cabinet.

I knew today was not the day, but I felt like I had made significant progress and was feeling more confident that something might eventually happen. I put the picture in my shirt pocket and patted it. I picked up my tool bag and walked to the door. I pulled out my business card from the Willbury and used my pen to write down the phone number of my efficiency for her. I handed it to her.

"You know," I said, "I live on site now, so if you ever want to call me when I'm not working, this is my apartment phone."

I could tell that taking the card was a big line she wasn't sure she should cross. By taking it, she was implying she might call. By refusing it, she was shutting me down. I had instant regret at the move.

I decided to punt and said, "You know, in case something breaks in the middle of the night, there is no sense in calling the emergency number and then having them call me." After I punted, I realized I should have just let it hang.

"Or if I decide I want my picture back?" she said, smiling broadly.

"No refunds," I said and patted my pocket again.

She opened the door, and as I walked out, she kind of did this half curtsy thing and closed the door. I rode the elevator down feeling really good about the situation.

I didn't see her the next day, but the day after that she called me at six o'clock, right after I came in from working.

"This is Lisa. Is this a bad time?"

"Not at all. I just got out of the shower and was relaxing a little bit."

She said, "I can call back later."

"No, its fine. What's going on?"

"Well, I was thinking."

I let it hang.

"I was thinking," she repeated, "maybe I *should* take some pictures."

"I agree."

"If, and it's a big if, if I decide to have them taken, do you want to take them for me?"

"Do I get a copy?"

"You already have one."

"I know. I'm looking at it right now."

"You're crazy."

"Just a little. But to answer your question, how about if I get some Polaroid film and we do this?"

She said, "Do you really want to?"

"Yes. I definitely want to."

"I'm not taking my clothes off," she responded, half-firm, half-flirting.

"I know, but how about lingerie?"

"Nope."

"Aw c'mon?"

"I think you just looked at that book too much, and have a thing for pregnant women."

"Maybe, but that doesn't mean you're not hot."

"I thought I was beautiful?"

"In this picture you're hot."

"Are you really looking at my picture right now?"

"Sort of."

"What does that mean?"

"It's hard to hold the picture and the phone at the same time."

"Why?"

I let my voice get a little huskier.

"I can't tell you," I said.

"Why not?"

"I just can't."

Lisa's voice got quiet and a little sultry now.

"But I don't understand."

"Let's just say the picture is now propped up where I can see it."

"Why aren't you holding it anymore?"

"I can't tell you." I was breathing heavy now in obvious distress. I wanted her to imagine me in bed, stroking myself to her picture. I had just admitted that I had a thing for pregnant women and hoped that my admission would give her an excuse to have an affair with me while her husband was neglecting her.

She said "Why not?"

Let's just say I am lying in bed in a towel. talking to beautiful woman on the phone who may or may not let me take pictures of her in lingerie, and it is very . . . exciting."

"Oh… so you're . . . busy . . .?"

"Does that bother you?"

"No, it's kind of flattering."

"And you don't mind me looking at your picture?"

"Does it make you happy?"

I was breathing flat-out heavily now, and there was no question what I was doing.

"Yes," I whispered, and continued in my pursuit of an orgasm.

She just stayed on the line and listened.

I made myself come, saying in a hushed tone, "Lisa, you are so sexy. Ahhh . . ." I breathed heavily into the phone, recovering from the orgasm. I caught my breath and said, "Would you call me again sometime?"

"Maybe."

"I shower every night after work around this time."

She said, "Good to know."

I said, "Can we still take pictures?"

"Yes."

I said, "I'll get film tomorrow so you can let me know whenever you want to do it, okay?"

"Okay."

"I'll see you later. I need a nap."

"I'll bet."

We hung up, and I cleaned up the mess. I constantly thought about fucking her for the next two days straight, waiting for her to call.

Finally, on Friday she called.

"Do you work Sunday?" she said.

"No," I said, and then she asked me if I would meet her in the park by the US Capital downtown about ten blocks away. I said

"Sure," I said. "Should I bring the film?

"Yes."

I said, "Why there?"

"So, you won't try and convince me to wear lingerie for you."

"What makes you think I would do that?"

Lisa said, "Do I really need to answer that?"

"No, I guess not."

She said, "It's Friday, don't you have a hot date tonight?"

I didn't know if she was fishing or teasing me because I gave her the upper hand.

"Nope," I responded. "Just a date with a picture of a beautiful woman"

She teased, "Is she pregnant too?"

"Well, she's pregnant, but there's no 'too' involved," I said.

"Aren't you tired of that picture yet?"

"Well, I wouldn't mind trading it in for one in lingerie, but I guess that's not happening any time soon."

"Or at all."

"It's okay. I have a great imagination."

"I'll bet you do."

I could hear mild excitement in her voice.

"Do you want to know what I'm imaging right now?"

"I don't know. That's a loaded question."

"If you want to know, I'll tell you."

She was silent and then said quietly, "Okay."

I said, "I'm imagining watching you undress and you don't know I'm there."

"Why don't I know you're there?"

"Because I want to see you in your natural state. I don't want you to be embarrassed. I just want to see your beauty with you relaxed. Then I want you to notice my reflection in the mirror, watching you, but you pretend you don't see me. You just keep brushing your hair and then you rub body lotion all over your stomach and breasts."

I started breathing heavily now and let her deduce I was stroking myself with her permission.

"Eventually," I continued, "you put on some very sexy lingerie and a bathrobe and come back into the living room, where I am supposed to be working on something. You see me nervous and can tell I'm hiding my erection. You can't help yourself because your husband is a fool, and you start letting the bathrobe fall open and let me have glimpses of your lingerie."

I was stroking hard and breathing rhythmically now, and she knew I was close.

"Then what?" she said almost in a whisper.

"Then you let the bathrobe fall open," I continued, talking out of breath, and let me see you. It's white lace and looks so good and . . . Ahaaaaa. Oh, God! Ahh . . . I'm coming . . ."

"Yeah," she said with a slight growl in her throat. I breathed heavily in recovery while she listened.

"You make me crazy," I said.

She said matter-of-factly but sweetly, "I didn't do anything but listen."

"And that's what makes me crazy . . . What time on Sunday?"

She said eleven, and we discussed where we would meet, and made the plans. Before we hung up, I said "Lisa?"

She said, "Yes?"

"Will you at least wear a see-through dress?"

"I'll think about it."

I said, "I'll think about it too."

"I think you've done enough thinking for one night. Goodbye."

We met at the base of the Lincoln Memorial. She was wearing jeans and a blouse, but had a large shoulder bag that I hoped contained a dress she could change into.

I smiled and said, "I got lots of film, even a couple packages of black and white."

"Well, I brought the camera, but I'm not sure this is such a good idea."

"Why not, it's a beautiful day, you're a beautiful girl…"

"I'm fat."

"Who says?"

"My husband won't even look at me."

"He's just got a thing. He'll get over it."

"No, YOU have a thing. He just thinks I'm fat."

I decided to change the subject.

"So, let's take some pictures, and we can talk about tearing them up later."

We walked towards the water. It was warm out. A breeze was coming off the Potomac and blowing her shoulder-length hair into her face. It was cute. I decided it would also make a good picture, and we set her up where the constant breeze pushed her hair slightly across her face and backwards. I wanted her to relax and didn't want to get too aggressive too soon. Things were progressing nicely, and I figured it was just a matter of time before we ended up in bed together.

After a few photos I said, "Did you bring a change of clothes?"

"I brought a sun dress, but it's a little breezy out here for it. It's pretty light."

"Perfect."

"For you."

I just smiled and said, "You can change in there," and walked with her to the welcome center, which had large bathrooms for the tourists.

She went in without argument and came out in a light blue, knee-length maternity dress that was, in fact, very thin. It was going to be interesting to see what would happen once we got near the water with the constant breeze. I took her first to the war memorials, loaded in one of the black-and-white Polaroid film packs, and we took some very artistic pictures of her with her hands on the memorials. Some tourists watched as we took the pictures. Lisa was both flattered and embarrassed at the compliments. I showed people some the pictures as they developed, and all in all, we had a good time.

We bought sodas from a vendor and sat on a bench, looking at our work.

"See, aren't you glad were doing this?" I said.

"I'm still fat."

"You're still beautiful. These pictures are good, and you will be glad in ten years when you find them in some box somewhere."

"Maybe."

I smiled. We sat for a couple of minutes, and then I asked, "So is your husband on the golf course, or is he working today?"

"He left on a plane to Boston. He has a conference. He won't be back until late Tuesday night."

"You didn't want to go?"

"No, it's hard enough being pregnant without flying in airplanes and sitting in hotel rooms all day. I hate airports."

I wanted to use the opportunity as an opening to get closer, but decided to just let it pass for now. She was relaxing with me as if we were just acquaintances, and she hadn't listened to me take care of myself on the other end of a phone line. I suggested we go over to a slightly wooded area behind the Jefferson Memorial, where there were large numbers of flower beds. When we got there, I put her on one knee pretending to pick flowers. The dress crept up her thigh and she tried to pull it down.

I said, "Leave it, it looks good."

She smiled and said, "Yeah," sarcastically, but she didn't pull it down. I stood on a short wall and took a couple more from above, as she was bending over to smell a red rose bush. Her dress had fallen open pretty far, and her enlarged breasts were pushing out against the too-small bra. The pictures weren't overtly sexual, but they were definitely interesting. She looked at them and at me.

"Well," she said, "I know which picture you're gonna want to keep."

"You never know. I might surprise you."

She smiled, letting me know that she knew that just because my mind wasn't all the way in the gutter, that didn't mean it wasn't rolling along the shoulder.

We finished both color packs, and one black-and-white pack. I had one more black-and-white, but we had done enough for one day.

I said, "We'll save this roll for next time."

"Oh, there's gonna be a next time, huh?"

"Sure, you're changing every week. There's gonna be a few 'next times.' "

I could tell she was pleased by my attention. I couldn't tell if she was as sexually aroused as I was, but I was pretty sure by her body language that if I could have checked, she would have been nice and wet.

I walked her to where she parked her car. She reached in and started it and turned on the AC.

She shut the door and said, "I'm going to let it cool down for a minute, I am sweating so bad."

"It's called glistening."

She laughed. "I'm pretty sure this is sweating."

"So, you're going to go home and take a shower too, huh?"

"Probably."

"Mmmmmmm…"

"Yeah, well don't get any ideas, I'll be showering alone, thank you."

"Awwwww..."

"You'll get over it."

I handed her the camera but kept the pictures and started looking through them.

"What are looking for?" she said.

I said, "Don't you want to find out if you're right?"

"Oh, you think you get to keep one, huh? That wasn't *officially* part of the deal."

"What if I say 'Pretty please?' "

"Okay, but only one, and if anyone ever sees it..."

I finished it for her, "You will kill me."

"Exactly."

I looked through and pulled out one she hadn't seen because I had distracted her and skipped over it when we were checking them out. It was her with the sun behind her, and it was shining right through the dress all the way to her crotch. She saw it and grabbed it, and said, "I haven't seen this one."

"I didn't want you to tear it up."

"I should."

I said, "You said I could have one. That's the one I want." I smiled to let her know it wasn't an order, but a request.

She handed it to me and said, "You may as well, you already have it embedded in your brain by now anyway."

I said, "Thanks," and grabbed it from her and handed her the others.

She got in the car and waved as she drove away. It seemed a little awkward to not talk about the next step, but there wasn't an easy way to broach it without us both being obvious about what possible events the next step might entail. I mostly just hoped I hadn't scared her off. It was almost three and I hadn't eaten, so I walked to a takeout, ate a sub, and thought about the day. I did come to one conclusion: I wanted to fuck her more than ever now.

Lisa Part 2

At six o'clock the phone rang. It was Lisa. She was talking in a slightly nervous tone.

"I was wondering," she said, "if you'd wanted to come up for dinner. I made a lasagna and forgot that Rob wasn't here so there's plenty."

"Can we look at the pictures again?"

"You are a little obsessed with pictures, you know."

"Well?"

"Sure, why not. But no funny business."

"Well, we do have a pack of film left. We could take pictures of you in lingerie."

"I don't think so."

"Not even one?"

"Well, if you behave yourself, we'll see. No promises."

"Deal. What time?"

"Seven thirty."

I knocked on the door at 7:31. She was wearing a long maternity dress that was smart, but not enticing. She instructed me to come into the eat-in kitchen, where she was finishing setting things up. There was lasagna and garlic bread.

"I'd offer wine," she said, "but since I'm pregnant we took it out of the house so I wouldn't even be tempted."

I said, "That's okay, I'm too young to drink anyway."

She had her back to me and stopped dead in her tracks. She turned around slowly and said, "That's right, you're just a kid."

"I'm not a kid."

"You're in between. Grown men don't look at pictures and get all worked up over nothing."

"First of all, yes they do, and second, those pictures aren't 'nothing.' You saw those people looking at you today. Those men thought you were sexy."

"How do you do that?"

"Do what?"

"You always manage to turn things around. It's . . . uncanny."

I laughed. "It's easy. You know I'm telling the truth, but you just don't want to admit it."

"Admit what?"

"That taking pictures makes you feel sexy."

"See there, you did it again. I'm not biting this time. Let's eat."

She turned around and continued gathering things for the table. When she turned back, she was trying to hide it but she was smiling.

"Okay," she said, "dig in."

I decided it was time to dial it back a little bit and ask her about other things: her family, where she went to college, other small talk.

After dinner was over, I grabbed our dishes and put them in the sink while she put the leftovers away.

As she was putting way the last of it. I said "Picture time?"

She looked around at me and said, "You don't give up, do you?"

I said, "Nope."

She said, "I don't think anyone wants to see me in lingerie."

"You promised."

"I said 'We'll see.'"

"Right, 'we'll see' you in lingerie."

"I just want one."

"Oh, for your personal collection, huh?"

"I'll swap the other two in for it, if you want me to."

She was quiet. I waited her out.

She said in a weak voice, "What if you don't like it? I mean, what if I come out and it's a big disappointment?"

"I think we both know that won't happen. How about this? We take one picture, and if you don't like it, we tear it up right then and there, and I won't bug you again?"

"Well, that's a big risk for you."

"What is?"

"If I like it, you get to keep pestering me for more. That's an incentive for me to lie."

I said, "I'm willing to risk it."

"You're not the one posing half naked."

"So, we have a deal?"

"Ughhh! I'll be out in a minute. No camera until I say it's okay."

I went and sat in the living room in an easy chair, from where I imagined her husband watched football games. I still wasn't feeling any guilt. I wasn't sure why. I think my desire to fuck her was overpowering my sense of responsibility. I decided to think about it later. I had more important things to deal with.

Lisa called out from the hallway, "Are you sure you want to see this?"

"Absolutely."

"I'm nervous. Turn down the lights."

I killed the lights in both the kitchen and the entryway. The living room had light showing through the drapes from the street lights. It was now dim, but there was plenty of light to see what I wanted to see. I sat back down and said, "Okay, let's see what you look like."

Lisa walked out in a white maternity teddy with white thigh high stockings. She was wearing lace underwear and bra underneath.

I said, "WOW." I semi-discretely adjusted myself in such a way that she couldn't miss it, but I still had deniability.

She said, "I'm nervous."

"We have to take a picture. You look hot!"

"I don't know."

I responded, "Please?"

She said, "Just one. Okay?"

I got out of the chair, picked the Polaroid camera and film off the counter, and loaded the film while she stood uncomfortably in the living room.

"Where should I stand?"

"You need to lie on the bed."

"No. That's too . . . too . . . too something . . ."

"It'll be fine."

"Ughh . . ." she said, walking down the hall and going into the guest room. "How about this bed," she said as she sat on the edge. "The other bed feels too wrong."

"This is fine." I was getting really turned on now, thinking this might be the night.

She said, "Where do you want me?"

I said, "Get on the bed on your knees with your hands at your sides."

She climbed on the bed as I asked, and I could tell she was really getting turned on by the whole ordeal.

She said, "Like this?"

"You need to take the bra off."

"No."

"I'll leave the room. We need the bra off; the picture will be incredible."

"No," she said with only minor defiance, begging a response from me.

"If I only get one picture, then it needs to be with the bra off. If you'll let me take more, I will take one with the bra on, and you can see what I mean."

"Okay, you can take two."

I instructed her where I wanted her, turned the lamp on, and then the overhead light off.

I positioned myself and then said, "Okay, look at that picture on the wall, and don't blink."

I took the picture and it came out of the camera, and as we waited for it to develop, I went over and held it up, standing close to her with my legs rubbing the edge of the bed. I could smell a whiff of perfume and that made me feel like she might think tonight was the night too.

Once it was developed, she said, "Okay that's it."

"Nope. We need one without the bra."

"This one is fine. This is too thin to not wear a bra."

"It was made to not wear one."

"Not for pictures"

"But nobody is going to see them, remember?" I said with a smile.

She said, "But you're going to see it."

"Which is why I want you to take off the bra."

"Okay, but that's it. No more. One picture without the bra and that's it."

"Okay."

"All right. Get out so I can change."

I went into the hall and closed the door.

I waited for a few seconds and said, "How's it going?"

"Don't come in yet!"

"I won't. I was just checking."

"Okay, you can come in."

She was back in the same place. This time, the bra was gone. Her nipples were large and dark, and you could see everything clear as a bell even in the dim light.

"I feel naked."

"You look beautiful." I put the camera up before she could protest. "Okay," I continued, "the same pose as last time."

She did as I instructed, and I took the picture.

I caught it as it popped out of the camera, set it down on the dresser and said, "Now one for you."

"I said one."

"This one's for you."

"Okay, but this is really it. Promise?"

We took another picture, and by then the other one was fully developed. She looked at it and said, "My God, I'm naked."

I said, "You're hot is what you are."

I could tell she was turned on big time now. She was looking at a picture of herself in a see-through teddy, fully exposed, while still on her knees on a bed in a see-through teddy.

I smiled broadly and put the camera down on the dresser and said, "We'll save the rest of the film for next time."

"Oh, there's going to be a next time, is there?" She was smiling.

"Unless you'd rather I just finish it now. There's like six left."

"No, this is enough for now. You need to take your picture and go, and I need to go put some clothes on."

"Can I watch?"

"No! You need to skedaddle."

"All right. I'll just head down to my lonely apartment and hope the phone rings."

"Or you could call a girl your own age."

"But I don't have pictures of them to look at while we talk."

She was chickening out. I could feel it. She was interested, but she was not quite there.

She said, "You think this is glamorous, huh?"

"As a matter of fact, I do."

"Well, you skipped over the part about my boobs being always tender and that I have to get up like clockwork every three hours just to pee."

"Well, that's a good thing."

"How's that?"

"It just so happens that one of my favorite fantasies is to have a beautiful woman call me in the middle of the night and ask me what I'm dreaming about."

"How often does that happen?"

"Well, it's never actually happened. That's why they call it a fantasy. But, you know, that doesn't mean it couldn't happen . . ."

"Git."

I smiled and left, taking one last look at her still in a completely see-through teddy.

The phone rang at one-fifteen in the morning. It was Lisa.

"Hello."

"It's Lisa."

"Hi, I was just dreaming about you."

"Sure, you were."

"Well, actually, I was sleeping, but I have been thinking about you all night. It was kind of like a dream."

"What does that mean?"

"Well, like if I was almost asleep and it felt like a dream. Is that close enough?"

"Maybe. What were you, um, 'almost dreaming about?'"

"I was giving you a bubble bath."

"A bubble bath?"

"Yes. We were in your apartment and there were candles everywhere. I was rubbing you down with the soap while you lay there in the tub with your eyes closed."

"Go on," she said. So, I continued for a while expressing my desire for her. I could hear her breathing deep, and I was too inexperienced to ask, but I was positive she was rubbing herself too. When I came, she growled, as if she came too.

When it was over, she said, "You have a very vivid imagination."

I said, "Is that a bad thing?"

"No, it's actually kind of cool. I just don't know how you think of all those details."

"It's easy when you have a picture for inspiration."

"Yeah, well that was a lot of inspiration for one picture."

We sat there in silence for a few seconds. I was thinking she wanted to say something, but if she did, she let the moment pass.

She finally said, "I'm going back to sleep now."

I said, "Can I ask you one question, and you promise to tell me the truth?"

"Maybe."

"Are you still wearing the teddy?"

"I plead the fifth."

"Ah . . . Inspiration; it's everywhere."

"Good night, Dino."

Lisa, Part 3

I didn't see Lisa at all the next day. I didn't want to lose our momentum, and I was feeling anxious. No matter how hard I tried, I couldn't concentrate. She felt so close yet so far, and I didn't want to have her slip through my fingers.

I shouldn't have worried. That night at six fifteen Lisa called. She was very nervous, but I could tell she was happy to hear my voice.

She said, "I've been wanting to call you all day."

"Why?"

"Because I want to ask you something."

I said, "You can ask me anything."

"Okay, here goes."

I stayed silent. I didn't know what was coming, but it sounded like it was going to be a good thing.

"First, do you really think about actually doing stuff like giving me a bubble bath, or is it just something you think about because it feels good?"

"No, everything I've ever told you is something I would love to ...um ... do."

"Okay," she hesitated for a moment, then continued, "well if I let you come over and give me a bubble bath, would you promise to only go as far as... Would you promise to, um, behave yourself and not ... you know, go too far?"

"I promise that you would be in charge in that department."

"You could never tell anyone."

"I promise I will never tell anyone."

"God, I can't believe I'm doing this. Okay. Do you want to come over tonight?"

"What time?"

"Nine o'clock, but remember your promise, and if I chicken out, you can't be mad at me okay?"

"I promise. I'll see you at nine."

I was on cloud nine. I knew playing with a married woman was playing with fire, but in my head, I was fulfilling the dream she had the first time I heard her talking to her friend by the pool. I didn't want to get involved in her marriage. I just wanted to fulfill her sexual needs without the baggage of a relationship. I felt oh so close. Nine o'clock couldn't come soon enough.

I arrived right at nine, freshly showered in a T-shirt and nylon running pants. She answered the door in a bathrobe.

She said, "Hi, c'mon in. Just so you know, I am this close to chickening out." She held her thumb and index finger a millimeter apart.

I said, "It's all fine, I just want you to feel comfortable."

She walked down the hallway and I followed. She stopped at the closed bathroom door and said, "Well here we are."

I just smiled.

She continued. "All right, we are really doing this. You go in and draw a nice hot bath and keep all of your clothes on. Got it?"

I said, "Got it."

She said, "And another thing. No matter whatever else happens, never kiss me on the lips, okay?"

I nodded.

"Promise?"

I said, "I promise!"

She opened the door and I walked in.

She said, "Let me know when it's all ready," and closed the door behind me.

The room had fifteen or twenty short fat candles lit. They were everywhere: on the back of the toilet, on the vanity, on the floor, even in the soap dishes. There were towels laid out, and a new bar of soap was lying in a washcloth. I drew the bath, making it pretty hot so it would last a while. I put in the little bowl of bubble bath she had left on the edge and chose the water height carefully, so that I could add more hot water later. I assumed we were going to be there a while.

I went to the door, cracked it, and said, "All set."

I then sat on the closed toilet lid. When she came in, she had turned off the hallway light so she was almost in the dark. She was wearing a white fluffy bathrobe that came to her knees and was getting a little too small around the middle but still covered everything.

She asked if the water was nice and hot and I said it was. She lifted a foot over the edge and stuck her toe in.

She said, "That's going to feel so good." I just kind of nodded in agreement. Lisa looked at me and asked, "Would you turn around?"

"Turn around?"

"So, I can get in."

"How about if I just close my eyes?"

"Please?"

I spun around and faced the other way and waited for her to tell me she was in.

"Okay, you can turn around."

I turned, and she was sitting in the tub facing me with her knees, stomach, and breasts out of the water. Her breasts were swollen, and I assumed they were probably much smaller before the pregnancy. Her skin was slightly tan from the pool. Even her stomach. I assumed there must have been a bikini at some point that I had missed seeing her in.

I said, "God, you are hot." She ignored the comment, but I could tell she was pleased that I was happy.

She said, "Ground rules okay?"

"Sure."

"Lift up that towel." I lifted the towel and underneath was a wash mitt that fit over your hand. "Put it on." I complied. "Now give me your hand." I stuck my hand out still not saying anything. She took my hand and dipped it in the water until it was wet and lifted it back out. She then took the new bar of soap and put it in the water and soaped up the mitten. She set the soap down and said, "I'm very tender, so be gentle, okay?" and put my hand over one of her breasts.

I gently rubbed the soap over her, being careful not to hit the nipple, which was larger than normal and stiff. It was actually fascinating to see the changes that nature does. I thought for a moment that her husband was an idiot for missing this. I used my other hand to pick up the bowl that had contained the bubble bath and dipped it in the water. I rinsed it a couple of times then used it to pour warm water over the breast I had washed and moved to the other side. She was watching my face the entire time. I just kept slowly caressing her with the soapy mitt. I pulled it away and reached for the soap.

She took the soap from me, got it wet, and lathered up the mitt again. I washed her arms, and moved up to her neck. I whispered for her to lean back as I went all the way up to her hairline under her ears. I poured the warm water over each side, and she moaned both times. I took the soap and put it in her hands to lather the mitt up again, which she did. She was watching my face, and I was staring at her body as if it were a work of art. I wanted to see how aroused I could get her. I was hard as stone and worried that I might come in my pants and not be able to perform if we went that far. I was hoping to fuck, but it was far from a done deal.

I moved next to her stomach, being very careful not to go too far down. I wanted to save the best for last. I moved in close with my face and washed her stomach oh so gently, acknowledging the precious cargo. I used my hand to rinse it off, and when I was done, I kissed it. She didn't mind at all.

I said, "I want to do your back," and she slowly moved to her knees. I just ignored the awkwardness of it.

She was now in the tub on her bent knees with her belly almost all of the way out of the water. I handed her the soap again and she lathered up the mitt. I started at the back of her neck and went all the way down slowly until I was in between her small ass cheeks. She let her head roll backward and was obviously enjoying what was happening. I put the mitt into the warm water and used it to rinse her back and butt. I then gently eased her back to where she was before, again ignoring the awkwardness of it again. I then gave her the soap, and she lathered up the mitt. I did both her feet and legs, up to her knees. I rinsed them off with my other hand.

I gave her the soap and she began to lather the mitt up again. She knew there was only one place left and she wasn't hesitating about giving me plenty of lather. I rested the mitt on one of her knees and used my other hand to add some hot water. I wanted to build up the suspense for what was coming next. I washed the inside of both of her thighs, then moved to the lower half of her stomach. I slid my hand down and immediately hit thick pubic hair that came up higher than I was used to. It threw my bearings off for a second, taking me a moment to find my place. She didn't seem to notice. I used the mitt to wash between her legs, making long strokes from her belly button all the way down until I hit the bottom of the tub. She repositioned herself, and we found a nice rhythm.

I was pretty sure I was hitting all the right places. It only took a couple of minutes for her to come. She put her hand over the mitt and held it there, moving her thighs in and out as she trembled and moaned. I just kept the pressure steady on her pubic mound and let her grind into the mitt. She knew better what she needed, and I was happy to just be a part of it. She lay back and relaxed from the stress relief. I had the urge to kiss her but I knew the rules. I just kept my hand there waiting for a cue. Her hands were still over mine, although they were relaxed now and just resting there. She was drunk with relief, and I didn't doubt that her husband hadn't had sex with her in six months. She slowly pulled her hands away.

"That felt so fucking good. I feel great."

I was completely surprised. I had never heard her utter a curse word, and this was a side I was thinking I might like.

I said, "You are so sexy. I am so turned on right now."

"That makes two of us."

I started to rub her a little bit, but she put her hand on mine and said, "I'm ready to get out."

"I'll get a towel."

She stood up, and I helped her step over the tub and onto the floor. It was technically the first time I had seen her naked, because she had climbed in the tub when my back was turned. She had a large pubic triangle that went up close to her belly button. She must have caught me looking at her.

"You'll have to excuse me," she said. "I can't reach to shave like I want." I just ignored her comment.

"Can I dry you off?" I said.

"That would be nice."

I placed a bath towel over her shoulders, then took the other towel and started with her ankles and dried her off while she dried her face and arms. I dried her back and ass while she did her stomach and between her legs.

I said, "Do you have moisturizer?"

"How did I know that was coming?"

"Do you?"

"Right behind you."

I looked over and on the shelf was some vitamin E massage oil.

I said, "Do you want to sit or stand?

"Stand."

I began at her ankles and calves. I took my time and rubbed it in well. I moved up and did her knees and her thighs about three quarters of the way. I was mostly behind her now, and rubbed the oil into the back of her thighs all the way to her ass cheeks. I pushed up a little and she moaned. I could see between her legs from the back, and I was fully aroused. I used both my hands and spread her ass cheeks and looked at her pussy. She knew what I was doing and allowed it. She leaned a little forward.

I looked around her and said, "Lean on the vanity."

She leaned and I could see everything. She was engorged and bright red. I put my fingers inside of her and she was soaked. She moaned audibly as I used one hand to finger her and the other to rub the massage oil into her ass cheeks. She pushed back against my hand hard. I rubbed harder. I began fucking her with three fingers while she rode back and forth against my hand. I was mauling her ass cheeks with my free hand. When she was close to coming, I got the sudden urge out of nowhere, and bit her ass cheek as I pumped her hard and rubbed her other cheek hard with my other hand. She came, and liquid came out of her, all over my hand and ran down her leg. She was growling now in an almost animal tone. She was bucking against my hand, and I just kept going until she slowed down like a train slowly coming into the station. I didn't know if it was female come, urine, or water from being in the tub, but it was sexy as hell.

I grabbed the towel and wiped up the spillage and then stood up and said, "I want to fuck you."

"Not here, in the guest room."

I opened the door and she walked ahead of me. She said, "Bring a towel."

I grabbed a towel and caught up with her in the room. She was lying back on the bed.

"How do we do this?" she said.

"Come forward a little," I said. I positioned her so that when I lifted her legs, she would be right at the end of the bed.

I stripped in about ten seconds and was inside of her in another five. I started fucking her hard and fast, and after only a couple of minutes, I realized I was too close and needed to slow down.

I said, "I need to slow down or I'll come.

She shouted, "Come."

I said, " No."

She repeated, "Come. I want to feel you come."

I lasted about another thirty seconds and filled her with come. She said, "Yes," the whole time I was doing my orgasmic thrusts.

I slowly slid out and put the towel that was on the bed in my place. She said, "I'm crying."

I said "Why?"

"I don't know. I just feel so good right now. I think I thought you were just messing with my head, but I really do turn you on. It feels so good to know I'm not ugly."

"You thought you were ugly?"

"My husband won't look at me."

"He's just confused. Once the baby is born, he will be all over you."

"What if he doesn't want me anymore?"

"Don't worry, he will."

She was still lying on her back with the towel between her legs, and I began caressing her knees.

I said in a soft voice, "Relax and enjoy the moment."

"Mmmm . . ." she said, closing her eyes. That let me know she was past the pangs of guilt or fear or whatever it was, and was there with me again.

I caressed her thighs and moved up to her stomach, rubbing my fingertips across her pregnant belly. I circled around and went down between her legs and inside the towel where it was pushed up against her. I ran my fingers through the wet pubic hair and teased the entrance as she moaned softly, obviously enjoying the moment like I had asked.

I kept my hand there, rubbing her gently, and made my way to the side of the twin bed so I was next to her, looking down on her. She was still flat on her back with her knees high, her legs spread wide, and her feet on the end of the bed.

I said, "I have a fantasy for you if you want to hear it."

"Uh-oh."

"Do you want to hear it?"

"Will I like it?"

"I hope so."

"Okay."

I began, "Well, the situation is this. You took a long hot bath, and then came in here to take a nap, so you didn't disturb your husband. You fall asleep and you wake up to realize that he has come in to check on you and decided to look closely at you while you were sleeping."

"I don't know about this."

I said, "Trust me," and continued. "You pretend to be asleep and are nervous, but it turns out he is looking closely and isn't leaving. He rubs his fingers gently across your stomach, then he slides his hand up and gently caresses your breasts, cupping them to feel the difference. He leans over and kisses your stomach."

I could feel her hips gently pushing against my hand, still rubbing the outside lips of her pussy, lubricated with both her and my fluids. I leaned down and gently kissed her stomach. I was talking in an almost whisper now.

"You could feel his eyes on you as he slid his hand down between your legs and ran his fingers through your pubic hair until his hand was right here." At that point, I slid two fingertips inside and teased her with some gentle but firm rubbing. She moaned audibly.

I continued. "You could hear him unbuckling his pants but didn't want him to know you were awake so you just lay there and let him touch you." I was rubbing her harder now with a solid but slow rhythm. She was beginning to push back against my hand, letting me know she liked where this was heading.

I leaned closer to her ears and whispered, "You could hear him breathing heavier now, and you were sure he was getting turned on." At this point, I took my free hand and put it in hers and said, "He reaches over and takes your hand and puts it on his cock to show you how hard he is." I slid her hand over and she reached for my cock and squeezed it as it finished engorging fully erect. I started thrusting harder and she stroked my cock with the same rhythm.

I whispered in her ear. "Do you want to feel your husband's hard cock inside you?"

"Yes." She pulled harder now.

"Do you want it inside you now?"

"Yes."

"Say it. Say, 'I want my husband's cock inside me now.' "

"I want my husband's cock inside me now."

I pulled my hand away, pulled the towel aside, and went and teased the entrance with my now fully hard cock.

"Say it again. Say you want his cock."

"Oh, I want his cock. I want his cock."

"Say, 'fuck me.'"

"Fuck me."

"Say it again!"

"Fuck me!!"

I slid myself inside and began fucking her hard right away. She put her hands down and touched the sides of my hips and thrust herself against me. I pushed her knees back and fucked her hard and steady. She was moaning steadily, almost humming in the pleasure

I said, "You love your husband's cock, don't you?"

"Yes."

"Do you love his cock inside you? Do you want his come?"

"Yes!"

"Then fuck him. Push your pussy against that cock."

She stared rocking hard against me trying to make me come. She was fucking me hard and loving every second of it. Her eyes were closed, and I was sure she was thinking about her husband, but I didn't care. It was me that made her this hot, and my cock she was fucking. I was inside her head and her pussy at the same time, and it was euphoric. It was taking me a long time to come, but she didn't seem to mind.

When I was getting close, I said, "Do you want to feel your husband come inside you?"

"Yes!"

"Beg for it."

"Come, baby. I need your come. Please, I need it so bad."

"I'm coming."

"Yes, baby! Come. Come. Come."

She was fucking me hard now. I came inside of her and thrust hard against her counter thrusts. The bed was saturated now with our wetness.

I could feel it running down my legs. It was an incredibly sexy feeling. I stayed inside of her for a long time. Her eyes were still closed. I slowly slid out as she drifted into a daze. I took the towel and cleaned her up a little, and then pushed it between her legs, kissed her stomach, took my clothes into the other room, dressed, and let myself out. I was sure she was going to sleep well. I knew I was.

Lisa, Part 4

Lisa and I began have sex almost daily for the next two weeks or so. She would page me and I would go to her apartment. She would be in her bathrobe ready for action. I always told her how hot I was for her. It was just like the first time I heard her talking to her friend Tammy at the pool. She needed sex. It was fun. I would have her pretend I was her husband, and she liked it. After about two weeks we were lying in bed after sex, and I was playing with her pubic hair covered in my come and her secretions. She was always beyond wet. She said it wasn't like that before she became pregnant and was worried that I was turned off by it. I assured her it was just the opposite. We were just making idle talk. She mentioned that she was getting "fatter" and felt like she was "fat and hairy" and wished she could reach to trim herself. I said I would trim her if she wanted.

She looked at me and said, "You're serious?"

"Sure. It would be fun."

"Fun?"

"Sexy fun, yeah. I want to."

"Really?"

"Yeah, why not?"

She thought about it for a minute.

"If I got embarrassed, would you stop?" she said.

"Of course."

"I'll think about it." We moved to other things.

We moved to other things. The next morning, she called me and said, "If

I get everything to, you know, trim me, can you come visit this afternoon?"

"What time?"

"Two."

"I'll be there."

She opened the door in her bathrobe and I went in. Her hair was still wet, so I assumed she was fresh out of the bath.

She looked at me and said, "This is weird."

"But kind of sexy?"

"In a weird way."

She led me to the guest room, which is where we always had sex. We never used 'their' bedroom. Deep down she did love her husband. I knew I was just pinch hitting. We never really talked about it, but I kept him in her fantasies, as a way of letting her know I knew the score.

She had everything laid out on the dresser: two pairs of scissors, three new ladies' razors, shaving cream, a bowl of water, baby oil and towels. There was also a giant bath towel spread out on the bed.

She said, "Are you sure you want to do this?"

I took her hand and put it to my crotch and said, "What do you think?"

She said, "You *are* weird, you know."

"I know. Lay down."

She lay on the towel and opened the bathrobe. She lifted her knees up. She was now spread wide open for my prying eyes to take in. I took one of the towels off the dresser and said, "Lift up." I put the smaller towel under her butt to catch the bulk of what I was going to cut.

"So how far do you want me to go?"

"I'm not sure. They're going to shave me before I deliver, so I guess we can go as far as you want."

"Have you ever been completely shaved before?"

"Once in high school. Usually, I just keep it ladylike."

"Ladylike?" I laughed.

"You know, a triangle trimmed neatly."

I said, "I want to shave you completely."

"I figured as much. If you want to, it's okay with me. It will just mean I won't have to deal with it until after the baby comes."

I said, "Well, you know, once I shave it, I'm gonna have to come back and do this once a week. Once you start you can't stop."

"Yeah, well we have to get through today first."

I ran my fingers through her pubic hair and she was already drenched. I was hoping this would turn her on. I was glad my instincts were correct. I started with the scissors and cut the hair as short as possible. She just lay there not saying anything. She was comfortable with me and her nudity now, so she wasn't nervous.

I said, "Do you have a hand mirror?"

"On the dresser."

I went over, and sure enough there was one she had obviously thought of that I hadn't noticed.

"Do you wanna see?"

"Yes."

I held the mirror so she could see herself, and she said, "Wow, what a difference."

"You haven't seen anything yet."

I took the mirror back and said, "Okay, you go back to sleep and I'll go back to work."

"Work, huh?"

"I am an artist. That's how we refer to our endeavors."

"Okay, go to 'work.' "

I covered her with the shaving gel and shaved her everywhere, rinsing the razor in the water and keeping her clean.

I said, "This is making me so hard; I might have to take a break and jerk off."

"Yeah, sure."

"Do you want to see it?"

"No, I believe you. I just don't quite get it."

"But you like that I'm a little wacky."

"Most of the time."

I went back to work. I was done with everything, except the most tender and vulnerable parts. I switched to a new razor and baby oil to make sure I didn't make a mistake. She was swollen from the pregnancy and the increased blood flow was making her very excited. I pulled and stretched the skin and removed every hair I could see. I rubbed baby oil all over the outside, and she was sucking in air from the good feeling.

"Are you done?"

"With the front. You need to turn over."

"No, that's too embarrassing."

"No, it's not."

"Yes, it is."

I thought for a second, and then said, "Please?" Sometimes a little was just enough.

"Do you really want to?"

"Yes."

"Ughhhhh . . . Okay." She slowly turned over.

"You need to be up on your knees," I said and she complied. Her ass was still small and looked even smaller now that her belly and breasts had swollen much more since the first time I had seen them.

I realized that I had missed more than I thought, so I pulled out the scissors and trimmed everything down low before I used the razor. I rubbed baby oil on her ass and upper thighs, where I had missed. She was nervous at first, but I kept rubbing the baby oil in while I was working. She started getting into it. When I was done, I began rubbing baby oil everywhere I had shaved. She was moaning audibly now. I was rubbing her clit with well-oiled fingers and running my other oiled hand all over her ass cheeks. She started pushing her ass against my hand, and I pushed back harder to meet her thrusts. I moved my fingers from her clit to inside of her. I used four fingers and began stretching the entrance out with the baby oil and her wetness. She moaned louder and pushed hard against me, grinding her ass in a gyrating motion against my hand.

Every time my hand slid down between her ass cheeks she would moan louder. I started going in closer and closer inside the gap, finger-fucking her with a solid rhythm now. She was lifting her ass up like a cat; I started teasing the entrance to her ass by running my fingers right over it. I took my hand away for a second and grabbed the baby oil and poured a stream at the top between her cheeks and caught it right as it got to the bottom. She moaned in ecstasy as I put a finger inside of her, and then she growled in satisfaction. I used both hands to fuck her. She came in about thirty seconds. She was out of breath but not finished.

She rolled over on her back and said, "I want you." I slid everything out of the way, kicked off my shoes, pulled my pants and underwear off, and was inside of her as quick as I could get there. She was fucking me more than I was fucking her. I had turned her on to a whole new level that I hadn't seen before. I fucked her hard. I lifted her legs to my shoulders and went in as deep as I could. She was rocking towards me with every thrust. She put her hand down and felt herself. I guessed that the smoothness made her feel sexy. I put my hand over her hand and pushed it to her clit. I started her rubbing it, then pulled my hand away and watched as she fucked me and got herself off. She came again with another growl, rubbing herself harder than I ever had. She was breathing short breaths as she lay back and collapsed, her hand still between her legs.

I hadn't come, but it didn't matter. She was done, and I would finish later thinking about it. I slowly slid out of her as she lay there. I took a towel and wiped her off. I realized how much wetness there was now that there wasn't hair there to absorb it. It was sexy. I put all of the shaving items back on the dresser, lifted up the bed sheet and draped as much of it as I could over her, and bent down and gently suckled a nipple.

She smiled and said, "I'll call you."

Lisa was getting close to her delivery date, and we were not having hour-long trysts like before. She was, however, as horny as ever. Once she walked into my office and shut the door.

"I need attention."

I said, "Lock the door."

"Is it safe?"

"I'm the only one working today. We're fine."

She locked the door, and I walked over and turned her around, and sat her up on the desk, sliding my hands under her skirt.

I said, "No underwear?"

"They're in my purse."

I touched her, and she was soaked. I bent down to go down on her.

"No, I need you inside me," she said.

I stood back up. She helped get my cock out and finished getting it hard. She leaned backwards and put her hands on the back edge of the desk. I put her feet on the two chairs in front of the desk and she held on while I pumped her hard. She came in about two minutes.

"Now you," she said.

I said, "I'm getting close."

She said, "I love your cock. I want to feel you come."

She was rocking forward and back as best she could.

She said, "Do you like fucking my pussy?"

"Yes."

"Are you going to come for me?"

"Yes."

I fucked hard for another twenty seconds or so and exploded inside of her. I slowed my thrusts down slower and slower. I slid out and went to my locker and grabbed a clean T-shirt and cleaned her up. She was so big now she could barely reach anyway.

"What was that all about?" I said.

"I don't know. I was just on fire."

Another time, she was coming in with groceries in this little hand truck carrier. We had gotten into the elevator together. As soon as the door closed, she grabbed my hand and put it down the front of her stretch pants.

"You have six floors to make me come."

I put three fingers inside of her. She was already soaked. When we got to the sixth floor, I popped open the panel with my free hand and turned the elevator off for another minute until she came. When the door opened, she said, "Thank you," and walked away, as if I had only carried her groceries.

She called me the day before she was supposed to have the baby, and we talked for a while about how this was fun but had to stop. We were both okay with it. She was in love with her husband and praying that he would want her physically again once the baby was born. She said he was great in every other way, but she couldn't imagine a sexless marriage if he didn't want sex anymore. I told her it was just a thing, and happened to lots of guys for some reason. I tried to convince her it was *because* he loved her that he was being too careful.

She had a six-pound, eight-ounce baby boy named David after his grandfather.

She gave me a going away present two weeks after she came home from the hospital. She called and asked me if I could come up, that she had something for me. When I got there, she answered the door, holding the baby. After the oohs and aahs, she went into the kitchen and handed me an envelope. I opened it and found ten naked pictures of her that she had taken of herself with the Polaroid camera.

I said, "Wow, this is a nice surprise."

"Well, I figured you might need something to look at in case I call you to say hi sometime."

"Sounds good to me. I get off at six."

"Ha, ha."

I smiled and looked at how much different she looked already. Her face had thinned back to normal and she had dropped a lot of the baby weight. She really was an attractive girl.

She said, "Dino?"

"Yes?"

"Thank you."

"For what?"

She pursed her lips and kind of shook her head. Then she said, "Oh, by the way, Robert is already trying to have sex, so I think everything is going to be okay."

"Good, that makes me happy. I knew he would come around."

After that, we would smile as we saw each other in the hallway or lobby, but she never called. I was okay with that. I had almost half the pictures and all of the memories.

Inez

I've been close to being in love twice in my life, and Inez was one of them. She was a recent college graduate with a job as a curator's assistant at the Museum of Natural History in Washington DC. I met her at a little place called Blues Alley. It is a semi-famous club in the heart of DC that was a visual disappointment to tourists because it was truly a genuine musicians' paradise. It was free of the Hollywood decorations, but there were plenty of old pictures of nobodies to the rest of the world, but legends to the locals.

I was there to see a pianist named Ron Elliston, who I had seen once before at a jazz festival. He was fabulous and really knew his way around a jazz piano. He was playing for a singer named Ronnie Wells, a black woman with a voice I would put up against Ella Fitzgerald. I noticed Inez, a smallish brunette, in the corner with a group of about five others, both men and women. They were all around my age, which was twenty-three. I couldn't tell if she was with a guy or not, but I was mesmerized by her smile and body language. She seemed to really like watching Ronnie sing and Ron play, so when intermission came, I went over and asked her what she thought of the show, as a way to start a conversation. She said she liked it and asked if I was a musician. I said I could sing and play a little guitar but had never performed. I said that I mostly loved watching talented people. She wasn't attached, and we hit it off right away.

She was a little shy, and I wasn't, so I took her in tow right up to the stage after the second set. I introduced myself to them, and then introduced Inez, and told them how much we both loved what they were doing. They were very gracious, as I was sure they would be. Inez was smitten with my confidence. I got her number and we met for lunch the following week on Capitol Hill, right near her work. We clicked. She was very reserved, had a good upbringing, and her goals were pretty much to be a curator someday and to be happy. She was also a virgin, and not the kind I had met at AU that lied about it to her future judge or CEO boyfriend. She said she just didn't want her first time to be with someone who was more interested in her body than her soul, and time got away from her.

We dated for almost six months before we decided it was time to get her past it. She was definitely in love with me, and I had feelings for her but didn't know if it was love or not. I felt like if it actually was, I would know it without question. I was honest with her about this, but I think she pretended I was in love with her, but just hadn't realized it. In the first six months we had done everything but go 'all the way.' She was shy but very sexual for someone who had never had sex.

We were coming up on the six-month anniversary of the time we first met at Blues Alley. She asked if we could make that night special. I said, "Sure," and she said, "No, I mean *really* special."

I knew what she was talking about and I asked her directly.

"Are you sure this is something you're ready for? I mean, I have to be honest, I really care about you, but you can do better than me," which was my chicken way of saying I wasn't going to marry her, or anyone, for that matter.

"I'm not interested in doing better than you, but I know the score. I want you to be the first. I trust you. Plus, we have already almost done it like a hundred times."

"I said, "Okay, where do you want to go to make it special?"

"The Greenbrier."

The Greenbrier is a resort on the Virginia-West Virginia line. She had gone there once before when she had a work retreat. I went camping with some friends and stopped in to see her while she was there. It was a beautiful place with all kinds of amenities, and private suites with fireplaces and hot tubs. It was pricey, but Inez was worth it. I said okay. She made the reservations; and on a cold day in January we drove through a snow storm to get there. They had had a lot of cancellations and upgraded us to a premium suite with a spa, two fireplaces, one gas and one real wood, and view of the valley. They also had so much food that was going to spoil that they made a buffet and allowed the guests to fill up plates and eat in their room if they wanted. It was great.

Inez was nervous as a cat. She had no reservations, she was just not a seductress, and I think she thought I expected her to be. She didn't want to drink because she didn't want to be drunk and not remember "every moment," but I convinced her to have a glass and a half of wine to loosen her up.

She had denied me sex for two weeks beforehand and didn't change clothes in front of me either. She said she wanted things as new as possible. I wanted it to be special for her but didn't want it to be too romantically special. I didn't want to feel like it was a trap. I remember feeling bad for having those thoughts and realize now those feelings are just a part of me, for whatever reason, and had nothing to do with Inez, or anyone else for that matter.

My mixed-up emotions notwithstanding, I wanted her badly. I imagined being inside of her all the time. I told her I fantasized about it, and she admitted that she did too.

We brought up a feast from the buffet and stocked the refrigerator, and decided we would nibble all weekend instead of having meals. I lit the wood fireplace with firewood from the snow-covered balcony. The view was wonderful when we arrived, but it was dark now and still snowing. I suggested we sit in the spa and watch a movie on the big screen TV. She said okay to that, but we couldn't be naked.

"I didn't bring a swimsuit because, um… it is snowing, and its January."

"Well, wear your boxers. I brought mine."

"Why did you bring a bathing suit?"

"In case we went in the spa… before…"

"Before what?" She was embarrassed now. It was very cute.

"Ha, ha."

"All right, I'll wear my boxers."

We put a movie on and went into the spa. It was wonderful. I reached over and cracked a window ever so slightly, so we had a combination of hot water, cold air, and dry heat from the fire stimulating us. Inez lit some candles, and all in all, it was a perfect setting. I had made a mountain of shrimp from the buffet, and we fed each other shrimp as we sat in the spa and watched the movie. The glass of wine, enhanced by the spa, made her a little lightheaded, but it did its intended purpose, and she wasn't nervous anymore. After the movie I turned the TV off with the remote.

"Well," I said, "it's time. Are you sure this is what you want?"

"Absolutely."

"Okay, well I guess we should retire to the bedroom then?"

"You retire to the bedroom. I need to go to the bathroom and get ready."

"Does that mean there is going to be a fashion show?"

"Maybe."

"I'll meet you in the bedroom in twenty minutes then?"

"Sounds like a plan."

She kissed me, hopped out, grabbed a towel, and disappeared into her bathroom. I went in the other bath, took a five-minute shower, brushed my teeth, put on the big fluffy bathrobe from the Greenbrier, took a condom out of my bag, tore the corner to save time later, and put it in the pocket. I then went into the bedroom with its giant California king-sized bed, dimmed the lights, and laid on the bed with my back against the headboard and my ankles crossed, waiting to see what she was going to surprise me with.

About five minutes later, I heard the bathroom door open and she said, "Are you ready?"

"I'm ready."

She eased out of the bathroom, leaving the light on, closing the door almost all the way giving me a silhouette that was absolutely stunning. She was wearing a full-length, sheer white gown that buttoned up the front and, as the light showing through proved, nothing else. She was a little over five feet and one hundred ten pounds. In the gap between her legs, I could see the light shining through, giving me a perfect outline. No sex, and not seeing her naked for a couple of weeks had served its purpose. I was stone hard and wanted her more than ever.

She went over to one of the bags and said, "I have a present for you."

"Now?"

"Yep, now." She brought me a small box, barely wrapped, and said, "Open it."

I opened it; it was a plastic case of birth control pills. I looked at her quizzically.

"Open it," she said.

I opened the case, and it was empty.

I said "I don't understand?"

She looked at me and said, "It's empty because I've been on the pill for six weeks. I don't want my first time to be with a condom."

I leaned over and kissed her and said, "Smart girl."

"I try."

I slid off the bed and stood in front of her.

I said, "You look gorgeous."

"Do you like it?"

"I like it."

I kissed her deeply. I held her face in my hands and purposely kept my erection from pushing into her. I needed her to know I cared about her. She was so different than so many other girls I had met. She was a sweetheart and unpretentious, and felt no need to impress anyone. She loved her work and she wanted to enjoy life without all the typical drama of girls our age. She also never made me feel guilty for not going to college to be some hot shot in the business world. She respected that I worked hard, even if it wasn't as a brain surgeon. I didn't know where we were headed, but I wanted to make this night special for her. We kissed for a long time. She was passive and receptive, and I knew she wanted me to control the night.

I was more than happy to oblige.

I slid my hands from her face to her sides and spun her around, still keeping my nagging cock from poking her. I walked her over to a giant double door closet that was also a giant mirror. The light from the bathroom was reflecting off of it, lighting up the front of her gown as she faced it.

I pulled her dark brown hair over her shoulders and kissed her neck while she watched in the mirror.

I whispered, "I want you so bad right now. I have wanted this night for so long."

She replied, "Have you?"

"Yes. You know I think about it all the time."

"Did you think about it like this?" She was leaning her head backwards, and I kissed her forehead.

I responded, "Yes."

"Really?"

"Yes."

She said, "I love you. I knew I wanted you to be my first the first time we kissed."

"Well, tonight both of our wishes are coming true."

I reached my hands around her neck and began unbuttoning the buttons of her gown. After I had unbuttoned the first few, I pulled it down over her shoulders and looked at her in the mirror; she was watching me watch her. I carefully moved my hips forward gently so my cock would graze her ass just enough for her to know what she was doing to me. The gown was silky and so sheer that the light shone right through it. She had smallish breasts with small areolas and tiny nipples. They were as stiff as I was and were poking through the gown. I unbuttoned two more buttons, and the gown dropped to her waist exposing her breasts to the mirror and my eyes. I slid my hands down her shoulders over her breasts and continued down until my hands were around her waist.

I rested my chin on her shoulder and said, "You will have to forgive me if I come before I even get inside of you. You look so beautiful, and I am so turned on right now I might explode."

She replied, "I would consider it a compliment."

"I'll do my best not to, but there's no guarantees."

I lifted the gown back up and buttoned the top button. I then walked her to the bed and laid her down on her back.

"Close your eyes and relax. I'll take it from here."

I picked up the remote control and turned on the gas fireplace, put on a light jazz tape with 1940s love songs, and turned off the bathroom light, so we only had the reflection of the moonlight on the snow from the bay window and the fire.

I went back to the bed and crawled next to her. I slowly unbuttoned all the buttons and opened the full-length gown exposing her body to me completely.

I gently kissed her forehead, then moved to her eyelids and cheeks. I ran my lips across hers but didn't stop to kiss, and then kissed the other cheek with more tiny, soft pecks. I moved down to her chin and neck, and then to her shoulders. Her arms were the only thing still in the gown, and I kissed the inside of her exposed arm and moved down and across her chest above her breasts. I did the same to the other arm. I skipped her breasts and began kissing her stomach down to her belly button.

I then went up and put my mouth to her ear and said, "You are so beautiful. I want to make love to you until the sun comes up."

"Mmmm..." was her only response.

I took my hand and gently put it on her upper stomach and slowly slid it upward to cup a breast. I put my tongue in her ear and squeezed her breast with moderate pressure as I licked her, eventually sucking on her ear lobe while I went from squeezing to holding my fingers outstretched and gently dragging the palm of my hand across her stiff nipple. She shuddered. I closed my hand back around her breast, and then did the same to the other side.

She was breathing very steady now. I could tell she was aroused and getting more so by the minute. I moved my mouth onto her breast and my hand onto her stomach. I suckled her nipple gently while I ran my hand down her stomach, across her hip, and down the top of her thigh as far as I could reach. I brought my hand back up and across her stomach and down the other leg the same way. When I reached the lowest point, I switched breasts, and then brought my hand back to her stomach. I moved my mouth down towards her stomach, as I slid my hand gently until I reached her perfect triangle of dark pubic hair that was always so neatly trimmed.

I began rubbing my fingertips through the curls, pulling up gently to stimulate her without touching anything directly. I sat up and repositioned myself so that I was lying face down between her legs. I kissed the triangle of hair to let her know where I was and where I was heading. I gently lifted her knees and put my mouth between her legs. I licked her lips and could taste the sweet wetness that let me know she was more than ready. I licked her gently as she moaned and then moved my mouth upwards to her clit. I teased there for only a minute. She was ready, and so was I.

I threw the bathrobe off my shoulders and arms and let if fall to the floor. I was stone hard and her body looked incredible in the dancing light of the fireplace. At twenty-three she was still flawless, and it showed. I put my knees on the bed and slid forward until my knees were against the back of her thighs. Her legs draped over mine and she moaned again, letting me know she was ready. I laid my cock on top of her pubic mound and slid it up and down with the base of it rubbing the outside of her pussy lips. I could feel the lubrication she was providing, making it slide easier with each gentle stroke. I leaned back and used it to lube the entire shaft, especially the head. I let my cock rest on her pubic area again and leaned forward.

"It's time," I said. "Are you ready?"

"Yes."

"Do you want me?"

"Yes!"

"Do you love me?"

"Yes!"

I leaned forward and kissed her deeply. I then pulled back and slowly and gently began to slide myself inside.

I had never seen her so wet. I had always fingered her with only one finger to save her for this moment, and it was worth it. I stopped half way in to let her body expand from the presence of my cock. I kissed her deeply again, and then began placing small kisses on her lips and chin in between her breathing. She had her mouth open from the pleasure of being stretched out for the very first time. I slowly slid the rest of the way in, lying there, supporting my weight on my arms as she became comfortable with my cock. I began sliding in and out slowly, watching the sheer pleasure on her face. She was by far the tightest girl I had ever been with, and it was hard not to come. She lay there and let me take care of her with my steady rhythmic motions.

After about three minutes she began uttering noises of pleasure that were unintelligible. She was starting to move her hips, and I could feel her pleasure building. She started repeating, "I love you. I love you," over and over as she thrust at me. I started kissing her lips as I thrust a little harder and with more determination.

"I want to feel you come inside me," she said.

"Not yet."

"Please."

"Are you sure?"

"Come inside me. I want to feel it."

"Okay."

I let the orgasm I had been holding back rise and explode inside of her with half a dozen full thrusts. I almost fainted for a few seconds as she moaned with pleasure at what had just happened. I came to a rest on top of her with my weight on my arms. I stayed inside of her and kissed her deep. She kissed me back more passionately than she had ever done before.

I whispered, "Was it worth the wait?"

"Yes... No... Yes. God, if I knew it felt that good. Oh, my God. Ask me later when I can think."

I kissed her gently on the lips, and then tucked her head into my neck and mine into hers. We lay there like that for a long time. I could feel myself getting smaller and was sure that between my huge orgasm and her excited wetness there was a wet spot the size of Lake Erie we would need to contend with.

I raised my head up and said, "Stay here, I'll get towels." There was no need though, she wasn't going anywhere.

I kissed her on the lips, and then slid backwards and off to the bathroom. I brought out two towels and a warm, wet washcloth. I wiped myself clean with one towel on the way back, and then used it to clean up the obvious mess that was running out of her now. She just lay there in bliss, letting me do what I was doing. After I got what I could easily get with the towel, I used the warm washcloth to wipe off everywhere there was wetness. I lifted her leg and wiped all the way down, and then put the fresh towel under her before I let her leg down again.

I tossed the other towel and washcloth onto the floor and lay beside her, leaning over her.

I said, "How are you doing?"

"Good, and you?"

"Great."

"Did I do okay?"

"What do you mean?"

"I mean, was I okay?"

"Okay, what?"

"You know, in bed. Was I okay?"

"I had to lift you up to clean my mess off of you. In fact, I'm pretty sure your gown is a goner. Does that answer your question?"

"I don't know. I guess so."

I realized she really was worried, even though we had fooled around at least a hundred times before.

"Inez," I said, "you were great. You couldn't have done better. Does that answer your question?"

"As long as you're not lying."

"Well, I ain't leaving," I responded, kissing her before she asked any more silly questions. I then closed up the gown and told her to get some sleep.

I said, "I'll check on you later." I grabbed the comforter off the chair and covered her up.

"What are you going to do?"

"Take a shower."

"Dino…"

"Yes?"

"Are we going to do it again?"

"Tonight?"

"Yeah."

"I'll let you know after my shower. I might need some sleep first."

"Okay."

We ended up having sex four more times in the next thirty-six hours. The fourth time she wanted to try "all the different positions" to see what it felt like, so we playfully experimented. She decided she liked "missionary" the best, so she could kiss me. It was a good weekend.

Inez and I enjoyed each other's company, growing more and more comfortable around each other. She was introverted and as bookish as someone who wanted to be a museum curator would be expected to be, but she also reveled in my ability to find humor in situations and make people laugh with a snide remark or quick quip.

Once I went to the museum to meet her for lunch and we were taking a walk around the Capital when we came across a press conference from an old pompous senator from New York. I don't remember his name, but he was an ass. I also don't remember what he was pontificating about, but it was bullshit, and the press was letting him get away with it. We stopped to listen for a minute as the press asked questions. When he said, "Okay, folks, that's it," I shouted, "Senator, one more 'yes or no' question?" And he turned and said, "Okay."

"Dino from the *DC Free Press* . . . Yes or no: Do you still take bribes from Exxon?"

"No!"

"Then you do their bidding for free?"

"No, of course not. Who are you again?"

His aides grabbed him and led him away as I hollered, "Somebody who knows a crook when he sees one."

I turned around and Inez was gone. I looked around and saw that she was sitting on a bench about fifty feet away. I went over and she looked up at me.

"You're crazy, you know," she said.

I said, "Are you mad?"

She said, "No, I can't stop laughing. How did you even come up with that?"

"I don't know, sometimes I just say things."

"To a US Senator?"

"Fuck 'em!"

We looked at the papers and news to see if anyone had reported my little outburst, but nobody did.

She had gone to private school and been raised by older conservative parents. We lied to them about us moving in together. It was more of a "don't ask, don't tell" situation, but they liked me well enough. I had left the Willbury and started working for an HVAC contractor as an installer. I had to carry AC units up and down stairways all day. It was hard work, but it kept me in great shape.

I liked the stability she brought to my life. After so many foster homes, it felt kind of nice to share a home where I was not on constant probation. Sometimes her shyness, which could have been an issue for others, was a plus for me. I liked pushing her boundaries in a good way. Once, we were in the shower having a good time soaping each other up and playing around before we fooled around, when she said, "Let me out for a second."

"Why?"

"I have to pee."

"Pee here."

"No."

"It's all pipes. Just pee."

"Let me out. I really have to pee. I had too much wine."

"Just pee."

"I can't"

"Why not?"

"Because you're here. Now, let me out or I'm gonna pee myself."

"Go ahead."

She was confused and embarrassed and really had to pee. She looked at me and pouted, expecting me to surrender.

I decided it wasn't going to be that easy. "I love that you keep the bathroom door closed. I love you for being a lady," I said. "But you're in the shower, and I'm giving you permission to pee. So, just pee. The water is on; no one will know."

"You'll know. I'll know." She was kind of dancing, now. She had obviously waited too long.

She said, "Turn around."

"Nope."

"Close your eyes."

"I'll tell you what, I'll look you right in your eyes the whole time, so I won't see anything."

"Please, I'm gonna pee myself." She was laughing now.

I just stared into her eyes and didn't blink.

She just looked back blankly, then she stared back at me and said, "Okay, but don't look."

She peed as the water ran over her and the world didn't end. When she appeared to be done, I said, "Feel better?"

"Much."

"Now was that so bad?"

"Wash my back."

We had a great time in bed after that. Who would have thought peeing in the shower could make people closer?

We had been together a little over a year when she had a crisis at the museum. A couple of months earlier she had been in the archives working late, and when she went back to her office to get her purse, she saw a woman she worked with who was a witch. The woman was in the director's office on her knees with her top off, giving the seventy-year-old guy a hand job or blow job—she wasn't sure which and didn't stick around to find out. They didn't see her.

She had heard some rumors about them, but never paid attention because she was there for the museum, not the gossip. The crisis came about because the director had to appoint a new director to replace himself, and this woman was on the list, even though she wasn't even close to qualified. Inez was upset because the word around the office was that this woman was a shoo-in for the job, and Inez was evidently the only one who knew that the rumors about the affair were true.

If Inez came forward, it might ruin her career because it was such a small community; however, if she kept quiet, then one of the good candidates would be cheated out of a position that they had worked really hard for and deserved. She was also sure that if this woman became director, it would destroy the department. She was really upset. She had no idea how to solve it. I told her she was too smart to solve it, and I offered my help. She looked at me and said, "Too smart? What does that even mean?" I told her that she was smart and educated, but that she had skipped the lessons from the street. I explained that she was so used to playing by the rules that she always consulted the rule book instead of her common sense for answers.

She said, "So how do we solve it?"

I said, "First, fuck the rule book. We will find another way to figure it out. Let's go to dinner and talk about it."

She reluctantly relented, and we went out to a local place we liked. She was very quiet and emotionally wrought with guilt. I said to her, "You're not even considering sacrificing your career for this are you?"

"I don't know. It's not fair for me to not say anything."

"No. It is not fair for you to give up your future because you worked late trying to do a good job."

"What choice do I have?"

"Do you trust me?"

"Of course."

"Then enjoy your dinner and stop worrying. And unbutton that top button."

"Why?"

"Because it makes you look worried, and if I'm worried that you're worried, I can't think."

"I love your brain. I just hope it works this time." She unbuttoned the button and relaxed.

I talked about other things and did my best to make her laugh. When we got home, she went into the shower, and when she came out, I went in. I crawled into bed with her.

"Did you think of anything?" she said.

"Not yet."

"He is making the announcement Friday; that's only three days."

"Inez."

"Yes?"

"Do you trust me?"

"I already told you, yes."

"Have I ever let you down?"

"No."

"Then go to sleep while I play with your boobs, and I will figure it out."

"What do my boobs have to do with it?"

"They help me think." I started unbuttoning her pajama top.

"You're serious?"

"Of course, I'm serious." I continued unbuttoning, and she let me.

I caressed her until she went to sleep and then buttoned her back up. When she awoke in the morning, I told her I had a plan.

"What is it?"

"Can you get me his private number, and let me know when he is alone so I can call him?"

"Yeah, I don't see why not, but what are you going to do?"

"Do you trust me?"

"I'm not so sure anymore. You're not gonna get me fired, are you?"

"No, but I need to know . . . is there any way they could have seen you when you saw them?"

"Absolutely not. All I could see was her face and hand buried in his crotch. I only knew it was him because he always wears the same pinstripe suits, and it was his office. All I really saw were his pants and stomach."

"Okay. You get me the number, and I'll handle it."

"What are you gonna do?"

"I'm going to call him and tell him I work for a person on Capitol Hill who is an old friend of his, who heard that there is an investigation about him and some woman. His 'friend' doesn't want to know whether it's true or not, but if it is, he needs to cover his tracks before it hits the fan. That should shut things down, and since he's retiring it should just be over."

Inez said, "Do you think it will work? What if he asks who told you to call?"

"I will say it's an old friend who would rather not get involved, and I am not authorized to say. What do you think?"

"Well, you're right, it's not in the rule book."

"Neither is rubbing breasts for inspiration, but hey, if it works, it works."

She called me around eleven and gave me the number, and said that he was alone. I went to the pay phone on the corner and made the call. He denied that there was anything going on, and asked me to tell his friend not to worry, but to please tell him thanks for looking out for him.

Two days later he appointed another person from the list to replace him. Inez was relieved and we celebrated in bed.

Inez, Part 2

We spent the next few months becoming more settled as a couple. I had been promoted to chief installer at work by the owner who liked that I never complained, and in his words was "always the first one to grab the heavy end of the load," instead of looking for a way to avoid it. Inez was really into her work, and she loved talking about all the things I never paid attention to. I hadn't realized how much work goes into a museum. It's not like decorating a hotel lobby, that's for sure. I wasn't sure where we were going. I did think I loved her, but it wasn't magical. I didn't know if it was supposed to be, but it sure seemed to be for her. We looked out for each other, got along well, and had a lot of fun times along the way.

Once we were lying in bed, waiting to fall asleep and she said, "Dino, can I ask you something?"

I said, "Sure, what's on your mind?" I wasn't worried or anything. I just assumed it was something about my past, growing up in foster homes, which she asked about a lot, trying to figure out what "made me tick."

"Would it be okay if I played with your dick?"

I busted out laughing.

I said, "No problem, in fact, you don't even need to ask."

"Why are you laughing?"

"I don't know. It's just not what I expected. God, I love you sometimes."

"Sometimes?"

"You know what I mean." I leaned over and kissed her gently on the lips. She slid her hands over my boxers and gently rubbed me through the cotton.

I said, "Do you want to have sex?"

"No, I'm too tired, but I want to take care of you."

"Well, you have my express permission to take care of me anytime you want. You don't even have to ask."

"Even if you're asleep?" She was stroking me now, and I was becoming fully erect.

"Why not? I touch you when you're sleeping."

"You do?"

"Sure, I slide the sheets down and graze a breast all the time, just to see the nipple pop up. I do it until you move your hand in your sleep and cover it."

"Is that all you do?

"I jerked off on you once."

She squeezed me too tight by accident and said, "You what? When?"

"Last summer at the beach." I took her hand and got her restarted on her endeavor.

"Why did you do that?"

"Remember when you got sunburned . . ."

"Yeah?"

"Well, remember we went back to the hotel room and you took two Benadryl for the sunburn, and I rubbed you all over with the aloe massage oil?"

"Okay. Go on." She was still stroking me so I knew she wasn't mad, just curious.

"Well, after being on the beach all day with you in a bikini and all those other girls running around, I was ready for 'action,' as they say, and then having you lie completely naked and passed out while I rubbed you with massage oil for two hours . . . Well, I couldn't take it anymore."

"So, you jerked off on me?"

"The 'on you' part was an accident."

"How do you figure?"

"Well, I was just kind of standing there at the end of the bed, looking at you naked with your legs spread and decided to, well, rub one out, to relieve the pressure, and when I came, I guess I was turned on more than I thought, and some of it landed on you."

"How much."

"Um...all of it."

"You're serious? Where did it land?"

I restarted her hand again. But she stopped.

"Not until you tell me where it landed."

"Everywhere."

"Not good enough. I'm not mad. I think it's funny. I just want to know." She was stroking me again but slowly.

"Okay. Most of it landed on your stomach right below your belly button."

"Where else?"

"On your left thigh."

"Where else."

"Oh yeah, and in your pubic hair. That was a big gob. It like floated on top."

"Did you at least clean me up or did you just leave me there?"

"Of course, I cleaned you up. It was fun."

"Show me."

"Show you what?"

"Jerk off on me."

"Really?"

"Yeah, I want to watch."

She took her hand out of my boxers and pulled the sheets away and then began unbuttoning her top. I watched her take her top off, then she lifted her hips and pulled her bottoms and underwear off and tossed them on the floor with the top.

"Okay, I'm ready. Get to work."

I laughed and said, "You're serious?"

"Of course, you owe it to me."

"How do you figure that?"

"Well, I think if a girl gets jerked off on, she should at least get to watch."

"Okay, but to be clear, you want it to land on you, right?"

"Right, then I want to watch you wipe it off." She was enjoying this new game, and I liked this side of her.

I said. "All right, I'll be right back."

I went into the bathroom and took off my boxers and T-shirt, grabbed the massage oil out of the vanity, put some on myself, grabbed a towel, and walked back into the bedroom.

"Well, here I am," I said, as I causally stroked my now rock-hard cock.

"Okay, do it just like at the beach. I want to see what I missed."

I walked over to where she was lying on the bed and took her ankles and gently pulled her down so her feet were just barely on the bed. I then moved one leg to the side, bending the knee so she was splayed out, giving me a full view between her legs.

I said, "Pretend you're asleep."

"How?"

"Close your eyes."

"Then I can't see."

"Just close them most of the way."

She did as I asked, and I stroked myself, knowing she was watching. I stared at her body intently, letting her know she excited me. It didn't take me long to come, and I leaned forward to make sure it spilled on her. I moaned and bucked as I came, my come landing on her left leg, hip, and torso. I looked at her face when I was finishing my last strokes, and she was smiling broadly with her eyes wide open. I closed my eyes, tilted my head back, and slowed my stroking down to a slow-motion crawl.

I was breathing heavy from the exhaustion of the orgasm. I reached down and grabbed the towel I had brought in and wiped myself off. "Are you ready for this part?" I said.

"Yep."

I wiped my come off of her gently and buffed her skin dry with the towel.

She said, "That was fun."

I said, "How fun?" and ran my fingertips between her legs to see how wet she was. She was soaked.

"Mmm..."

I kneeled down and started gently licking her. She was incredibly turned on, and I decide to turn the tables. I stopped.

I said, "My turn."

She said, "Your turn? For what?"

"To watch."

"Oh, no."

"C'mon. You told me you do it sometimes. Let me watch."

"No way."

"Okay."

I licked her a little more.

Then I said, "At least put your hand down here so I can pretend."

She said, "Okay, but that's it. I'm the shy one, remember?"

"That's it. I promise."

She put her hands down until they were at the top of her pubic hair line and let them lay there. She began toying with the hair ever so gently while I licked her.

I said, "Imagine you're doing it and I'm watching."

I didn't wait for an answer, but went back to suckling her. I was watching her hands intently for any sign that she might be doing as I asked. I saw her push down on her stomach with her one hand and pull the other slightly back. I licked her a little more.

"Imagine you are all alone in the house and you are so horny you can't take it." I said. "You start rubbing yourself, and I come home early and see you from the doorway, but you don't know it." I licked her a little more. She was arching her hips now. I said "Now imagine you have your head turned to the side and you notice me from my reflection in the mirror. I have my cock out and I am stroking myself watching you."

She moaned, and I wet my fingers in her pussy and then used them to rub her clit while I put my mouth over her fingertips and started licking between her fingers. She put her fingers in my mouth and played with my tongue, obviously fully into things now. I sucked her fingers and moved my mouth closer to her pussy, with her fingers following the suction. I took my other hand and used it to put her fingers all the way in my mouth. I was licking her palm with three of her fingers in my mouth as I rubbed her clit with my hand. I then slid her hand out and onto her pussy, never breaking contact and licked her clit through her fingers.

Her hand was passive, and I used my hand and mouth to use her hand as a tool to rub the entire clit area in a circle the way I imagined she did when she was alone. She went from passive to helping, and within a minute or two she was rubbing herself full force while I licked the tops of her fingers and rubbed her thighs. She exploded in an orgasm and squeezed her thighs around her hand as she found the right spot to keep the orgasm going. She laid there in bliss while I gently stroked her body. I slowly got up and covered her with the sheets and let her fall asleep while I took a shower.

Within a few weeks I had her riding on top of me while she was rubbing herself into some incredible orgasms. It was fun.

They say all good things must end, and I guess our relationship was no different. There was no fight or even a break up. On the same day that she got offered a job as Junior Curator at a museum in San Diego, I was informed by my boss that he was selling his company, and he had secured me a management position with the new owner that was going to double my salary and get me in as a future right-hand man. I knew that Inez and I had to split when she said she would pass up her offer and stay in DC with me. That let me know that she loved me, but the reality was, that put me in a quandary. I loved her too much to let her do that, but not enough to make the same sacrifice for her.

We spent an entire night talking and laughing and crying, and at the end of it all we decided that we were perfect first loves for each other. But just like all first loves, we both needed to find the real thing. In her case she needed to find someone who wanted a family and kids, and a super smart successful wife. In my case, I needed to find out what the magic she felt for me was like. The maturity of the breakup has never escaped me.

We both spent the next few weeks before she left worrying about each other. We made love in the dark, always in missionary position, with a lot of kissing. We took baths together, and it was as if she was going off to college and would be back at the end of the semester, instead of leaving forever. She showed me brochures and explained to me about how her first project was to set up a display for a sarcophagus, which is an ancient coffin and has nothing to do with an esophagus, which is your throat.

Sort of.

I helped her pack her stuff and bring it to a shipping warehouse in Maryland, and then the next day I took her to the airport. As soon as I saw the plane leave the runway and go over the Potomac River, I felt like I had made a huge mistake. I shed tears and wanted to chase her.

I fought it for a few weeks, but after talking to her on the phone a few times, I realized we had done the right thing. She needed to have her life, and as much as I cared about her, I would have never been able to stick it out. She married three years later. She has two kids and a husband that adores her the way she deserves. That gives me peace.

Shannon

After Inez left I threw myself into my work at my new job and started making good money. I kept the apartment. I was going to get a roommate, but since I could afford it, I decided to live alone. I started playing more guitar and singing, and actually got to a point where I could sing enough to pass at most campfires. When spring came around, I started helping Larry at the marina on weekends. After hibernating all winter I was looking forward to the open air. He occasionally booked me as a boat hand for some wealthy clients who wanted to take their boats sailing, but didn't want to do all the work. I worked with a guy named Ronnie who was about thirty-five. He and I were equally skilled, but because he was ten years older, he made sure I deferred to him when we dealt with clients. I didn't care. I enjoyed the sailing and the expensive boats, and there were usually a few decent looking women along for the ride.

I was almost over Inez, but was not looking to replace her. In fact, I was making sure that any woman I showed interest in was someone I could never fall in love with. I didn't like the hurt, and I never even had the magic to balance it with. Not caring whether a relationship would develop into anything made it easy to talk to women. It gave me an honesty that turned out to be a double-edged sword. While some women hated that I was a confirmed bachelor, others saw it as a challenge and tried to fuck me into submission. It was a weird couple of years in that dating scene.

The first woman I had an actual affair with after Inez left was thirty-eight, divorced, wealthy, and banged me like a piñata. I met her on a weekend when Ronnie and I were deckhands on a large sailboat owned by a lobbyist. We left Alexandria for a sail down the Potomac River to the Chesapeake Bay and back. There were no politicians on board, but there were a lot of congressional staff that were getting properly schmoozed.

I had been out a few weekends already, so I was tan and also fit from moving HVAC equipment around the warehouse every day, staging it for my crews. Shannon made no bones about letting me know that she liked what she saw. Ronnie saw her checking us out and called "dibs." I rolled my eyes and went to work. It's easy to screw up and tear a thousand-dollar sail, or worse, get somebody hurt. Ronnie took every opportunity to flirt with her, and she ignored him and tried to flirt with me, which I at the time presumed was to get Ronnie to back off. She was, after all, at least a dozen years older than me, and lots of guys closer to her age were weaving in and out, refilling her wine glass and chatting it up with her. Besides, I was there to work, and if it didn't get done, we were going nowhere fast. Literally.

She left us and socialized for a while with the others, and I concentrated on keeping the boat rolling through the warm spring air. We took the boat to the bay, came back and docked in Alexandria, where everyone went to dinner dockside at the Harbor House restaurant. It was a swanky place, and the dozen or so people went to get their obligatory lobster dinner on whatever company the lobbyist with all the money worked for. As they were departing for the restaurant, Shannon came up to me and said, "Are you coming for dinner?"

I said, "No, I'm the help. Besides, I need to get everything squared away." Ronnie came over to see what she was saying.

"You're sure?" she said. "I can get you in."

"No, thanks," I said. "I appreciate it, but we have a lot to do."

"Okay, Dino," she said. "It was nice meeting you."

I was surprised that she knew my name and she noticed. She didn't say anything but smiled, letting me know that she was truly interested, and not just trying to avoid Ronnie. When she walked down the gangplank, Ronnie said, "Bye," and she just waived over her shoulder at him and took a sip from her wine glass, as she walked to the restaurant to catch the others.

Once she was out of earshot, Ronnie said, "Dude, I called dibs."

I looked at him and said, "What is your problem? I didn't say shit to her."

"Yeah, right."

He went back to work in a bad mood like I had stolen his sure thing.

When we were almost through, and he was still sulking, I said, "Why don't you head out and I'll finish up."

He didn't need to be told twice. I continued working as it was getting dusk. I closed the last footlocker of equipment, and when I turned around, there was Shannon holding a covered plate.

"You didn't want to come to dinner, so I brought dinner to you."

"You didn't have to do that."

"I know. I wanted to."

I lifted up the tin foil, and there were two lobster tails and a small bowl of butter.

"Wow, lobster," I said.

"You like lobster?"

"Of course."

"Good, eat up."

I sat on the bench on the dock with the plate in my lap. I began to remove the tin foil when she pulled a bottle of beer and napkins out of her pockets. She was wearing white shorts, a white polo shirt, and a white spring jacket. I got the impression she came from money and breeding. She sat down next to me, picked up a lobster tail, cracked it with her hands, and expertly slid it from the shell. I was glad she had done it because I was going to do it a different way, which surely would have made a mess and looked pretty ignorant.

I opened the beer and took a sip, picked the lobster tail off the plate, dipped it in the butter, and took a bite as butter ran down my chin.

She dabbed it with a napkin and said, "So, what do you do when you're not sailing?"

"My day job is running an HVAC place in DC."

"Married?"

"Nope."

"Girlfriend?"

"Nope."

"Gay?"

"Nope."

"How often do you work out?"

"I don't."

She put her had around my bicep and said, "Where did you get these?"

"The old-fashioned way; I move AC equipment around all day."

"Where do you live?"

"DC, off 16th Street Northwest."

"I live in Chevy Chase. We're almost neighbors."

I dipped the lobster tail in the butter and managed to get it in my mouth without spilling anything.

"Where in Chevy Chase?" I said.

"Right off of Bradley and Connecticut."

"Wow, we are close."

"Can I bring you to my gym and show you off to my girlfriends?"

I looked at her strangely and said, "Show me off?"

"Yeah. They all have these fit guys, and I always end up with old fuddy-duddies. I want to make them jealous."

"Are you asking me out on a date?" I was intrigued and realized I was horny as hell.

"Sure, why not?"

"Okay."

She picked up the second lobster, split it like the first, dipped it in butter, and put the tip of it in my mouth. I bit off and chewed. She took a bite for herself and then dipped it twice more and fed it to me until the lobster tail was all gone. I smiled at her and wasn't quite sure what to do next when she said, "You have a little butter on your chin. Let me get it."

She licked my chin and then kissed me. She immediately put her hand on my stomach and pushed on my abs. I felt intimidated and excited at the same time. I was in good shape, but I wasn't some body builder, and I didn't know what she was dragging me into. I kissed her back as she ran her hands all over my stomach. It had been a few weeks since I had been with anyone, and I was instantly hard. We continued to kiss for a few moments.

She said, "So you're coming to my gym right? It'll be fun. My girlfriends will be so jealous."

I kissed her again and slid my hands inside her blouse and cupped her breast. She slid her hand down and let it rest on the bulge in my pants but didn't grab me.

"Just so you know, I don't sleep with guys until the second date."

"Okay."

"But since we kissed, this qualifies as the first date."

She dragged her hand over my cock and stood up. She bent back down, putting one hand on each of my thighs and kissed me one more time. I slid my hands inside her jacket and cupped both of her breasts. She slowly pulled away from the kiss and whispered in my ear, "I'll call you."

She stood up and I let my hands fall away. As she was getting up, she ran both her hands on my crotch and right across my cock again. She smiled, obviously proud of getting me aroused.

As she walked away, I said, "I need to give you my number."

She turned halfway around and said, "I already got it," and scurried away. I went home, jumped in the shower, and washed my cock first, so it would leave me alone.

The following Saturday at 11 a.m., I pulled into the driveway of a house that was about twice as big as a bank. It was right off of Bradley Boulevard in posh Chevy Chase, a mile from the DC line. The house was very impressive, but it was only one of hundreds, all sharing the commonality of freshly landscaped lawns, multiple car garages, and hired help.

I parked next to a Jag convertible. There was a newer Range Rover under the portico. The three-car garage was closed, so I couldn't tell if it was full or empty. I made the assumption that Shannon lived with her parents. This just didn't seem like the kind of place she would reside. I imagined the inside would have a Steinway piano in the parlor, a library with a rolling ladder, and lots of oak or mahogany paneling everywhere. I wasn't that far off. The piano was a baby grand and it was in the living room with lots of modern furniture that looked out of place among all of the ample wainscoting and oak trim everywhere–everywhere, of course, except the curved stairs; they were marble with an ornate white metal railing that went up about twelve feet or more to the second floor.

A Hispanic woman answered the door, and I told her I was Dino, here to see Shannon. She invited me in and led me through the living room to an outdoor covered porch, overlooking the backyard pool and the neighbor's backyard and pool.

"Ms. Shannon will be right down. She upstairs."

I was wearing nylon workout pants and a T-shirt and felt awkwardly out of place among all the elaborate furniture that also smelled of old money. I sat and casually watched the neighbor's gardener weed a flawless flower bed. I didn't notice Shannon come in until she was right in front of me. She was wearing a black sports bra and matching workout pants, so thin and tight that my imagination didn't even have to shift out of first gear. She leaned over, and we kissed cheeks. I'm not sure if that was her decision or mine, but she was glad to see me.

"This is a very nice home."

"Thanks. I hate it."

"What?"

"I hate it. I only have it because it was in my husband's family, and I got this instead of half his business."

"Why don't you move?"

"It's a long story. Are you ready to work out?"

"Sure."

"Do you mind if we have a light lunch first?"

"That would be fine. Do you want to go out somewhere?"

She said, "No, I told Rosario to make us crab cake sandwiches. She makes the best. Is that okay?"

"Yeah, great."

I could tell she was used to getting her own way. I knew I was there for the sex and not a replacement for Inez. She was a person to have fun with, but nothing more. That was fine. I was quite sure I was just a tryst for her, and in a few weeks, she would be off to someone else to make her feel young.

"Do you want the tour?"

"Okay."

She turned around and walked back into the living room through the double doors.

"Well, here is the living room. In here, we have the dining room. It's too small for a house this big, but what can you do?" She walked into a hallway past a small kitchen and said," This is the galley."

She kept walking, and about the time I figured out that the galley wasn't the main kitchen, she walked us into the main kitchen, which was large enough to use for a restaurant if you wanted. There were two built-in refrigerators, a giant stove with six burners, two wall ovens, and enough counter space to hold a feast for twenty. I smiled at a woman I presumed was Rosario, fixing our lunch.

Shannon looked over her shoulder at her and said, "Don't forget the wine."

I said, "Wow."

She nodded casually and said, "It's dated, but it will do."

We continued around the first floor, which had a library, a sitting room, a servant's bedroom, and a giant atrium that overlooked the pool from the opposite side of the house.

"I spend most of my time in here."

There was a table and chairs with a set up for two. She motioned for me to sit, and I did. I poured a glass of water from the pitcher into a glass and filled hers. As I took a sip she said, "So, do you want to know why I hate it?"

"I do."

"Well, Larry, my husband . . . scratch that—ex-husband—grew up here. I lived about a mile away in Kenwood. We hung out at the country club together, and when we ran into each other at the pool after college, we decided we wanted to live happily ever after. We had a big wedding at Congressional Country Club, and since his parents had just moved to Florida, we moved in here. We have a kid. Fast forward ten years, and he fucks my best friend, takes my kid, and tries to bankrupt me."

"What does that have to do with the house?"

"Well, when I found out what was going on and consulted an attorney, I found out she couldn't talk to me because he had already interviewed her, and it was a conflict of interest. So, I went to another. Then another. The son of a bitch had 'consulted' every divorce attorney worth a shit in the entire county, so I couldn't hire them. Meanwhile, he locked in Mike Freelander, a goddamn jackal, and I was stuck with a nobody from Rockville. His lawyer went for the jugular. He had his girlfriend give a deposition that I caused them to get together because I seduced her, and they only became lovers after commiserating about my infidelity."

"You slept with her?"

"Yeah, he watched, for Christ's sake. Anyway, my lawyer, bless his soul, figured out at the last minute that Larry had used this house as collateral for a loan for his business and had added my name on the mortgage without my permission. The judge ruled that even though his parents gave the house to him, that when he added me to the mortgage, which was for more than the house was even worth, that it became half mine. He had a choice of selling his family's home or letting me live in it until I get my settlement for half his business."

"Then what?"

"Then I buy a condo here and in Florida and follow the sun."

"What about your kid?"

"Jewels? She is twelve and living with them. I get her every other weekend and two days during the week. She hates me."

"Why?"

"Andrea saw to that, and still does. She sides with Jewels on everything and undercuts me every chance she gets."

"Andrea's the new wife?"

"Andrea's my ex-best friend, his new wife, and my nemesis."

At that moment Rosario came with our lunch. We had a small salad, a crab cake sandwich, and what looked like freshly made fries.

I was curious about this whole new world I had never been in and asked, "So how did it happen?"

"I was a dumb ass. I thought that Andrea and I were close, but it turns out she was just a gold-digging whore who used me to get my husband. We went everywhere together. She would come with us to Florida. We would fix her up on dates, and then when it inevitably crashed, she would cry on Larry's shoulder, and I was too stupid to realize she was just scheming and waiting to come in for the kill."

I started eating some fries, waiting for her to wind down a little bit, but she just grabbed the bottle of wine and poured herself a large glass and started drinking it down while she continued her story.

"Andrea and I were best friends. We even slept in the same bed, naked and drunk, and never did anything. We would party and have a good time. Larry would come home and sleep in the guest room because we were both blotto and passed out on the bed. The three of us hung out all the time when Andrea was between guys. Anyway, Larry used to ask me all the time about whether Andrea and I ever fooled around, and hinted that that it would be cool with him, as long as he could watch. So, like a dumb ass, I mentioned it to Andrea, and she was all for it. The sly bitch said that it was cool with her as long as Larry thought that she didn't know he was watching. So, I told Larry that I was going to seduce her, and he could watch from the veranda but couldn't let her know he had watched. Andrea and I got really drunk, watched some porn, and we gave him a show that no man deserves. He was thrilled, and then next thing I know they were hanging out without me, and it didn't take long to put two and two together. By the time I confronted him, it was too late; she had already turned him against me and stolen him."

"I'm really sorry. That must have been tough."

"Fuck 'em. Fuck 'em both! He has three years to get me my settlement, or I can sell the house. I'm just biding my time until I have my life back. Meanwhile, I'm going to enjoy myself as best I can."

She had already finished the first glass of wine and was refilling her glass. She took a big gulp and said, "Let's eat. Then we work out."

We made small talk while we ate. She asked me normal questions about myself, but mostly relayed lots of stories about her own antics. I was thinking about an old saying I heard around the warehouse from the older guys. "Never stick your dick in crazy." I was about to ignore their advice.

After lunch she said, "Are you ready to work out?"

"Yep, how far is the gym?"

"Twenty steps."

I looked confused.

She saw my confusion and said, "Downstairs. The house comes with its own workout room. I don't hate 'everything' about it."

I followed her down a long flight of steps, past what I would find out later was a screening room, past a wine cellar, and into a workout room similar to what you would find at a nice hotel, complete with a hot tub, bar, and big TV in the corner.

I asked, "Where's the bowling alley?"

"His parents didn't bowl. If they did, there would probably be one."

"Can I ask how they got their money?"

"Sure. His father had built roads in DC until he made his big score by paying people off to get the contracts to do all the paving for the metro construction."

"He paved parking lots?"

"*He* didn't do anything. He never got his hands dirty, except counting money. His father, Larry's grandfather, was the one who started the business in the 1930s. He was a bricklayer who worked his ass off for his family. Larry's father and uncle took what he built and learned how to make deals that made everybody rich."

"Is that what Larry does now?"

"Mostly he tries to stay one step ahead of the banks and two steps ahead of the IRS. First generations earn it, second generations multiply it, and third generations spend it. Never marry a third generation."

I digested that for a minute. I couldn't tell if she was bitter at who he was or that she wasn't a part of it anymore. She was definitely a little out there, and I had my guard up, even though I figured there was nothing to be worried about. I was looking for sex, and it would either happen or not. It happened.

Shannon said, "Let's stretch first," and began bending in all kinds of different positions that made me want to fuck crazy, regardless of the consequences.

I said, "It must be nice having your own gym."

"It's no fun unless you have someone to work out with. That's why I belong to the Washington Sports Club. I'll take you there. It will be fun. Plus, everyone will be jealous. You won't mind if they think you're my boy toy, will you?"

"Boy toy?"

"It's a compliment. It means a younger guy who really knows his stuff."

"His stuff?"

"Spot me." She went and laid her back on the bench press, and I stood behind her head as she lifted the weights and did reps. I wanted to find out a little more about the whole boy toy thing, but figured things would fall into place soon enough. Besides that, her tits and crotch looked great from this angle. She was stronger than I thought, and I imagined she must have spent a lot of time at the gym.

She did three sets of ten, and then said, "Your turn," and we switched.

I set the weights a little heavier and laid down. She took her place where I was, and I began doing reps. I did the first set, and she said, "Pretty good." I looked up at her and realized her pussy was right in my face. I could see the outline of her lips through the thin material. I didn't know what kind of fabric it was, but I could tell it was expensive. It was obvious that there wasn't any underwear between my eyes and paradise either. I did two more sets, looking back at her each time and not hiding the fact that I was admiring her body. I sat up and she said, "Now me again." She lay back down as I readjusted the weights. She did a set of ten reps and put the weights back in the cradle. She tilted her head back and put her hands on the sides of my legs.

"Do you think I'm pretty?"

"I wouldn't be here otherwise." I was swelling less than a foot from her face; I was pretty sure she could see the movement.

"Will you say it?" she said.

"I think you're very pretty."

She slid her hands around to the front of my pants, very near my cock, and started rubbing the front of my legs with her fingertips.

"Do you think I'm sexy?"

"I think you're very sexy."

She moved her fingertips over until she touched my cock through the nylon. I was hard at this point, and when she realized it, she moved from her fingertips to her hand and pushed the palm of her hand over my cock and squeezed gently.

"Can I see?"

She reached up and put her fingers in the waist band and slid my pants down my thighs. I pulled off my T-shirt. She reached back up and grabbed my boxers and pulled them down to the same spot. I was now standing over her with her on her back on the exercise machine; my hard cock inches from her face. She pulled me forward and slid backwards at the same time and put me in her mouth. Her head was now laying over the back of the machine with it supporting her by her neck. She took me out of her mouth and teased the tip with her tongue.

"Fuck my mouth."

I took my cock in my hand and bent forward, resting my other arm on the bar with the weights and slid myself into her mouth. She found the angle and put her hands behind my legs and pulled me forward until my cock was buried all the way in. She used her hands as a cue for me to pump forward and back at a tempo that turned her on. She took her hands from behind my legs but kept her mouth on me and pulled her sports bra up over her tits. Then she lifted her ass and started trying to pull her pants down. It wasn't doable, so I pulled out of her mouth, undressed quickly, and went around and helped.

Once her pants were off, she reached her arms up and grabbed the weight bar and used it for leverage to lift both her legs up 90 degrees and then open them for me. She was completely hairless. She was also tan all over with no tan line to be found. She had flawlessly smooth skin and had obviously had the hair removed with some high-dollar method I had never heard of. I went down and began licking her in my traditional "lick the butter off the popcorn," and then advance to the "Tootsie Pop" fashion, but she had other plans.

She closed her thighs around my head and pushed me in further between her legs. I took the cue and began sucking and licking aggressively as she rubbed her tits and moaned. After a couple of minutes, she said, "Fuck me." I slid backwards, got to my feet, straddled the bench, and slid inside of her while I was standing and she was lying back. She put her legs straight up and rested her ankles on my shoulders and tortured her nipples while I fucked her hard. I had made myself come in the shower before I came over so I wouldn't be too excited, and I was glad I had. Her need to be fucked was very exciting, and it was hard to not keep from coming. I kept going for a long time, as she moaned from the pleasure of it all. I slowed down to rest a little and catch my breath.

"I want to turn over," she said.

I slowly pulled out, and she flipped over and lay face down on the bench with her legs hanging over the sides. She bent her knees and moved them forward, allowing me to guide myself back into her and continue.

She put her hands behind her and spread her ass cheeks apart and said, "Slap me." I slapped her ass.

"Harder!" she said. I slapped again.

"Harder." I slapped again.

"Harder."

I slapped again and she said, "I'm going to come, don't stop. Harder." I fucked her and kept slapping her ass as she slid her hands down to the back of her thighs. She was fucking back at me now and finally exploded in a bucking orgasm as I spanked her ass. Once the bucking slowed, I stopped with the slapping, but kept pushing in and out of her with determination. We slowed down together until she let her knees buckle and put all of her weight back on the bench.

She groaned, "Oh God, that was good."

I was still inside of her and still hard. I hadn't come. I began slowly sliding in and out very gently as she lay there and moaned.

After a couple of minutes, she said, "You're going to kill me," and started moving in sync with my slow deliberative thrusts.

"Do you want me to stop?"

"No, this is how I want to die," and she began pushing back on me harder. After about thirty seconds she stopped and said, "That's enough, I'm exhausted."

I slid out slowly and picked up a towel. She grabbed it out of my hand, lifted herself off the bench, shoved it under her, and laid back down.

"Why don't you get in the shower, and I'll join you in a minute."

"Okay."

I looked around, and sure enough there was a door that opened into a giant bathroom with a giant shower with a bench and dual sprayers.

I went into the shower and was rinsing myself off when she joined me with a tall glass of wine in her hand.

"Did you come?"

"No. I held back. It was more fun fucking you than coming."

She reached down and took the soap from my hands.

"Well, let's see what we can do to even the score."

She started rubbing my cock with the soap, and it began swelling right away. After a minute or so I was fully erect, and she turned me to face one of the jets and rinsed me off. She then turned me around so the jets were on my back, dropped to her knees, and began sucking me while looking me in the eye.

I put one hand on her shoulder and the other on her head. She took the hand off my head and slid it to her shoulder.

"I've got this," she said, taking my cock out of her mouth. "You've done enough work for one afternoon."

She then put me back in her mouth and looked up at me while she gave me a very pleasurable and highly-skilled blow job. It only took a couple of minutes for me to come, and I squeezed a little on her shoulders to let her know, but she just looked me in the eyes and moaned as she coaxed me to a great orgasm. As she felt me ready to explode, she pushed her knuckles into the underside of my ball sack hard, causing pain and pleasure at the same time. She must have found my prostate. I released, and she took it all in her mouth.

After I was done bucking, she pulled out and moved her head to rinse her mouth out in the shower stream. She stood up, and took the soap off the ledge and went back to soaping me up as if the blow job was just a mild distraction. She turned me around and washed my back, taking too long on my butt cheeks. She reached around and washed my cock again.

"Your turn," she said, handing me the soap.

We both turned around so I could wash her back. It was a little confusing with two jets from two different angles, but it worked. I started at her neck and worked my way down. Her tits were smallish but firm and full. I moved in close behind her and soaped up her stomach and between her legs. I then moved to her back. I knew we were both spent, and this was just some nice icing on a delicious cake. When I got down to her ass, she bent over, and I washed her from the back. I got a very nice look at all of her private parts. I could tell that she enjoyed being washed, probably more from an exhibitionist standpoint than anything else, but I didn't mind looking, that was for sure.

She stood back up and rinsed off. "I'll meet you upstairs. Take your time," she said, turning to me and stepping out. She grabbed a big fluffy towel and walked away, drying herself off.

I got out a minute or two later, dressed, and went upstairs. She was out on the portico porch, wearing shorts and T-shirt with no bra.

I said, "That was fun."

She looked up at me from her magazine and said, "I am going to sleep like a baby tonight, that's for sure."

I sat down and Rosario came out and stood in the doorway. Shannon looked at her and said, "Wine . . ."

She looked at me and said, "For you?"

"Coke."

Rosario left to get our drinks and Shannon said, "You're tired too, huh?"

I just smiled and said, "Satiated, is more like it."

"So?"

"So . . . what?"

She said, "So are you coming back or did I scare you off?"

"Oh, I'm coming back."

"Good. How about Monday night we go to the gym, so you can meet my friends, and then we can come back here for showers?"

"Sounds like a plan."

Rosario showed up and we made small talk for a while as we rehydrated.

After a few minutes I said, "I guess I'll see you Monday. Do you want to meet here or at the gym?"

"Here. Seven work for you?"

"Sounds good." I stood up to leave.

"Dino," she said.

"Yes."

"Bring a toothbrush and change of clothes. You're probably gonna be really tired after the workout."

"And the shower?"

"Especially the shower."

She stood up and walked me to the door. She kissed me, putting her tongue in my mouth and massaged my cock gently. I realized that was the first time we had kissed all day. I kissed her back.

"Monday?" I said.

"Monday."

I walked to my pickup truck while she watched. It was nice to be wanted.

On Monday, we went to her gym. Her showing me off made her as giddy as a school girl. It was a little confusing to me because I was just a regular looking guy in "okay" shape. After a few minutes, things fell a little more into context. Her girlfriends were all dating older guys with money, all except a woman named Karen, who had a guy who couldn't have been more than twenty and a workout king. Shannon saw me as the perfect crime: a younger guy who was old enough that he could be attracted to her and not her money. She did her best to try and give me a boner that would have been obvious to all if she could make it happen. She was going a little bit overboard, so before she embarrassed herself, I decided to help her out. One of her friends, Olivia, was giving me a little bit of a nonchalant third degree while Shannon was on the treadmill.

She said, "So what attracted you to Shannon?"

Without missing a beat, I nodded to her on the treadmill.

"Have you ever seen a nicer ass than that?" I responded.

She was quiet for a minute and said, "That's it?"

"No, I like what is connected too well enough."

"So, you met on Harold's yacht?"

"Yeah. I couldn't take my eyes off of her."

"Really?"

"Yeah. Sometimes you just meet someone and get turned on for them, like its pheromones or something. I don't know. Whatever it is, I just want her every time I see her. By the way, you're not gonna tell her any of this, are you? I don't want her to think it's just her body. I mean, she's cool to hang with too."

"No. I wouldn't ever say anything."

I went back to watching her on the treadmill while Olivia watched me.

When I was sure she was looking, I adjusted myself so she would think I was nursing an erection. I kind of was, so it was easy.

We worked out a little more and went into our respective locker rooms to get our gym bags, as we were saving the showers for her house. When we left the building, heading to her Jag for the mile ride she said, "You do know Olivia can never keep a secret?"

"It was an educated guess. What did she tell you?"

"That you were rubbing your dick, watching me on the treadmill."

"That's it?"

"No. She says you're infatuated with me, and I better watch out because you might be a stalker."

"Oh, great. I was just schmoozing her because she was being nosy."

"I love it!"

"You don't think I'm a stalker, do you?"

"Of course not. You just learn fast how this whole thing works."

"What did you say when she said that?"

"I said you can fuck for an hour straight without losing a hard-on, be ready again in twenty minutes for round two, and that I didn't care if you were a serial murderer as long as you fucked me first."

"I guess round one goes to Shannon?"

"Yep."

When we got back to her place, she did everything in her power to make sure she had plenty of stories to tell at the gym. I also found out that when she said she liked to fuck for an hour straight, she really meant it.

The next two weeks were crazy. We couldn't get enough of each other. We went to the gym, restaurants, even clothes shopping at Lord and Taylor, where she tried on lingerie, picking the first room so that all the men waiting for their wives would get a nice view. She had me come in and watch while she changed. The female attendant, a woman about forty, said very nicely that only one person was allowed to use the dressing room at a time, and Shannon replied with authority and dismissively that only one person was "using it," the other was just watching.

The woman sensing that she had a possible problem on her hand said, "Okay, but please make it quick."

Shannon was standing there in front of me, naked and holding in laughter. I had never been around someone so extroverted and thoroughly enjoyed the games. I also, of course, enjoyed the sex. She was, far and away, the most sexual person I had ever met. Her life was one big cock tease.

After about three weeks as she walked me out to my truck at her place. She said, "Can I come visit you tomorrow at work?"

I said, "Sure, to what do I owe the honors?"

"I want to see all the guys you've been bragging to about the older woman you're fucking."

"I don't kiss-and-tell."

"Liar."

"Seriously, I mean they know I'm hanging out with you, but I haven't given them details."

She almost pouted. "Well, that's a stupid rule."

"You want me to tell them?"

"Sure! In fact, I want you to let them have a peek." She reached into her bathrobe pocket and pulled out a white envelope. It was full of Polaroids she had of herself topless and naked out by the pool. She said one her girlfriends took them one day when they were drinking.

I perused through them and said, "What do you want me to do with these?"

"Well, if you promise to give them back, I will let you take them to work and show them to your buddies. Then I'll come in for lunch, and we can see how nervous they get."

"Are you sure?"

"Absolutely."

I looked her right in the eye and said, "I'll do it. All I need is permission."

"I give you permission to show your friends pictures of my pussy. How's that?"

"Done."

I put the pictures in my gym bag and climbed into the truck. She leaned in and kissed me as she shut the door. She was smiling wide as I drove away.

The next day, I pulled the envelope out of my gym bag and showed it to three of the guys in the office. I didn't tell them that she knew I was showing them, but I did say she probably would get turned on if she found out. I didn't let them know she was taking me to lunch either.

Shannon came in around eleven thirty wearing a micro mini skirt and blouse that was tied at the waist. The top barely covered her breasts. I saw her coming and went in the back, so the guys would have to greet her. You don't get too many women walk-ins at HVAC places, so when she came through the door in a skirt and no bra, they fell all over each other to help her. None of the three put two and two together until she asked for me.

Tommy came to the back and said, "She's here," in a hushed tone.

"Who?" I said, and kept looking at the paper I had picked up.

"You know," Tommy added, "the woman in the pictures. She's here!"

"What . . .?" I leaned around the corner and saw her and said, "So she is." I grinned back at Tommy, and walked out to greet her.

She said, "Hi handsome."

I smiled and said, "Well, don't you look nice." She beamed.

"I was nearby, so I figured I would stop and say hello. I left that envelope in your gym bag yesterday and wanted to get it before it got lost. Do you have it with you?"

"I think so . . . Let me check." I walked to my desk, picked up the gym bag, and pretended to go through it so she could eye-fuck my coworkers.

After an exaggerated few seconds, which my buddies were sure was me pretending it wasn't right on top, I pulled it out and said, "Here it is, safe and sound. I told you I wouldn't lose it."

"I know, thanks," she said, placing the envelope on the counter and putting her hands over it. "Can I steal you for lunch?"

I looked at the guys and said, "Can you guys adjust to cover for me?"

"Yeah. Sure. No problem."

I wanted to laugh at the giant charade, but I kept it to myself. I came around the counter, and as we walked out the door, she grabbed my ass, knowing the guys were watching hers. Outside, I climbed into the passenger seat of the Jag with its top down, and off we went to lunch at a local café, so she could tell me how exhilarating it was to know they had seen her naked. She downed two Manhattans and promptly got tipsy.

We had lunch, and I drove on the way back to my work. I pulled into a space at the far end of the lot, figuring I would give her a long kiss goodbye where they could see, but not so close that they could see everything in case she did something crazy. I had already seen about fifteen times that she wasn't wearing panties. She had sobered up a lot, but I wouldn't put anything past her at this point. It was a smart decision. I got out of the driver's seat and opened her door. She put one leg out and opened her legs wide. I said, "Just so you know they're watching from the window."

"Good."

"You're nuts."

"Maybe a little."

I put my hand out to help her out of the low-slung car. She stood up and pulled me in for a kiss. I kissed her back and ran my hands up and down her sides, more for her and the guys than me. I liked that she was like this at the time. The newness of the experience and ego boost was definitely a confidence builder for me. She rotated me around and pushed me down into the passenger seat, saying, "Stay there and help me put the top up."

"Okay," I said.

She went around, sat in the driver's seat, and started the car. She pushed a button on the dashboard and the top started closing. When it finally fell down to the windshield, I reached up and pulled it into place, latching it. As soon as I locked the latch, she turned the car off and proceeded to climb over on top of me with her facing the rear of the car.

"What are you doing?"

"Fucking you."

"It's broad daylight."

"Then you better come fast."

The truth was that other than the guys in the window, it was pretty private. I guess I figured that since she already had my cock out and it was rising to the occasion, I would go along and enjoy the ride. She spit on her hand and stroked me until I was fully hard, and then slid herself over me. She was soaked, and I slid in easily. I reached over to the door and found the seat switch and laid my seat backwards as she rode me up and down. I was sure the guys were straining very hard to see what was going on through the little rear convertible window. I came quickly but only a little, as it was an awkward position. She pulled me out and wiped herself on my shirt.

I looked down and laughingly said, "What are doing?"

"It'll ruin my skirt. Besides, it's your come anyway."

"When you're right, you're right," I said.

She finished and rolled off of me, pushed a button on the dash to make the trunk pop, and said. "Would you be a doll and get my gym bag?"

I closed myself up and got out of the car, looked at the window to see three very happy faces, and got her gym bag out of the trunk. She took it, opened it, grabbed a small workout towel, and shoved it up her skirt.

She grabbed another one and said, "You want one?"

I laughed and said, "Nah, I'm good."

She said, "I'll see you Friday?" as she put the bag on the passenger seat.

"Yes. I'll call you. Thanks for, ah, lunch."

"You're welcome."

I leaned in and kissed her quickly on the lips, and then backed up a little and watched her drive away. Needless to say, when I went back into the office, I was the subject of lots of questions, jokes, and typical male camaraderie. I didn't hate it.

Our entire relationship was based on sex. We both knew it would run out of steam at some point, but it hadn't yet, and we were both happy with that. I didn't know if she was truly oversexed or if there was just a void she was trying to fill and had found a formula that worked for her. I have my guesses, but I still don't know for sure.

One night we had gone out to dinner and then retired to the giant bedroom in the giant house she hated. She lay next to me on the bed.

"Can I tie you up?" she said as casually as if she were asking for the remote control to the TV.

"Well, that depends... What happens after I'm tied up?"

"I want to tease you and see how long you can hold out before you come. It will be fun I promise."

"Fun? It won't involve my butt, will it?"

"No, I promise." She crossed her heart, like she was in fourth grade.

"What are you going to tie me up with?"

"My bathrobe belt."

"So, you've done this before?"

"No, I've just wanted to."

"Okay, but I wasn't kidding about my butt."

"Stop worrying about your butt. Get naked."

I took off my clothes and tossed them on the floor, and laid spread eagle in the middle of the bed. She came back with a bathrobe belt and tied my wrists to the ends of the bed. I could have easily gotten away, but there wasn't any need to tell her that. It was after all her fantasy. She didn't tie my feet at all.

"What now?"

"You'll see." She went into the bathroom and came out a couple of minutes later in black stockings, a garter belt, and a push up bra. She was carrying a bottle of massage oil.

"I like."

"Good."

She went to the other side of the room, and turned off the lights from the wall switch, and then came back and turned on a lamp on one side of the bed.

She stood in the diminished light and said, "Now let's see how long you can hold out without making a mess."

She set the massage oil on the nightstand and climbed on the bed, and sat on my stomach. I was already hard. She slid backwards, and I felt the top of my cock poke her back. She slid forward and checked to see that my wrists were still tight, and as she did, her pussy was almost above my mouth. I lifted up my head to kiss it and she pushed my head back.

"I'm in charge, remember?"

"Ughh . . . "

She sat back down and reached behind her, and touched my cock.

"Well, look who's got a hard-on. Is that from looking at me in my little outfit?"

"Yes."

She ran her fingertips over my balls and up my cock, then pulled away.

"And you want to taste my pussy?"

"Yes."

"Do you like my pussy?"

"Yes."

"Is it sweet?"

"Yes."

"And you want me to let you taste it, don't you?"

"Yes."

"Say 'please.'"

"Please."

"Please what?"

"Please let me lick your pussy."

"You want to lick it? I thought you just wanted to taste it. Do you want me to let you lick it too?"

"Yes."

"But if I let you lick it, you might get too excited and come. We can't have that."

"I won't come, I promise."

"I don't know. It feels pretty hard to me." She slid her fingertips up and down the shaft again and teasingly said, "You're going to have to settle for a little taste for now. I don't want you to come until I'm ready to let you." She took her hands and spread her pussy lips and said, "Stick out your tongue." I did as she asked. She lowered herself down, and I rose my head to meet her halfway. She pulled back and told me to lay my head down. I complied. "Now stay there and stick your tongue out." I stuck my tongue out again and she pulled herself open with two fingers and lowered herself onto my tongue for a couple of seconds and then pulled back. "I think that's enough for now."

"No!"

"You want more?"

"Yes."

"Do you promise to keep still?"

"Yes." I stuck my tongue out again, and she lowered herself on me and began fucking my tongue. I was surprisingly getting very turned on. It was hard to keep from moving my head up to tongue-fuck her. After about fifteen seconds she pulled away and said, "Close your mouth." I closed it.

"Don't open it! Okay?" she said again.

"Okay."

She put her hands on the headboard and watched as she lowered herself onto my mouth like a mask. She rubbed herself on my face. She slid from my chin, over my nose, and then back down again, covering me in her wetness. The smell was raw, sexual excitement, and I was getting harder by the second. She lifted up and went down again. She then pulled back and rotated herself around until she was facing the complete other direction, and I watched as she lowered her pussy on to my face from the new position.

"Keep your mouth closed." She took the tip of her tongue and touched it to the head of my cock; it was like an electric shock. She pulled herself away and said, "It looks like somebody doesn't have much willpower."

"Fuck me."

"But I'm not done rubbing my pussy on your face."

"Let me lick you."

"No, I don't think so." She was obviously enjoying herself.

"Please, I'll lick it so good."

"How about if I let you kiss my ass? Do you wanna kiss my ass?"

"Yes."

"Okay."

Shannon swung her hips around and put her left ass cheek right over my mouth and said, "Okay, kiss my ass."

I started repeatedly kissing her ass cheek, over and over. After about thirty seconds she pulled away and turned to the other side and said, "Do you want to kiss this side too?"

"Yes."

"Say it."

"I wanna kiss your ass."

"Okay, that was sincere." She lowered her ass cheek within reach, and I did the same as the other side. She pulled away and said, "That's enough for now." She climbed off, and then while still on her knees and leaning over me said "Do you want to suck my nipples for me? They're lonely."

"Yes."

"Are you going to suck them really sweetly? That's what they're in the mood for."

"Yes."

"How can I believe you? You're pretty excited."

"I promise."

"You promise what?"

"I promise to suck your nipples so sweetly. I'll make them feel so good."

"But what if I let you suck them and you come? What then?"

"I won't come, I promise."

"Do you promise not to come until I let you?"

"I promise."

"Okay." She lowered her bra and placed a nipple into my mouth, and I suckled it as gently as I could. I felt it get hard under my lips as I wet my mouth and didn't use my tongue. She slowly pulled away and replaced it with the other one. She was moaning as I did this, and I knew she was as aroused as I was.

After a few seconds she pulled back, reset her bra, and then lay down beside me with her head at my waist. She ran her hands up and down my thighs and said, "I'm afraid to touch you. I don't think you can hold back like you promised."

"I can. I promise."

"Well, I'll touch you, but you better not come until I say so."

"I won't. I promise."

She took her hand and ran it under by ball sack and lifted up hard. She took her other hand and slid it between my cock and my stomach and made a fist around it. She let go of my balls and pointed my cock towards the ceiling. She took her index finger from her now free hand and said, "What do we have here?" and took a drop of pre-cum off the tip of my cock. "It looks like somebody wants to come."

"Let me fuck you."

"No, you're too excited. You would come too fast."

"I won't. I promise."

"No, I don't trust you. Your too excited from tasting my pussy and kissing my ass."

"Please. I won't come until you let me."

"No, I think I better just use my hand and play with you to see if you really have the willpower you say you have."

"Okay, use the massage oil."

"Oh, I know that will make you come."

"No, I won't come. I promise."

"I'll tell you what. How about if I let you lick my pussy while I tease your cock, and let's see how long you can last?"

"Yes."

"Say you want to lick my pussy."

"I want to lick your pussy."

"And you won't come until I say it's okay?"

"I promise."

She climbed on me again and said, "Wait until I'm ready."

She positioned herself over top of me in a sixty-nine position and lowered her pussy to my face.

"Okay," she said, "you can lick me, but you better be good, or I won't ever let you come."

I began licking her pussy furiously. She put her hands on my knees, ground her pussy on my mouth, and had a quick orgasm. She lifted up and then came back down on my face soaking it with her pussy juices. It was all over my face and went inside my nose, making me almost come from the sensory overload of her raw, sexual excitement. She stayed there for a few seconds, and then lifted up.

"And you didn't come," she said. "Good for you." She climbed off and said, "Well, since you did so good, I think maybe, just maybe, I might let you come."

She picked up the bottle of massage oil and poured some into her open hand. She got on her knees between my legs and rubbed her hands together with massage oil. She took my balls in one hand and my cock in the other and slowly began sliding her hand up and down while she rolled my ball sack through her fingers like a bag of gold. I laid there with my eyes closed and enjoyed the torture. She was slowly gliding her hand up and down, squeezing harder with each pass.

She said, "Did you like licking my pussy?"

"Yes."

"How about when you sucked my nipples?"

"Yes."

"And I know you liked kissing my ass. And do you like fucking me?"

"Yes."

"But you can't fuck me tonight. You are just gonna have to settle for a hand job. Is that okay?"

"Yes."

"So, you don't want me to climb on top of you and fuck you?"

"No, fuck me, fuck me."

"No, I don't think so. This is too much fun."

"Make me come!"

"What's the matter? Have you had enough?"

"I want to come."

"Well, you can't always get what you want. You are pretty hard though. I would probably enjoy putting this in my pussy."

"Yes, put it in your pussy."

"I can't do that."

"Why not."

"Because you would like it too much."

"Make me come."

"Say 'please.' "

"Please, make me come."

"You wanna come?"

"Yes."

"Okay, but don't come until I say it's okay. Promise?"

"I promise."

She started stroking me at full speed now while she was massaging my balls. I started humping back at her and was getting close.

"Don't come."

"I won't."

"But you want to?"

"Yes." She stroked harder until she knew there was no turning back and said, "Okay, let me see you come." She kept stroking faster and harder, all the time massaging my balls hard. I ejaculated toward the ceiling in at least four, maybe five or six huge spurts. Shannon said through her teeth, "Yes, come, I want that come, give me that come," and kept stroking until it was all out.

As I was laying there about to pass out, she slowed her hand down and used it to smear the come all over my stomach. She climbed up and kissed me on the forehead and said, "That was fun. Don't go anywhere." I closed my eyes and relaxed, and about a minute later felt a warm wet washcloth cleaning up the mess we made. She untied the bathrobe and covered me with a comforter. We both slept through the night.

A month or so later Shannon took me to Florida for a two-week stay with two other couples in a place they called "The Compound." It was owned by a giant DC law firm and the partners were able to use it. Shannon and I were the youngest of the six people. By that time, we were "dating, but not a couple," as she explained to her friends, which I took to mean she didn't want me fucking anyone else, but she wasn't my girlfriend. I was fine with that. She was so different from Inez that I felt like I was in a whole different world. I liked the sex and the fun, and even the intrigue of hanging out in a world that was like a soap opera, especially since I wasn't the villain or the victim.

The two other couples were in their mid-fifties. At twenty-five and thirty-eight, we were kids compared to them. The men kept their eyes on Shannon, and I thought it was going to mean trouble, but evidently the other women liked the libido boost and sexual overtones Shannon brought to the vacation.

They all drank to excess. I wasn't a teetotaler, but never really saw the benefit of being drunk since I didn't need "liquid courage" to be myself. I preferred the light buzz of a couple of beers or glasses of wine. The first couple of days I hung out with the guys, but it was obvious they were more interested in golf than being with their wives, and I was more interested in being with Shannon than them. They did pump me for information, so I pretended to be discreet and gave them just enough info that they could tell their wives and have it get back to Shannon to feed her ego. I told them her tits were "picture perfect," and that I had never been fucked by a woman as good as she does it. It took less than twenty-four hours for that gossip to get back to Shannon. She was ecstatic.

As the days passed, she became less and less discreet. The three women and I were out back at the pool one evening while they guys were inside watching baseball. The three girls were sitting on the lounge chairs getting pretty drunk, and Shannon was getting loose with the innuendo. The other women, Tara and Denise, didn't seem to mind. They kept saying they remembered those days and told Shannon she better enjoy me while she can because you never know when I might discover sports. Tara said that the Super Bowl was the downfall of half of women's sex lives. She said once men found out they could get ninety percent as much fun as sex with ten percent of the effort, they did the math and that caused the invention of the "weekend widow" during football season. Denise chimed in, "And basketball, soccer, golf, baseball, and tennis..."

Pretending to be more intoxicated than I was, I said the only sport I liked was to see who could make who come the most times in one night. That got Shannon started about my stamina, and the women ate up the conversation. It went from bad to worse as they trashed their husbands, which really made me question why anyone would ever get married. Denise kept referring to Bob, and dumb me, after about the fifth time, said, "I thought your husband's name was Don" They busted out laughing and had to explain to me that 'Bob' stood for "battery operated boyfriend."

They continued to get trashed, and at some point, Tara asked to see my "cock of steel." I was in the pool at the time, and there wasn't any steel to be found, so I acted shy and hoped it would blow over. It didn't. Shannon was egging me on. I leaned over the edge of the pool for a kiss and whispered that I wasn't hard, and nobody wants to see that. Shannon took that as a challenge and dropped into the pool, and began to massage my cock underwater in the semi-darkness.

Denise said, "Are you playing with his dick?"

Tara said, "Oh, goody."

"I want to suck it in front of them," Shannon whispered in my ear. My head said, "No way," but my cock said, "Let's do it," and I began to swell to a full erection.

"Do you want me to get Denise to pull her tits out?" Shannon continued. "I can do it."

"Sure."

"Denise, do you want to see it?"

"Sure, go for it." Tara squealed a little, and they both laughed.

"Okay, show him your tits."

"Nope."

"C'mon, you want to see him, don't you?"

"I just want to see if it's all you said it is."

"Go ahead Denise," Tara said. "Show him, then you can take credit for his boner."

"Should I?" She looked back at Tara for support.

"Just go for it."

Denise undid her bikini top and pulled out her oversized and artificially enhanced tits. I had to admit they looked great. Shannon was stroking me firmly now, and I was sufficiently hard enough to be seen without embarrassment. I'm just average, but I figured my audience was used to older potbellied golfers, so I wasn't worried.

Shannon whispered, "Go ahead, give them what they want."

I said, "Are you going to help?"

"Of course."

I had been standing in water just above my waist, and I walked over about three feet. I stood on one of the steps to walk out of the pool. This brought my cock, still in my bathing suit, to the water line. Shannon put her hands on my butt and coaxed me up another step. At this point, my suit was bulging with an erection. I didn't know if Shannon was really going to suck it in front of them or not, but the idea of it was a turn on. I looked over their shoulders and could see the TV was still on through the sliding glass door. I assumed their husbands were still watching baseball.

I said to Shannon, "You take it out."

Denise was sitting there with her top around her waist, watching, and she said, "Not there, you're too far away."

I stepped up and out of the pool with Shannon behind me, rubbing my ass. I walked over until I was standing in between their lounge chairs in front of two reasonably attractive, very drunk women who most likely hadn't seen a twenty-five-year-old cock in over twenty-five years. Denise was staring at my crotch and leaned forward in her chair. Tara was laid back in the chaise lounge, sipping her drink with her ankles crossed, smiling.

Shannon said, "Last chance to take it back."

Tara said, "We're waiting."

"Here we go," Shannon said, dropping to her knees and putting the palm of her hand over the bulge in my suit as I stood there. She put her fingertips on my waistband and slowly pulled them down, pushing my cock downward until the waistband was right over my now pointing straight-forward cock.

"Get on with it." It was Denise. She was obviously ready for whatever was coming next.

Shannon gave a solid tug and pulled my suit down until it was stretched across my thighs.

She said, "Ladies, I present to you 'youth.'" She put her hands on my cock and stroked up and down causally as the women watched. Tara was leaning forward in the chaise lounge now, obviously interested in the show.

Denise said, "Our own private bachelorette party."

Shannon said, "Feel it," to Denise. She didn't need to be asked twice, and she reached out and took it in both hands, like she was going to play tug of war.

"Nice. Very nice."

Shannon said, "Rub your tits on it."

Tara said, "No, your husband's fifty feet away."

Denise responded, "We're at a bachelorette party. It's okay," and she pushed her tits on my cock and rubbed up and down. Then she took her tongue and licked the head for a second and hopped back in her chair, laughing like she had just pulled off the crime of the century and gotten away with it.

Shannon turned to Tara and said, "Your turn," as she put her hand on my cock and turned me towards her.

Tara looked up at me and I said, "It's okay with me." Tara leaned forward, looked at my cock, then she looked me right in the eye as she made a fist around it. She stroked me, letting me know she knew her way around one. She let go almost right away and turned to Shannon, and said, "If he knows how to use that, he's a keeper."

Shannon said, "Say goodbye," as she started pulling my swim trunks up.

Both women said, "Goodbye," and my cock disappeared back to its resting place.

Shannon exclaimed, "We're going to bed. Don't wait up." I shrugged and let her lead me away by the hand. Shannon was very proud of herself, and we had fun sex, laughing out loud as we played around. It was a good vacation.

I had always heard that even great sex gets boring after a while, but it just wasn't waning with Shannon, even after almost nine months. I did realize she was fragile, though.

We once ran into a waitress I had had a small fling with before I met Inez, and Shannon became very insecure. She wasn't jealous exactly. She just wanted to know every detail of our relationship. How many times I fucked her? What was she like in bed? Did she let me come in her mouth? Did I think about her? I realized that she was so insecure that she thought the only interest I had in her was for what was between her legs. Why else would I date an older woman? She knew I didn't want her money. I wouldn't let her buy me things. I told her if she bought me presents, her friends would think I was there for the gifts instead of how hot she was. That made her happy, but made me realize how mixed up she really was about her self-worth.

I tried to get her to talk about different things. She was smart and educated and could be funny in a lot of different ways, but she was just stuck in the mode that she had gotten screwed over by her ex. I tried in vain to show her how well off she was. She didn't have to work, could buy most things she wanted, and would have a pile of money in a couple of years when her husband came through to get his house back. None of it was good enough. I found out that she wasn't nearly as sex crazed when she was married and only became that way after they split. She said she became that way after meeting some guys who actually "knew how to fuck." But the truth as I saw it was that she did get screwed over by her husband, and was trying to prove to him and herself that he was the one missing out.

One evening we were in a restaurant in Georgetown in DC, and across the room was her husband's business partner. Shannon had me hold her hand, like I was hopelessly in love. She ran her fingers through my hair and kissed my fingers like our conversation was about marriage or true love or whatever else he might assume that she hoped would get back to her ex-husband.

She didn't want him back; she wanted revenge. She wanted him to find another woman and leave her former best friend, so her nemesis would feel what it was like to lose. I felt bad because I surely didn't love her and couldn't fix her, which meant I *was* just there for the sex. Sometimes I felt like a scoundrel.

We had been together about a year and a half when I decided to make myself busy and put some space between us. At first, it was probably what she wanted, too, but then once she realized it may have been my idea, she became very insecure and very sexual, trying to lure me back. It worked for a short while, but then when I pulled away again, she became resentful, and in a preemptive strike told me she needed her space. I let her win the tug of war by letting go of the rope, and as much as I missed the sex, I was happy for my freedom.

Hayden

I decided to concentrate on my career for a while, which turned into a few years. I occasionally dated someone I met, and occasionally had a one-night stand or a wild weekend with someone I barely knew. I had had sex every time I wanted it with Shannon, and as much as I wanted to be, I wasn't addicted to having it like a schoolboy. I was now preferring to have it like a bottle of fine wine. Enjoying it, savoring it, remembering it. At almost thirty, I thought I was finally growing up.

When I was thirty-one, I opened my own small heating and air conditioning business. It was just me and two guys as installers, but I was landing contracts left and right by just being fair and honest. It was such a crooked business that it was actually easy. Way easier than I thought it would be anyway.

I met Hayden when I was giving a proposal for her boss' new heating system for his new house addition. She was his personal assistant; thirty, with straight, jet-black hair and long legs. When I first saw her, she was talking to another contractor, and she was, apparently, giving him a hard time about something she wasn't happy with. I saw that as a reason to be careful. It turns out I was wrong. It was him who was giving her a hard time, and she was almost in tears when I sat down at the table in the garage to explain my proposal to her. It was hot, and she was dressed in a dark skirt and blouse that was getting soaked in sweat from the heat. I again misjudged her, and thought she was just another woman with a chip on her shoulder because of the frustration of trying to navigate the male, blue-collar world.

It turned out her boss ran a popular DC magazine and she was a publishing assistant, hijacked to do his personal errands because he owned the place. She did it hoping it would be a stepping-stone to something she really wanted. She knew nothing about building a house, plumbing, electrical, heating and AC, or dealing with contractors. If I were dishonest, I could have sold her anything at that point.

She introduced herself to me and said, "I have to confess, I know nothing about HVAC, and so if you can just look at this other proposal and tell me what the differences are so I can tell my boss, that would be great."

She handed me the proposal, and I looked at it. It was way less quality than I was offering at twice the price. I could have easily added ten thousand dollars to my estimate, still be the low bid, told her mine was the better quality, and laughed all the way to the bank. I could have done that, but that would have been dishonest. So instead, I told her the truth, not only about the proposal, but about how she was going to get taken advantage of.

I ended up taking her to lunch, and then meeting with her the next day to look at all the other contracts she was involved with. Two days later, she fired the electrician and the stone mason. Two weeks later, she had rebid the roof and saved another ten thousand dollars, and two months later, we were an item.

We got to know each other by her calling me all the time with questions on how to handle problems that came up. I knew most of the inspectors, some of whom loved to give people a hard time. I asked them to call me with any problems, so I could get her straight. I told them she was in over her head, and if there was a problem, it wasn't her trying to cut corners, and I would help her get through it. She had never had to deal with government power trippers before, and I made her life a thousand times easier. We hit it off well.

She was a regular girl with natural looks. She wore only a hint of makeup, and the construction site notwithstanding, knew how to dress smartly for every occasion. I had to step up my game to fit in, but that was okay with me since I was now a business owner who needed to show a slightly different face to the public anyway.

We went to a lot of events, due to her connection at the DC Journal, the magazine she worked for. I saw a lot of semi-famous people, and it was fun. She had a natural, approachable way about her, and we always seemed to manage to get into the front of the room or line.

She was a gentle lover. To her, sex was about our ability to find a romantic satisfaction to go along with our orgasms. It wasn't boring sex; it was close sex. I loved going down on her and making her come. I would wait until after she was out of the shower so she was relaxed and felt "clean." I would then lay her out on the bed and tell her to relax. I would take my time and listen to her breathing and watch her fingers as they opened and closed. I let her use me as a tool to achieve satisfaction, and she knew it made me feel good to make her feel good. She used to talk about how much harder I came if I made her come first. After Shannon and a lot of short-term flings, I guess something different was what was next in store for me to confuse me about who I was.

We dated for two years but never managed to fall in love. It's said that when you meet a girl her first compliment to you is that you are "so funny." A month later it changes to "Why is everything a joke to you?" That sort of happened to us. We didn't fight, but it was obvious that she was getting impatient with her career, and me telling her to be patient was not supportive. When I realized she was withholding sex from me as a tool, I started looking for an exit strategy. Neither of us was looking for marriage anyway. She was still looking for a career break, and I was still building my business.

We had a sit down one Saturday morning, and for the first time since we met, she went off on me and called me every name in the book. She told me I was bad in bed, obsessive with money, never understood her feelings, and was selfish. Then she broke down crying and told me she didn't mean any of it, and loved me, and we should try and work it out. When I said that I thought splitting up was the right thing for now, she went off the deep end again, and brought up some more stuff, including my growing up in foster homes and "dating nymphomaniacs to feed my ego."

It was a long day. I packed my stuff and left with her telling me she was sorry one minute, and then calling me a cold bastard the next. We had four months left on the apartment, and that Monday I went to the landlord and paid it all in advance. I didn't want to give her any reason to do anything but remember me fondly.

I got a letter from her almost a year later telling me she was getting married, and that the real reason she went crazy was because she thought I might be the one, but I never stepped up. I wished I had known that before I went on a binge fucking every girl who would fuck me because I thought maybe I was a piece of shit. In fact, two weeks before I got the letter, I had run into Shannon in Georgetown and went back to her new condo with her.

Shannon, Part 2

I was hanging out at a club called LuLu's in Georgetown. Shannon was there with a group of friends. I wasn't in a mood to talk to her, and it had been almost six years, so I discreetly headed for the door. I walked about two blocks, trying to decide what to do next, and ducked into a strip club called the 2020 Express, on M street. I sat up front and ordered a beer. I, as always, enjoyed watching the naked girls. I wasn't ever really turned on by the girls or their moves, but a beautiful woman's body is always a welcome sight. Kind of like a rainbow or the sun coming out from behind a cloud.

I didn't see her come in. I had presumed I had made a clean getaway, or that if she had seen me, she didn't care enough to chase me.

"I thought that was you."

Without turning around I said, "How are you Shannon?"

"Good. I finally got my settlement and have a nice new condo in the northwest, right on Wisconsin."

I turned and looked at her. She was a little older now but still fighting age as best as could be expected.

I said, "That's great. I'm glad for you." I wasn't cold. I was neutral. There was a part of me that wanted to fuck her, and a part that wanted to run before I got sucked in. She didn't seem to notice or care about my thoughts and just assumed I was happy to see her.

"So, I see your trucks around once in a while. It looks like you're doing okay."

"Yeah, I have three trucks on the road now. I'm doing all right."

"Are you 'taken' yet or still trying to decide who gets you?"

"I'm just doing the bachelor thing. Relationships don't seem to be in the cards for me. How about you?"

"You know I'm a narcissist. If I don't constantly get new lust, I go into depression."

I had been taking turns looking at her and the twenty-something beauty on the stage. The 2020 Express was known as the "classy" gentleman's club in DC, and the girls were almost always tens. Shannon was watching the girl too when the waitress came, asking if she wanted anything. She ordered a Manhattan while I chose another beer. I told the waitress to put Shannon's drink on my tab.

We watched the tall blonde dance, and Shannon leaned over and said, "So you're the perfect age now. You can get girls like that and girls like me with no questions asked. It's the perfect crime."

"Well, if I could figure out a way to get both at the same time . . . *that* would be the perfect crime."

She ignored me and said, "Do you ever think about me?"

"Occasionally."

"Are they good thoughts?"

Before I could answer, the waitress brought our drinks. Shannon began downing hers quickly. The music wasn't loud. It was classy but it was loud enough that there was obviously not going to be any meaningful conversation. I was kind of glad for that. I could tell she was interested in me, although I didn't know whether she was feeding her ego or protecting some latent insecurity. Either way, I was quite sure it had very little to do with me or my abilities in bed. I wasn't discounting my skills; I just knew that she had a constant need to be satiated in order for her to stay sane.

I pondered her question and decided one more roll in the hay for old times' sake might be fun. After all, she would be worried about whether she had aged and would probably want to make sure I had a great time. I had gained some skills along the way since we split, so I thought maybe I could turn the tables a little bit and have some fun in the process. The song ended and the dancer started gathering her stuff as a new girl was coming out. I turned to her.

"Do you mean," I said, answering her question, "when I'm on the verge of an orgasm and need something to help me over the edge, or when I'm sad and lonely and the phone's not ringing?"

"Wow! Um... I guess both."

"Well, I never look at the phone to see if it's gonna ring, and I do occasionally think about what you would do if I put you over my knee and spanked your bare ass with a hairbrush."

She opened her eyes wide, digesting that, and then downed the rest of her drink and waved her glass to the waitress as she was walking past. I assumed if she was ordering another drink, she wasn't too offended.

"What do you think I would do?"

"Beg for mercy, but get turned on, just like in the movies."

"I'll have to think about that one."

The music started and the new girl began her quick striptease to the crowd. She was a natural redhead with a deep red pubic triangle, which was rare for strippers as most were bare nowadays. I figured that was her "thing" to make her desirable. I know I liked it. The waitress brought her Manhattan, and she went to work on it as we watched "Molly" sway to the beat on the stripper pole. She was more sensuous than the first girl and a pleasure to see. As we watched, Shannon inched closer and was rubbing her leg up against mine. Five years ago, she would have already been rubbing my cock, and I decided she was worried more about her insecurity than feeding her ego.

Shannon leaned close to my ear and said, "You like this one, don't you?"

I turned and got a little closer to her ear than I needed to be and said, "I'd like to watch the two of you together, that's for sure."

She leaned back and said, "I wouldn't kick her out of bed for eating crackers."

I laughed, and we went back to watching Molly do her stuff. Each girl does three songs and then works the crowd for tips. When Molly's set was over and she came in our direction, I gave Shannon a five and said to put it in her G-string. She saw it as a dare, and when Molly got close, she waved her over and made a big production about it, getting lots of attention from the other guys, mostly older, in the room. I asked Molly if she did private lap dances and she said they were fifty dollars. Shannon looked at me, I couldn't tell if she was insulted or just surprised, but I said to Molly, "If I buy one for my friend here, can I watch?"

"You betcha."

Shannon's jaw dropped, and this time it was a dare.

"What do we do?" she said to Molly. Molly pointed to a stairway and said, "Up there. See Roland and tell him you're there for me."

I caught the waitress as we walked over to the staircase and told her we would be back, and she nodded. We went up the steps and saw Roland, a very large bouncer on a stool with a baseball bat in plain sight behind him. I presumed he rarely had to use it, if at all. He pointed to the second opening, and we went into a small room with a curtain for a door. I presumed that was so Roland would have no obstructions between his bat and an unruly gentleman, should the need arise.

The room was old school-classy with a nice leather chair with arms like a fine dining room might have. It was wallpapered and had fake artwork on the walls like you would buy at a hotel sale.

Shannon said, "Well, this is something I've never done before. What are the rules?"

"The only rule is, she's in charge, and she calls the shots. If she wants you to touch her, she will put your hands on her, so just sit back and enjoy."

Shannon sat in the chair and set her purse on the floor. She was wearing a sheer blouse with a darker bra underneath, which was something you were seeing more and more of in the club scene. Her skirt was below her knees but slit right up the center almost the entire way. She had pulled it apart at the slit, and I was within an inch of seeing all the way up. I looked into the hallway and saw Molly coming towards us.

I said, "Let me pay her now," and left Shannon in the chair while I met

Molly. I said "Fifty?"

"Yeah," she replied.

"Okay. Here's a hundred. Please do me a favor, and rave over her body. She's a little insecure because you're so young and pretty, and she needs the ego boost. Okay?"

"Gotcha."

"Thanks."

Molly walked in and said, "Well this is a pleasant change of pace." Shannon beamed and looked at me. I had taken a place, standing in the corner with my arms crossed. I just smiled and winked.

Molly said, "Before we get started the rules are, I do all the touching, and you only touch me where I allow you." Then she turned to me and said, "And you just get to watch. Got it?"

I said, "Got it," and smiled at her.

She leaned over to Shannon and said, "I'm jealous."

Shannon looked at her puzzled and said, "Jealous?"

Molly said, "Yeah, jealous. I get to get you all turned on, but then he gets to take you home and fuck you."

"Is that the plan?" Shannon smiled again and looked at me.

"We'll see."

Molly said, "Ace that bra."

"What?"

"Ace that bra, you're gonna see me naked. The least I can do is get a good look at you."

Shannon reached in her blouse and undid the center clasp, and then somehow pulled the bra out of her sleeve. With it gone her tits were completely visible through the sheer blouse. Molly took off the Redskins T-shirt she was wearing as a dress, and was now standing there stark naked. She pushed a button on a boom box on the shelf, and the Tina Turner song "What's Love Got to Do with It" came on. She bent over and pushed her bare tits against Shannon's through the blouse and began whispering things in her ear. I moved slightly to the left and was looking at Molly's beautiful pussy from behind. Her skin was milky white with no tan lines. It was exciting mostly because of the exoticness of it. She pulled back and turned around, putting her ass on Shannon's lap and her hands between Shannon's legs and up her dress. I couldn't tell if she could reach all the way, but it was close. Shannon was liking every second of it.

I leaned over a little bit further to watch Shannon bite her lip and gyrate her hips as Molly rubbed herself into her lap. Molly stood up and turned back around, dropped to her knees, and lifted Shannon's knees as high as she could reach, exposing Shannon's pussy to both of us. She rose from her knees, and spreading her own legs, stood with Shannon's legs over hers and put her hands on the back corners of the chair, placing a breast right into Shannon's mouth.

Shannon sucked it, and Molly said, "Oh god, I should be paying you."

She pulled out and switched breasts. After a few seconds, she slid back down to her knees, and then with a quick jerk she tipped the chair backwards until it hit the wall. I looked to see why it didn't tip over and realized they had installed a wooden catch strip in front of and behind the rear legs so it couldn't slide, only pivot. Molly put her wrists under Shannon's knees and lifted her legs up over the chair's arms. She was completely exposed now, and there were no panties.

Molly, still on her knees, moved forward and began biting the inside of Shannon's thighs, just above the knee. She pulled back and said something to Shannon that I assumed was a compliment, because Shannon smiled from ear to ear. The song began to wind down, and Molly let the chair come back to earth. She let Shannon's legs drop and then whispered something in her ear again. Shannon undid her blouse, and Molly suckled both her breasts for a good ten seconds after the song was over. She gave Shannon a quick kiss on the lips, turned, and gave me a big smile, which I returned, letting her know she did great.

She said, "I go back on in ten minutes. Will I see you downstairs?"

Shannon said, "Absolutely."

I was sure Shannon was drunk with both alcohol and passion at this point. She picked up her bra as if figuring out how to put it back on without removing her blouse, and I took it from her and started to put it into her purse.

She said, "What are you doing?"

I said, "You're in a strip club. Give the men a thrill."

She said, "Ya think?"

"Yeah. They all saw you shove money in her G-string, and they also saw us come upstairs. Let 'em fulfill the whole fantasy by seeing how great your tits are."

I guess she couldn't argue with that logic, so she opened her purse and threw the bra inside.

We went back downstairs and took our seats. The waitress came over, and I ordered another round. We watched a dark-haired girl with a tattoo of an angel on one shoulder and a devil on the other do gymnastics on the pole, which made me feel even more like Molly was in fact exotic. When the drinks came, Shannon went right for hers, and I sipped mine. I figured after we watched Molly one more time Shannon would want to take me back to her new condo, and I needed to be able to drive.

While we were waiting for the brunette to finish, Shannon discreetly looked around the room to see who was staring at her barely-covered tits, which was pretty much everybody in the room. Her nipples were dark enough to be seen from across the room, and her breasts were white compared to the tan on the rest of her body. I presumed she no longer had a place to sunbathe topless at any more.

Molly came on and was openly flirting with Shannon. I didn't know if it was just good for business or not, but she had the entire room convinced, including me, with her new "crush." Shannon was mesmerized by the attention. I leaned over and whispered in her ear that everyone was staring at her and Molly, imagining that the two of them were fucking. She smiled and kept looking at Molly.

I continued whispering to her. "Open your legs and let your skirt fall away. Give these old men some visual Viagra."

She smiled and slowly opened her legs, pivoting like she was leaning over towards me, letting herself fall open further as she stared at Molly dancing on the pole, giving her too much attention. About ten men were now going back and forth, looking between Shannon's legs and Molly on the pole. You could feel the tension in the room.

We stayed for Molly's set, and when she came back around again, I gave Shannon a twenty and she placed it in the G-string very slowly as the room watched. We told Molly we were headed out, and she said to come back soon. All eyes were on Shannon as she walked past with her tits in a see-through blouse and a smile on her face.

She had downed her last drink in a big gulp before we left for the ten-minute ride to her condo. Once we got in the truck, I realized she was pretty drunk. When we got to the condo, I pulled up to the door so she had to walk as little as possible. The doorman, a boy about eighteen, opened the passenger door of my truck, and as she spun around. The look on his face was priceless as he saw her breasts in all their glory. She climbed out of the seat, and I realized he was probably getting a good look between her legs too. I hopped out, laughing to myself, and helped him help her semi-stumble to the bench.

He said, "Is she okay?"

I said, "Yeah, she had one too many."

Shannon interrupted and said, in slurred tones, "I'm fine. I just need to sit for a second." I asked him where I should park, and he looked at my truck and said, "Just put it right there, if anyone asks I'll tell them you are a plumber or something on an emergency call."

I slipped him a ten, and parked the truck off the side of the driveway. When I got back, Shannon was sitting there, waiting for me, and he was leaning against the wall ready to open the door. I noticed he had positioned himself to get another shot up her skirt as she stood. I made sure I kept my back to him so he could enjoy himself. I was eighteen once too.

When we got to her condo on the twelfth floor and opened the door, I was taken aback at how nice it was. Her settlement must have been large to afford this. I was also wrong about a place to sunbathe. The balcony was a good size, and you could see all the way across to Virginia, which was five miles away. I took her to the bedroom and was contemplating leaving.

"Aren't you going to spank me?" she said.

"Maybe another night. You're pretty drunk."

"That's why you should spank me. I shouldn't get drunk. I do bad things."

"Like show your pussy to the doorman?"

"And kiss girls."

"You didn't just kiss her; you sucked her tits."

"That was fun! Are you gonna fuck me?"

"Like I said, you're pretty drunk."

"But you need to spank me. There's a hairbrush in the bathroom."

I thought about it for a minute and realized maybe she was actually pretending a little bit. She was definitely impaired, but I had seen her down way more and not be this far gone.

I said. "I'll tell you what," I said. "Let's take a shower, and if you sober up a little bit, I'll put you over my knee and spank you."

"And fuck me?"

"We'll see."

She stood up and wriggled out of her skirt and undid her blouse just fine, which let me know she was only half as drunk as she was letting on. We got in and took a quick shower. She "miraculously" sobered up a little bit, and as she dried off, I put my boxers back on.

She said, "You're getting dressed?"

"No, I just don't want my cock poking you while you're over my knee."

"Are you really going to spank me?"

"Like you said, you've been a bad girl."

"I've never been spanked."

"Not even as a kid?"

"Never."

"Well, no wonder you're so whacky. You need a little discipline."

"And the boy becomes a man and gives it to me?" She was smiling broadly at the thought of it.

"Something like that. Do you still have a bathrobe I can borrow the belt from?"

"Oh, so you're getting even, huh?"

"Maybe."

"And you're going to tie me up and spank me?"

"No, I'm going to spank you, and then tie you up."

She wasn't pretending to be drunk anymore. She was too turned on. She went over and opened the door to a closet and came out with a strap from a bathrobe and handed it to me.

"Do you have more?"

"Do you need more?"

"Yeah."

She dutifully went back and came back with one more and roll of wide ribbon like you would wrap a birthday present with. "Will this do?"

"Oh yeah."

I took them and tossed them on the bed. I then went to the bathroom and came out with a hair brush and a bottle of baby oil. She looked at the baby oil and said, "What's that for?"

"To rub in when I'm done. It will soothe the pain."

"Oh, is that how it's done?"

"That's how it's done."

She stood there for a second, perhaps wondering if this was real or not and then said, "What now?"

I sat on the edge of the bed and said, "Drop the towel and bend over my knee from this side. I'm left-handed."

She said, "Here goes nothing." She dropped the towel and lay naked over my lap.

I said, "Do you want it bareback or with the hairbrush?"

"You're in charge. Which one is gonna teach me a lesson?"

"I guess I'll start with the brush and finish bareback. Are you ready?"

"I don't know."

"Are you a bad girl?"

"Yes."

"Did you let strange men look at your pussy?"

"Yes."

"And you liked them looking, didn't you?"

"Yes."

"Then we need to punish you."

I slapped her ass with the hair brush semi-hard to see how she would react. She squealed in pain with a hint of pleasure, and I wasn't sure whether to go harder or softer. I went harder. She squealed again, this time with more pleasure. I hit her ten times until her ass was cherry red.

I said, "See what happens when you show strange men your pussy? You get punished."

"But you told me to."

"I was testing you to see if you would do it. You're a bad girl." I smacked her ass again two more times. "And you liked them looking, didn't you?"

"Yes," she responded meekly.

"And what about that doorman? You liked letting him look at your pussy too, didn't you?"

"Yes."

"And I didn't tell you to show *him*, did I?"

"No."

"Now you get it bareback, do you know why?" I said, setting the hairbrush down.

"Why?"

I put my hand between her ass crack and rubbed my fingers outside of her soaked pussy teasing it while she squirmed.

"Because when you got in my truck to come here, that meant that from that moment on this pussy belongs to me, and I didn't give you permission to let anyone look at it, did I?"

"No."

"But you let him look, didn't you?"

"Yes."

"And that makes you a bad girl, doesn't it?"

"Yes."

"Okay. Take your punishment like you're supposed to and I'll rub your ass with baby oil to make it feel better. Got it?"

"Okay."

I spanked her hard seven or eight times. She was jumping and squirming from the pain and the pleasure. I stopped and let my hand rest on her ass.

"Okay. You took your punishment, so I'll rub you with baby oil, and make you feel better. Would you like that?" I said.

"Yes."

"Are you gonna be a good girl?"

"Yes."

"Okay. You relax and let me take care of you."

I picked up the baby oil bottle from the bed and rubbed it on my hands and all over her ass gently, and then as she calmed down and the redness went away, I began manipulating her ass cheeks slowly but aggressively, allowing my fingers to go down between her pussy lips but not inside. She was squirming in place and wanted my fingers inside her. I didn't go inside and just kept rubbing the outside. I had other plans for her. I slowed down and then stopped with my hands on her ass.

I said, "Time to tie you up."

She said, "You're serious?"

She was obviously turned on and up for anything at that point. I lifted her off of my knees and said, "Lay in the middle of the bed."

She went and lay on her back, waiting for the next instruction. I used the ribbon and tied her wrists to the headboard while she lay there in silence. I then took one bathrobe belt and tied it around her knee. She looked at me puzzlingly, but when she saw me tie the other end to the headboard instead of the foot board, she realized that she was going to end up with her legs spread wide with her knees up, splayed for whatever I wanted to do. She just allowed me to finish restraining her.

I went to bathroom and grabbed a small towel and put it over her eyes.

"What are you doing?"

"Whatever I want. Do you want another spanking?"

"No."

"Then be patient."

"Okay."

I went down between her legs and played with the wetness with my fingertips while she moaned. I then began licking her pussy gently and pulling away, torturing her. She wanted to push herself to my mouth, but I pulled away just out of reach.

"Do want your pussy licked?" I said.

"Yes."

"Say 'please.' "

"Please!"

"Please what?"

"Please lick my pussy."

"I don't know. You were a bad girl. I don't know if you deserve to have your pussy licked. Will you be a good girl if I lick your pussy?"

"Yes, I promise."

"Will you only show your pussy to people I let you?"

"Yes, I promise."

"Will you suck my cock for me?"

"Yes."

"Can I come I your mouth?"

"Yes. Please, lick my pussy."

"Okay."

I licked her pussy for a while until she was getting close to an orgasm.

"I think that's enough for now," I said.

"NO! I wanna come. Please, don't stop."

"No, I think I need my cock sucked for a minute, it's lonely."

"She opened her mouth, and I slipped my cock in. She moved her head up and down on me as fast as she could. I took one hand and held the towel in place over her eyes and used my other hand to play with her tits while she gyrated her hips, wanting to be touched. I pulled my cock out of her mouth.

"I want to rub my cock all over your tits. Is that okay?"

"Yes."

"Do you like this?"

"Yes!"

"And I could come on your tits, if I want?"

"Yes!"

"Can I come in your pussy?"

"Yes!!"

"Can I come in your mouth?"

"Yes, anything, just make me come. Please!"

I put my fingers inside of her, and she was gushing wet. She began humping my hand and moaning. She wanted to come so bad, but I just kept bringing her close and then stopping.

"Ughhh . . . You're killing me . . ."

"I know. I haven't decided whether I'm gonna make you come. You've been a bad girl."

"Please!"

"Do you want my cock inside of you?"

"Yes, I want your cock."

"Well, you need to suck it for a minute to make sure it's all the way hard. Are you going to suck it good for me?"

"Yes, I promise I'll suck it good, I swear."

"Okay, let's see how you do. If you do a good job, I'll put it in your pussy."

"Yes, yes!"

I slid myself into her mouth, and held her head with my hand while I went in and out, making sure her eyes stayed covered with the towel. She opened her throat and let me glide all the way down. I pulled out of her mouth.

"That was good. It's all hard. Do you want it in your pussy now?"

"Yes."

"Okay."

I got between her knees and slid myself inside of her. She was pushing herself towards me, and I began pumping hard right away. I spread my legs about a foot apart and went up into a push-up position and pumped her hard until she came. I kept pumping until I was ready to come, and then pulled out and shot my come all over her stomach, tits, and even some on her mouth. She squealed in laughter and pleasure and tried to lick the come from her chin with her tongue. I climbed up and wiped my dick all over her tits and then put myself into her mouth and she sucked hard just to make sure there was nothing left. I pulled out and went and got a towel and wiped the come off of her while she was still tied up and her eyes still covered with the other towel.

"Oh, my God! That was so good. Fuck!" she said.

I went over and turned off the lights, and then told her to lay there and relax while I untied her. I did so and left the towel on her face for last. When I slid it off, we were in the dark room, lit only by the city lights and the moon.

She looked at me and said, "My boytoy is all grown up."

"Does that disappoint you?"

"God, no."

I said, "So do you want to do this again sometime?"

"Sure! I'll make sure I'm a bad girl, so you have a good reason to come over."

"Sounds like a plan," I replied, tucking the towel I had removed from her face between her legs. "Sleep well."

"I will."

I got up dressed and left while she dozed. That was the last time we ever had sex. We crossed paths but it was casual, and it was as if we both realized we should go out on a high note.

Deena

Over the years, I've had a few relationships that never actually ended up in bed. A lot of women have rebound sex just to make sure they are still desirable, and it is fun. But sometimes it's not good for the woman. Plus, I truly never wanted to hurt anyone.

I was in Atlanta at a trade show when a woman named Deena threw herself at me, going as far as getting me up to her room. Once we got there, she confessed that she had never had an affair, but that she was in a sexless marriage. Part of me wanted to be the scoundrel, but there was something about her that made me feel like she was more lost than looking for a good time. She was drinking heavily, talking about her marriage as if to justify what she was about to do, and talking like she was vulnerable when she was in fact the aggressor. I decided to talk with her for a while to see where things led. She said that she and her husband were arguing all the time about his long hours and money. She felt neglected and distanced herself from him. Now, he just treats her like a roommate. She said she had no idea how to get things back to where they were.

I ended up going only as far as rubbing her shoulders. I let her talk for two hours about her woes. In that time, I found out that she had turned him down for sex with excuses, and it backfired, and now he doesn't give her any attention. She was in decent shape and pretty enough, and she said until she pulled back, they had a decent sex life. After a while, she realized her and I weren't going to have sex, and we began talking about how to fix her marriage.

She said, "How can I just tell him I want sex now? What if he turns me down?"

"Do you think he will?"

"I don't know, it's been almost a year."

"And he isn't cheating?"

"I don't think so. I think he just gave up."

She said she wasn't the kind to seduce somebody; it would look fake or ridiculous, or "something," and it had been going on so long that she couldn't even bring it up. She was sure he was angry at her for shutting him down, and she had no clue how get past it. She said it would feel weird for them to have sex now. I suggested they both get completely drunk and let nature takes its course. She said he didn't drink, and she had never been sexually aggressive in their fifteen years of marriage. She was really depressed, and said her girlfriends' advice was always the same: cheat.

I tried to change the subject. I was at a loss for advice because whenever a woman went from wanting me, to letting me, to me asking for sex, I headed for the exits. I know that sex is more important to men than women in most cases, but I also know that once someone loses interest it is really hard to get it back. I had slept with too many women who told me exactly that. I had had trysts with women who had great-looking, rich guys in their lives, but they were in my bed, and a lot of it was that we both had a need for sex and affection, and an equally strong desire to not be locked into something that could go bad. I found myself in bed many times with women for the simple fact that we both knew there would never be any love or magic between us. We both felt "safe" with the situation. It made for some great times and few fights. When things were over, if we were both honest, then we were both happy, kind of like an extended vacation with good memories.

Deena was crying softly. She said I was a nice guy, and that she was glad I was there to talk to. That was her way of letting me know that not only were we not having sex, but the official lie would be that I was just a shoulder for her to cry on. I felt bad for her. She was just too shy to make the first move, and her husband was too afraid of rejection to do it. I told her I did have one idea.

"Tell me. Please!"

"Are you willing to lie a little to get things going again?"

"I don't know, maybe. I mean I'm here in a hotel room with a man who's not my husband. What kind of lie would I have to tell?"

"Well, you will also have to act."

"Act? Act how?"

I said, "Well, it's kind of crazy, but it might just work."

"Tell me!"

"Okay, here goes... your too shy to just seduce him or jump his bones, right?"

"Oh, yeah."

"So, here's my idea... First, you go to a doctor and get a prescription for Ambien."

"Why?"

"Let me finish... so, you get the prescription. You tell the doctor you can't sleep, and that you tried one a girlfriend gave you, and it worked like a charm."

"Why would I take sleeping pills?"

"You aren't going to take any sleeping pills."

"I am so confused."

I laughed as I realized I was talking nonsense, mostly because I was still hatching the plan in my own head as I told her.

"Okay, so here is the deal. You tell your husband you can't sleep, and that the doctor is giving you Ambien. You tell him you're a little nervous because it has made people sleepwalk and not remember it. Make a couple of jokes about how somebody went outside and washed their car in the middle of the night, so if his car is waxed, he needs to let you know so you can dial it back."

"But why would I..."

"The first night," I interrupted her, "you pretend to take it. You also pretend to talk in your sleep, and if he wakes you up you have a nonsensical conversation with him, and then deny it in the morning. Keep it light, like ask him why the cat is wearing his hat, or does he know which side the bread is buttered on. Then pretend to fall back to sleep, and if he tries to wake you, act like you're in a deep sleep. The key is to keep it light, so it's funny, not scary. If he overreacts, then pretend to take the pills but just sleep normal."

"Why?"

"Because you are going to evolve from silly dreams to sex dreams, and then you are going to climb on him and have sex with him in your fake sleep, hopefully within a couple of weeks. Once that happens, you go back to sleep, and in the morning just say you're in a great mood but don't know why. Hopefully, once things are jump-started the engine will keep running."

"I'm scared. What if it doesn't work?"

"Only one way to find out. Do you have a better idea?"

"No."

"Then at least think about it."

We talked a little more, exchanged numbers, and I went back to my room. I pleasured myself thinking about what I had just missed. Deena started calling me almost every afternoon. I would do paperwork while we talked. After a couple of weeks, she went to the doctor and got the prescription. She was into it now, and it was officially "the plan." She said no one knew about me or the plan, not even her girlfriends. She said it was weird how they would have heard all about what might have happened with us in her hotel room, but not this. Deena said she kept our plan to herself because she didn't know if it was too wrong, or if it was because if it worked, she would never want her husband Peter to get wind that it was a set up.

She had been telling him that she was waking up constantly at night, and that explained the doctor visit and the prescription. She told him she was taking the pills, and laid the ground work about the side effects. She told him that if she was vacuuming the rug to go ahead and let her finish before waking her, and then laughed. She said that the first night she was too nervous and just slept normal without doing anything.

The second night she mumbled loudly around one a.m. to see what he would do. He woke up and gently tried to wake her. She pretended to fall back to sleep, but then started again a few minutes later. She said she asked him if it was daylight-savings time yet because she needed to feed the cat. Deena said it worked like a charm. The next morning, he asked her about it, and she told him she didn't remember anything. We talked for an hour. Deena was all excited that this plan might actually work. Being somewhat of a scoundrel, I had a good time pumping her ego and telling her, in no uncertain terms, what I would have done that night if I believed she really wanted to have an affair. It made her regain some much-needed confidence. I gave her scenarios of all the things she could do, guilt free, while "under the influence," and she was getting very excited about the whole thing.

She called me the next day a little early, and she was very excited.

"I think it might work."

"Yeah, what happened? What did you do?"

"I walked around the house naked, turning on all the lights."

"What did Peter do?"

"He asked me what I was doing. I said I was looking for my sock."

I laughed. "Then what happened?"

"He took me back to our bedroom and tried to get me to put on clothes. I told him, 'no,' and that I was too hot. Then I went and crawled into the bed naked."

"Was that it?"

"No. Once I was in bed, I waited for him to get in, and then I asked him where my clothes went."

"What did he say?"

"He tried to get me to snap out of it, but I just stayed in character."

"Then what?"

"He put my pajama bottoms and top on me."

"That was it?"

"He was turned on. I could feel his, you know, when he rubbed against my leg."

"His cock."

"Yeah, that."

"And that was it?"

"This morning he asked me how much I remembered, and I said I didn't remember anything. He told me I was walking around the house naked and he had to dress me."

"Was he upset?"

"No, he thought it was funny. He said he was going to get me an ankle bracelet in case I started wandering the neighborhood. He was in a good mood too."

We talked a little more and then I said, "You know what comes next don't you?"

"Sort of, but I'm not sure what to do."

"Can I make a suggestion?"

"Please, do."

"So, tonight, assuming he is in a good mood, you go to bed as normal. At about one or two a.m. when he is asleep, figuring you're okay, you quietly take off your pajama bottoms and get yourself excited, and then start moaning like you're having sex. When he wakes up and tries to wake you, you say to him, "Remember that time we . . .""

"We what?"

"This is where you fill in the blank with some time you had some really hot sex with him."

"At the lake. We did it on the dock in the dark."

"There you go. You tell him you can't stop thinking about it. Then you reach under the covers and grab his hand and put it between your legs, right into your wetness. If he pulls away and doesn't want you, pout and act like you are going back into a deep sleep, and then we will figure out a plan B. The odds are that he is going to keep it going. Just remember, you can do whatever you want if he rolls with it. In the morning, act like you had another great night's sleep and see how it plays out."

"I'm scared."

"You want to save your marriage, don't you?"

"Yes."

"Then get over it."

"So, I guess I'm really going to do this?"

"You don't want to do this?"

"No, I just want my husband back."

"Your enjoying this, you know how I know?"

"How?"

"Because I can hear it in to your voice. I would bet a hundred bucks you're wet right now."

"Oh, you think so?"

"Tell me I'm wrong."

"There is nothing wrong with me trying to save my marriage through... creative means, right?"

"You go get him. Call me tomorrow."

Deena called me the next morning as soon as Peter went to work, and told me they fucked all night. She called me almost every day for about a month filling me in on how things were getting better.

I gave her the best advice I could. She faked taking the pills as a way to liberate her sexuality, and Peter loved it. She said she told him after a couple of weeks she didn't need them anymore, and they just kept things going. I told her she had pulled off the perfect crime. As far as I know they are still together.

Sandy

A few months later, I slept my way into a three-year relationship.

I had been keeping to myself for a while. I wasn't losing interest. I was just feeling like the girls I was meeting were a little too jaded, and while I didn't think I wanted a relationship, I had lost interest in having sex for the sheer sport of it. I wanted to be remembered as the guy that got a girl to open up and give up all her secrets because I was safe. That often takes an emotional commitment on my part. At that point, that was something I had no interest in giving. So, instead of yet another series of one-night stands and weekend flings, I just kept to myself. I wondered again if perhaps I should have made more of an effort with Inez.

After my sabbatical for solitude, I ended up sleeping with a client. Sandy was a thirty-nine-year-old lawyer. She was a couple of years older than me, but it didn't seem to make any difference to either of us. She worked for the IRS and had purchased an old house in Arlington, Virginia, and contracted me to do the HVAC upgrades. I had been there about a dozen times, checking on the situation as we were working with her other contractors doing the retrofits as the work progressed.

We had always flirted a little bit, as is my nature, but I was always professional and careful not to cross any lines. Sometimes, however, temptation takes over, and you let nature takes its course.

I had called her on a Wednesday and set up an appointment at nine-thirty the next morning to measure her return ducts in the upstairs hallway so I could get them ordered. The phone call was normal. When I arrived, she opened the door in a towel with wet hair. She said that she forgot I was coming, and to come on in. She was slender with light brown hair, and when she turned around and ran up the steps with the towel barely covering her ass, I immediately felt like it was going to be a good day. She hollered for me to follow and go ahead and get the measurements. She went into her room and closed the door. I went upstairs in the hallway with a screwdriver and a measuring tape to get what I needed. She opened the door, standing behind it with two hands peeking around and said, "I have coffee. Help yourself. I'll be down in a minute." I said, "Thanks," and went to work.

She left the door ajar, and I naturally kept one eye on it just in case I might be rewarded, and I was. She walked past it naked, giving me a nice profile, and then with her back to me, she pulled a dress over her head and shook it into place while I stood down the hall and watched. She walked out of sight, and I put my arms up to measure while keeping an eye out. A second later, she came into view with a pair of sandals, and put her hand on the dresser to brace herself while she slipped them on. She came out into the hallway and said, "Are you getting what you needed?" My immediate *thought* was, Almost. I realized she didn't have enough time to put on any underwear and was definitely intrigued by the possibilities waiting for me downstairs. I answered that everything was fine, and that I was almost done. She said, "I'll see you in the kitchen," and went down the steps with me looking at her ass. She didn't look back.

Five minutes later, I was sitting in her kitchen, having a cup of coffee. We talked a little about the progress on the house, and she said she was home for the day because she was catching a plane at four o'clock to visit her parents for a week.

After a couple of minutes of easy talk, she said, "So, I guess the rumors of women answering doors for workmen in their towels isn't just a myth, huh?"

"No, it's not a myth. It happens."

"How often does it happen to you?"

"Not as often as I would like, but it's always a nice surprise."

"So, how often do you end up sleeping with your clients?"

"Now, that's more of a myth."

"So, you don't seduce all those lonely housewives?"

I laughed. I could tell she was fishing and trying to get me to make a move.

"I don't ever seduce a client."

"Never?"

"Never. Now, they occasionally seduce me, but I never make the first move."

"Why not?"

"Well, it's their house, and if I were to make a mistake, or read a signal wrong, it could cost me my business. So, I just wait until they seduce me. Fortunately, I'm an easy mark."

"You are, huh?" She was smiling, and then continued. "How do they do it… seduce you, I mean?"

"Well, they usually try and guess my situation to find out if I'm single or available by making small talk. They might let me know they're interested by flirting or telling me their situation. Sometimes, they even answer the door in a towel."

"Does that mean they want to sleep with you?"

"No, that's just one sign. They might do something else like get dressed with the door cracked and not wear underwear, hoping I'm watching, but that still isn't enough for me to make the first move."

"It's not? That seems pretty bold to me."

"Oh, it's bold, but I still need more."

"Like what?"

"Well, like she might ask me if I think she's pretty."

She said, "That's a loaded question. She might not want to hear the answer."

She was getting anxious now. This was a slow dance, chess match, and she was enjoying us putting each other in check.

I said, "That's true. She might not, but I do my best to put them at ease so they know I would never say anything to hurt their feelings."

"How do you do that?"

"If I don't want to sleep with them, I tell them I think they are very pretty, but if my girlfriend asks, I will deny I even heard the question."

"What do you say if you do want to sleep with them?"

"I tell her that she is pretty in a hot kind of way and hope that doesn't offend her."

"Why would that offend her?"

"It shouldn't, but it's complicated. I need plausible deniability if things go bad."

"Plausible deniability? I haven't heard that term since law school. Have things ever gone bad?"

"Well, I have been asked the question, 'Why don't you love me,' more than once. It's tough when someone thinks they love you, and you just don't love them back. Basically, I'm kind of a respectable scoundrel."

"Respectable scoundrel. That's a new one."

"Well, it's not pretty, but its accurate."

She was quiet for a minute. She sipped her coffee, looking at me and was pondering things.

I asked, "What are you thinking?"

"I was just wondering what you would say if I asked you if you thought I was pretty."

"Do you want the answer?"

"I'm not sure."

"I'll tell you."

"That's what I'm afraid of."

"What are you afraid of?"

"That you'll tell me you have a girlfriend."

"You're not afraid that I will tell you I don't?"

"No."

"And you're not afraid that I will tell you I think you're hot?"

"I wouldn't believe it, but I wouldn't be offended."

"What if I told you that I watched you put that dress on and knowing that you're naked underneath is making me crazy? Would that offend you?"

"Well, what do you mean by crazy?" She was smiling broadly now.

"Um... excited, I guess."

"Are you excited?"

"A little bit... no, a lot..."

"Really?"

"Really."

She took a sip of her coffee and looked me right in the eye and said, "Can I see?"

"See? Whether I am excited it or not?"

"Yeah. I want to see." She was the one with confidence now. She had just put me in check again.

I said, "I'll show you mine if you show me yours."

"You've already seen mine. Now, it's my turn."

I pondered the situation for a minute and realized I was ninety-nine percent hard anyway; so why not?

I stood up and said, "You really want to see?"

"Yep."

"I'll do it."

"I'm waiting."

I unbuckled my pants and slid them down over my thighs and was standing there in my boxers. She was sitting in a chair with her coffee cup in her hand at eye level with my hard-on, straining the front of my boxers.

She looked up at me and said, "Well, I'm still waiting."

I pulled the waistband forward and pulled myself out in all its glory. She took a sip of her coffee and put the cup down.

"Can I touch it?"

"Sure."

She grabbed it with her fist and gently stroked me up and down. She then took her other hand, and picked up the coffee cup, took a swig, and put her mouth over my cock, with the hot coffee making my cock even harder. She looked me right in the eye as she began going up and down with her mouth on my cock. I put my hands on her shoulders and let her take control for a minute.

Then I said, "Let's go to the bedroom."

She took me out of her mouth and said, "Okay," and put my cock back into my boxers. I pulled my pants up and started for the stairs.

When we got to the staircase she said, "In here," and pulled me into the first-floor guest room. I sat down on the end of the bed and pulled off my T-shirt and kicked off my shoes. She kicked off her sandals and pushed me gently back on the bed. She lowered my zipper the rest of the way and pulled my shorts down and off. As she reached for the boxers I reached for her dress and lifted it up and tried to pull it over her head. She leaned over and helped me get her naked. She then pulled my boxers off, and we lay on the bed on our sides with our heads on the pillows and kissed. She crawled down and put me in her mouth again.

After about thirty seconds I said, "I want to taste you." She sat up on the bed and climbed over me into a sixty-nine position. I could smell her sweet scent of arousal, and the taste was just as sweet. I licked her with a lot of passion. She was pushing herself on me, and I could tell she was having trouble concentrating on pleasuring me.

I said, "I want to be inside of you." She obviously wanted the same thing.

She turned around, and as I lay on my back she climbed on and inserted me inside. I lifted my hips to give her maximum depth. She began riding my cock with a steady rhythm, and placing her hands on my chest, she pumped me hard. It was obvious that she had found a sweet spot. I just kept myself in place so she could hopefully make herself come from her own thrusts. Her head was tilted back and her eyes were closed. She had very pretty, smallish breasts with very small nipples. I reached up and touched them, and she shivered. They were taut and sensitive. She started grinding harder, and I could see her chest become red above her breasts, all the way up to her neck. She came hard, rocking hard in waves.

Putting more and more weight on her arms and my chest, she let the passion subside. She collapsed onto my chest and put her head on my shoulder and tucked herself into my neck. She was smaller than me, and it was a perfect fit.

I said, "That was nice." She just moaned, and then started slowly riding me some more.

I could tell she wanted more, but was too spent to do the work. I turned her over and managed to stay inside of her. I lifted her knees to her chest and fucked her hard. She laid there and just moaned quietly from my efforts, enjoying the thrusts.

After a few minutes I said, "I want to come."

She said, "Yes I want to feel it."

I lifted myself up and thrust as hard and as deep as I could, coming with powerful thrusts as I growled out loud from the pleasure. She kind of squealed with excitement as she ran her arms up and down my sides.

I collapsed onto her and braced my weight on my elbows. "That was fun," I said, looking her in the eyes.

She said, "It was even better than I imagined."

"Than you imagined?"

"Uh… yeah…"

"Cool."

"Cool?"

"Yeah, I didn't think girls imagined things like that. I assumed that was a guy thing."

"Well, now you know. I guess the secret's out."

I laughed and kissed her on the lips. I slid out and rolled over on my back. I said, "So how did you imagine it?"

Without missing a beat, she said "Which time?"

"It was more than once?"

"Do you want the truth?"

"Of course."

"Well, I wanted to sleep with you the first time you came over. The way you sized me up, it was like you could read my mind. I mean, you were like looking at me and not hiding the fact that you were looking, but you weren't like a perv. It was like you knew what I was thinking."

I was flattered and thought to myself she wasn't wrong.

She continued, "In fact, truth be told, you're the reason I didn't stop taking my birth control pills last month."

"What?"

"When my boyfriend and I broke up, I stayed on the pill for a few months to see if we might get back together, but once I realized it was completely over, I was ready to stop taking them, and then . . ."

"And then?"

"And then came you. You show up, and you're all tan, and it was like you knew I needed sex, and that's when I began imagining how it would happen."

"So, why today?"

"Because you're almost done. You hadn't made a move, and I only have another week before I have to decide whether to take the pills for another month."

"So, are you going to keep taking them?"

"Are you going to keep coming over for . . . coffee?"

"Take the pills."

We started seeing each other, mostly for dinner and sex at her place. She was almost insatiable. She said that she was always that way at first, because she went so long between relationships, rarely had flings, and never knew if things would last. We sort of fell onto a relationship without ever really discussing the formality of it. I could tell she was monogamous because of our conversations. Finally, about a month and a half in, she asked me about it. We were lying in bed around eleven one night, and I was getting ready to head home.

"So, are we . . . exclusive yet?" she said.

"Do you mean, am I sleeping with anyone else?"

"Or... dating or whatever..."

I could sense that she was struggling to ask a question she didn't want a negative answer to. I decided to make it easy for her. I rolled onto my side, facing her as she lay on her back.

I whispered in her ear, "You are the only woman in my life right now, and I am not looking for anyone else. I haven't slept with anyone since about two months before we had our little 'towel incident'; however, that fat Spanish maid at the bus stop does wave to me in the mornings when I spend the night, so..." She rolled on her side, and put her arms around my neck and hugged me.

"I had to ask. I didn't think anything. I promise."

"So, this isn't about that Spanish maid? I could have gotten away with doing her in the bushes?"

"Go home."

And just like that we were dating.

We started doing the dating things, and making plans together. She lived across the Potomac River from me, so we didn't see each other every day, but we talked most nights and were together most weekends. She would stay at my place or I at hers. Because we weren't together every day and sometimes apart for three to five days at a time, the sex stayed fresh. She wasn't wild in bed, but she was always in search of the next orgasm. She talked about how she didn't lose her virginity until college and that she had gone a couple of years without any sex with a man at least a couple of times. She said that she wanted to have a tryst, but it was hard for her conscience to allow it. She said that didn't stop her from having sex, and she had a cigar box in a bottom drawer with a few toys she used for the lonely times. She said she didn't use them when she had a boyfriend because the real thing was worth waiting for if it was only going to be a few days. I discovered a few months in that she had a much more active imagination than I first thought.

We were lying in bed early one evening when I was going to spend the night. She was wearing one of my T-shirts and little white cotton briefs, and I was gently rubbing her breasts.

She said, "Why are you always so fascinated with my breasts? They're tiny."

"They're sexy."

"If we were both twelve."

"I like them."

"Why?"

"Because they are so sensitive to my touch. I can always tell when you like what I'm doing."

"I wish they were bigger."

"So, you toss quarters into wishing wells and hope for the best, huh?"

"No, I just wish they were bigger, that's all. Sometimes, I just fantasize about having big ones and . . ."

"And what?"

"You know."

I said, "I don't know. Why don't you tell me?"

She just shook her head as if I was being ridiculous and moved my hand down in between her legs. I decided to do some detective work. I started teasing the hair between her legs and then I said, "So who do you fantasize about having sex with your big boobs?"

"That's a secret."

"Why? I don't care. Do you think I don't imagine having sex with some girl on the subway or crossing the street?"

"Yeah, but you're a guy. You can get away with it."

"Well, if you remember, counselor, *you* are the one who brought 'imagination' into evidence the very first time we had sex. So, you can't plead the fifth, now."

"You watch too many cop shows."

She was very wet now. I could tell she liked the idea of confessing her thoughts to me but was just a little shy. I was getting aroused myself to find out what went on in the dark corners of her mind. I continued with my interrogation.

"Okay, let's just start with what we do know. We know you imagined having sex with me. So, what other guys working on the house were in your mental Rolodex?"

"Nobody you would know."

"So, then there were some?"

"Not some, just one. I don't want to talk about this." Her hips said otherwise.

"Sorry, too late. You're on the witness stand, sworn in, and you will be held in contempt of court if you don't answer."

"Are you going to throw me in jail?"

"No need."

"Why is that?"

"Because, just like Jack Nicholson in the movie, *A Few Good Men*, you want to confess."

"Confess what?" She was really hot now.

"C'mon, the court is waiting. Who's the mystery guy you wanted to have sex with? Or did you have sex with him?"

"No, I didn't have sex. I just thought about it... I was still dating William."

I had my fingers inside of her now and was slowly fingering her.

"So, I need details. Give."

"You really want to hear? I'm embarrassed."

"Trust me, I'll seal the file so no one ever sees it." She laughed and put her hand down and repositioned my hand a little bit.

"Okay," she said, "his name was Paulo, and he was an Italian guy around twenty who was breaking up the cement on the driveway last summer. He barely even spoke English."

"So, what happened?"

"Nothing happened, at least not in real life. He was just so good-looking and tan, and had these muscles that you never get from going to a gym. This is embarrassing."

"Too late. So, did you at least hit on him?"

"No, I just watched him work from the window. It was like a hundred degrees, and he was soaked in sweat and dust, and he was taking water from the water cooler and pouring it over his head. I just kind of hung out in my room and watched him work. That's all."

"That's all? Bullshit. You're all wet now just thinking about it."

"That's because you're rubbing me."

"So, you're in your room, all wet, watching an Italian Adonis in one-hundred-degree heat pour water over his sweaty muscular body."

"Adonises are Greek."

"Ah-ha! So, you don't deny that you were wet on the day in question?"

She laughed. She was still aroused but more relaxed as she realized I was truly interested in the details.

"Okay, I'll tell you, but you can't judge me."

"Okay, courts dismissed. We are officially off the record. Now, give."

"Well, like I said, I was watching him work, and after a while he took his shirt off."

"And . . .?"

"And he looked even better without it."

"So, what did you do?"

"I stole his shirt. I mean, I put it back, but he put on a fresh shirt and forgot his sweaty shirt on the fence, and I brought it into the house."

"What did you do with it?"

"I don't want to tell you."

"Why not?"

"It's too embarrassing."

She was pushing herself onto my hand now. She was completely turned on, and I could tell she really wanted to tell me everything, but was worried about how I might react. I slid over and pushed my erection-filled boxers into her side and put my head on her neck and whispered in her ear.

"Tell me babe, I want to hear it all."

"You won't judge me?"

"I promise."

"Okay, I took the shirt inside and put it to my face and smelled it. It was just so… masculine. I took it upstairs and … finished what he started."

"That's not embarrassing."

"But that's not all."

"Okay, what else?"

"Well, that's when William and I were having problems, and he had been begging me to come over and, you know, fool around, so I called him and told him to come over and take a Viagra first."

"And, of course, he came running."

"Yeah, and…"

"And what? It's okay." I was still buried in the nape of her neck and fingering her in a steady rhythm.

"Well, we had sex, and after a few minutes, I rolled over on my stomach and, well, I pretended he was Paulo."

"That's nothing to be embarrassed about."

"But, but… I had the T-shirt under my pillow, and I pulled it out and buried my face in it while he was screwing me, and I came like four times."

"Did you tell William about the shirt?"

"God, no. He thought it was all him."

I took my hand from between her legs and pulled her underwear down as far as I could reach. I climbed up and pulled them the rest of the way off. I took her body and rolled her over and pulled her shirt up over her ass. I pulled off my tee shirt with one pull, and put it in front of her. I slid my boxers off and then climbed on her and slid myself inside. Once I was in, I lifted my legs outside of hers and squeezed her legs shut and then whispered in her ear.

"Tonight, I'm Paulo. You have big tits, and this is Paulo's shirt." I pushed the shirt to her face and began fucking her with solid steady thrusts. She began moaning right away. It only took her a minute to reach the first orgasm. She reached two more before I couldn't hold out any longer. It was a fun night, and set the stage for a lot more fun in the bedroom.

We were both in a good place for the moment. We were both getting what we needed and without any pressure from the other to move the ball forward, as so often happens in relationships.

I guess that made Sandy my most normal relationship, except that we never moved in together. We both liked our space and were used to living alone. Her ex, William, had wanted children, and she didn't, which is why their relationship ended. I don't think either of us thought too much about the long term; we were both enjoying the present, and the months just slipped away. We never fought, and there was never any real tension. She went on vacation a couple of times with her girlfriends, and I was all for it. When she asked me what I wanted her to bring me back my answer was always the same: "Tan lines. Tasty, tasty tan lines."

She knew I trusted her, and she trusted me. I always looked at women. I still do. It makes me happy. It's no different than a gardener looking at flowers blooming in someone else's garden. It's just nice to see them. I never "picked" one, though. I was happy with her.

She was quietly sexual, which I liked. I was always coaxing her to go the next level of passion. I convinced her that I liked hearing all the fantasies she had gone through "in the lean times." Once she realized I was into it and not judgmental, she just needed a couple of glasses of wine to tell me all the thoughts that no one on the planet would have guessed were in her head.

Learning from the Paulo encounter, I would lay there in bed and fondle her while she told me about all the different fantasies she had had over the years. She said that in college she had majored in pre-law and minored in masturbation because she didn't have a boyfriend and couldn't do the one-night-stand thing.

About a year and a half into the relationship, I won a free trip to Greece, which was really just a bribe from a big HVAC company to make sure I kept them as my primary supplier. We went to Mykonos. I was looking forward to the topless Europeans who frequented the nearby Paradise Beach. We arrived in the late afternoon and had a wonderful first night, sleeping with the windows open and the warm, salty air reminding us we were on vacation. The next day we went to the beach, and as expected there were lots of sights to see. Sandy was in a tiny bikini, and I told her I was okay if she wanted to go topless or even naked, but she declined, and I didn't push the issue. I didn't want her uncomfortable. It was a nice day, and the beaches were as spectacular as promised.

When we got back to the room around four o'clock, I went into the shower and she went after me. When she came out, I went to dry her off and hopefully have our first of what I wanted to be many sexual encounters on the trip. She, for the first time in the relationship, rebuffed me. She kept the towel draped around her and said, "Maybe later." She picked up her clothes and went to the bathroom to change, which was really strange because she had no qualms about being naked in front of me. I let her go and went over the day in my head to try and figure out what might have upset her. She wasn't mad, but there was something wrong. I thought the typical guy thing that her period had started, and she was either embarrassed or afraid I would be disappointed.

I put on underwear and nylon sweat pants and waited for her to come out. She was fully dressed for dinner, except shoes. I waited to see if she was going to say anything and she didn't.

"So," I said, "Are you hungry?"

"Sure." She wasn't short or complacent, but there was something on her mind.

"Are you okay?"

"I don't want to talk about it. I'm fine. Let's go to dinner."

I said, "Sure, but whatever it is that's bothering you can tell me. We may be in Greece, but I'm still me. You can tell me anything." I was leaning towards her period starting.

"I'm fine. Really." She needed to be let off the hook, and I let her off. Whatever it was would come out soon enough. She wasn't a brooder.

"Okay. Let's have some lamb. A guy on the beach told me about a place called the Molyvos Taverna, which is only a block away. It's still early so we should be able to get a table overlooking the ocean."

"Sounds nice," she said and was back to her normal self. I let the other go.

We walked down the two-thousand-year-old sidewalk to the five-hundred-year-old building and got a nice table, where we could see the ships going by out in the Mediterranean. We had a nice dinner and talked about renting scooters to drive around the next day. She drank a traditional drink called Ouzo that is 40% alcohol with lots of sugar, which delays the effects. The waiter warned us that it would hit us a little later and to make sure we weren't driving. She was only about a 120 pounds and had two. By the time we got back to the room she was wasted. It was still early, so we sat out on the balcony that overlooked the city as the sun began to set. She was very drunk and talking about how beautiful the country was, and said she had always wondered why ancient Greece collapsed. In her inebriated state, she decided it was because with all of this, who would want to go to work?

"That's a pretty good observation for a drunk girl."

"Are you mad that I'm drunk?"

"Not at all. I'm enjoying it."

"Good, because I like being drunk sometimes. That Ouzo is good!"

"Well, if you're happy, I'm happy."

"I'm sorry we didn't fuck." That was the first time I had ever heard her use the word outside of the bedroom. I thought it was funny to hear it, and it also let me know how drunk she really was.

"Do you want to know why? Because I want to tell you."

I had decided it was her period and said, "Sure, go ahead."

I was completely surprised by the response.

"I hate my tits."

"You what?" I was laughing.

"I hate 'em, hate 'em, hate 'em. They're too small, and I don't want you thinking about other girl's tits while you're fucking me."

I was really laughing now. She was truly wasted, and there was nothing coming out but the truth.

I said, "I love your tits. They fit your body perfectly."

"If I was just starting puberty."

"They're not that small. You were just inundated today with all those topless women."

She interrupted me, "YOU were the one who was inundated. I saw you looking at all those giant tits. All tan and, and, and big!"

I busted out laughing. I said, "So you think I like big giant tits huh?"

"Of course, that's what all guys like."

"Not all of us. I'm more interested in what they are attached to."

"Yeah, well you can't titty-fuck titties if they don't even touch."

I was laughing uncontrollably, now.

"Titty-fuck? I didn't even know you knew that word."

"Everybody knows that word, and all guys like doing it."

"That's not true. Not all guys…"

"Have you ever titty-fucked a girl?"

"Of course, but…"

"But you've never titty-fucked me, you know why? Because I don't have any tits."

"You have tits." I was trying to think of a way to change the subject before it went south but couldn't do it.

"I don't have tits. I have titty wannabes."

I laughed again, but I was realizing she was, in fact, describing how she felt, and it saddened me a little for her to feel that way. She did have small breasts, but they were beautiful on her small frame and they were also a big part of our sex life. I was just always of the opinion that a woman has no control over her breast size any more than I did of my cock, so why should the sexes judge each other on what nature gave you?

"So, I don't get to play with them anymore?"

"Why would you want to?"

"Because it makes my dick hard to look at them, and I like having a hard dick."

"Yeah, right."

"Pull 'em out and I'll pull out my dick and you can watch it get hard."

"Nope. They're too small, and I'm sleepy. Besides, even if you got hard you couldn't titty-fuck me anyway." She closed her eyes, and in about two minutes, she was passed out.

I carried her to bed, wondering what she would remember the next day. I wasn't upset with her. I just wanted to find a way to make her feel better about herself. She was very pretty and had nothing to be ashamed of. I figured that although I felt adequate with my cock, if I was strolling on a beach with guys swinging baseball bat-sized dicks, I might feel a little dejected too.

The next morning, she woke up only a little hungover. I got out the massage oil and rubbed her neck and feet hard. It was a surefire way to get rid of a headache from dehydration. She perked up. I went out and brought us back some breakfast.

I asked, "So do you remember last night?"

"Maybe. I'm not sure what was real and what was a dream."

I said, "Well, why don't you tell me what you remember, and I'll tell you want happened and what didn't?"

"Doubtful."

"You don't want to know what happened?"

"Happened?"

Bad choice of words. "What we talked about."

"Can we pretend last night didn't happen?"

"So, you do remember?"

"Sort of. Can we just . . . forget it?"

"Sure. Are you up for renting scooters?"

"Sounds good."

We had a great day. Went to an early dinner and came back and had really nice romantic sex. I didn't do anything different than we had done in the past. I wanted her to assume that I wasn't thinking about what she had said, or any other woman's breasts. I did my best to make the sex about us, and Greece, and closeness. Afterwards, I did try and think a lot about what I could do, so she didn't have to feel the way she did. We had a little wine and went to bed early.

In the morning, I went for a walk and talked to the concierge at the hotel, and asked about less-populated beaches where locals frequented. It was the tourists who came for the topless beaches more than the residents. He gave me some choices, and I bought two pairs of wrap-around sunglasses and went back to the room.

I said, "I found us a nice private beach only the locals know about to go to today. What do you think?"

"We can go back to Paradise Beach. I'm okay."

"I want to go somewhere where it's less crowded."

"And it has nothing to do with my drunken confessions you haven't talked about?"

"Absolutely not."

"Okay, we can go where you want."

We packed up and had one of the million taxis take us to Paraga Beach, about half an hour out of town. It was quiet, sparsely populated, and beautiful. We appeared to be the only obvious tourists there. I saw a couple of topless women, but, by and large, everyone was clothed. I had brought a cooler with a bottle of wine, Sprite, ice, cheeses, glasses, and grapes. I had a plan. I was going to get Sandy drunk and then get her to take her top off and wear the sunglasses to see if the men checked her out. I didn't know if it would work, but it was worth a try.

I waited until noon and then opened the wine. I started plying her slowly until she had a nice buzz going, and then began feeding her grapes. I teased her with stories of how two thousand years ago she would be a Greek goddess and have young, strapping servants feeding her grapes and refilling her wine glass, wishing they could have sex with her. She was enjoying the thoughts, and when I thought she was sufficiently lubricated, mentally and physically, I pulled out the sunglasses and said, "Here put these on."

"Why? I'm already wearing some."

"Because these are wrap around, and no one can tell what you're looking at. The men wear them so they can check out the women."

"Why would I check out women?"

I thought maybe I had gotten her too drunk, but she corrected herself. She continued, "I have no interest in checking out these men. I'm good."

"I want you to do something for me."

"What?"

"I want to see you go topless, and I want to watch other men check you out."

"Why would you want me to do that?"

"Because you're mine, and I want to see them jealous."

"Nobody wants to see me. This is just about the other night."

"Please?"

"Nope. Nobody wants to see me."

"Then prove me wrong. Please?"

"You really want me to do this?"

"Yes, I really do."

She reached over and grabbed the sunglasses, took hers off and put the new ones on, reached back and untied her top, and pulled it off over her head in one swift motion.

"You've got fifteen minutes to try and find anyone who wants to look at me."

"Deal."

I put my sunglasses on and lay back with my head tilted like I was asleep. I wanted anyone walking past to feel comfortable enough to look without having to be too discreet. I needed for Sandy to see proof that she was attractive.

After about two minutes a man and his wife walked past. She was wearing a one-piece suit with large boobs, and her husband made no bones about checking Sandy out. When they were out of earshot I said, "Dino one, Sandy zero."

"You have twelve minutes. Enjoy it while you can."

There was no one nearby, so I refilled her glass and lay back down. Within the next ten minutes, at least a dozen people walked by, and all of them, including the women, took a good look at her lying there. Her nipples were taut from the ocean breeze and she really did look good. She was small, but she was well proportioned.

I asked, "Will you keep the top off for a while longer?"

"Just a little while." I was sure my little escapade had worked. I waited until another dozen or so people walked by with the vast majority making a point of looking, and then I said, "We need to go back to the hotel."

"Why?"

"I need sex."

"We had sex last night."

"Yeah, but that was romantic sex. I need animal sex."

"Animal sex?"

"Yeah. Get your stuff."

"Okay."

She stood up and put her top on while facing the crowd of people down beach. We grabbed a cab back to the hotel.

When we got to the room, she said, "I'm going to take quick shower before you defile me."

"No way. I want you smelling like the beach."

"But..."

"But, nothing. I want you."

I walked over to her and took off her sunglasses and unwrapped the sarong that was over her bathing suit. I took her top off and pulled her to the bed.

"What are you doing?"

I took off my T-shirt, kicked my tennis shoes off, and pulled off my swim trunks, exposing my hard cock. I picked up the bottle of massage oil and put it in her hand.

I lay on my back on the bed and said, "First, you're going to play with my cock while I suck your nipples, then we're going to fuck."

"But, I'm all sweaty."

"Yep."

I lay there holding my erection, pointed towards the ceiling and she said "This is crazy, you know."

"I know. Now, rub."

She got on her knees on the bed next to me as I slid over. She opened the massage oil and poured too much on me and immediately had to rub it all over to spread it out. While she was doing that, I pulled her to me and began suckling a nipple. She moaned a little bit, and I could tell she was turned on too. I was sure she liked being looked at. Who wouldn't?

I switched nipples while she rubbed me all over. There was too much oil, and she was rubbing it on my legs and balls, taking attention away from the shaft, which was probably good because I was now really aroused, and wouldn't want this ending in an accidental ejaculation.

I said, "I want to lick you."

"But I've been at the beach."

"I don't care. I want you."

I put my hand down and slid her bikini bottoms down over her ass, and she took her free hand and got them off the rest of the way. She climbed over my face as she kept stroking me. I helped position her and buried my face between her legs. It was sweetly pungent and incredibly arousing. She was soaking wet and tasted good. I licked her as she stroked me. She had a quick orgasm, which let me know she was probably aroused from going topless.

I said, "Put me inside of you."

She let go of my cock and turned around. She reached through her legs and grabbed my cock, sliding it in while she purred in satisfaction.

As soon as she was settled in place I said, "Put your hands on the headboard." She did, and I said, "Now tease me with your nipples while you fuck me."

She began fucking me and lowered a nipple into my mouth. I suckled it gently, and then after almost biting the nipple, I lifted my head up and licked the entire breast aggressively.

She pulled back and switched to the other side, and I repeated my routine. She was fucking me in a steady rhythm, which was for her benefit not mine. She was enjoying this every bit as much as I was.

I dropped away from her breast and said, "Sit back so I can see you."

She let go of the headboard and leaned back, putting her hands on my chest. She began rocking back and forth in long hard strokes.

I said, "Look at me." She opened her eyes and saw me staring at her chest.

"Now, close your eyes."

She closed them. "Now imagine its midnight and we are on the beach fucking in the sand."

I continued, "Rub yourself." She put a hand down and started rubbing her clit while she was fucking me.

"Are you imagining it?"

"Yes."

"Now, imagine all the men who looked at your tits are watching you right now and what it would do to their cocks."

"Ahh… ahh. I'm coming. I'm coming…"

I said, "They all want to watch you come. They want to know how tight your pussy is. They can see how stiff your nipples are getting."

"Oh, fuck. I'm coming…"

I reached up and played with her nipples hard. That took her over the edge. She rocked back and forth on my cock hard, and her hand was full speed on her clit. She was riding a wave, and I knew what she was imagining. It took all of my self-control to not come and ruin it for her by going soft. She collapsed on me and said, "Oh, God. That was so good!" She lay there for a minute and then slid off of me, crawling up to lay in the nape of my neck and tell me that she was going to sleep for a week.

I said, "Don't go to sleep just yet."

"Why not?" she asked, half asleep already.

"Lift up a little." She lifted up and I put a nipple in my mouth and suckled gently.

I said, "Just stay there. This will only take a minute."

"What?"

I put the nipple back in my mouth and began jerking myself off while I suckled her nipple. She watched for a few seconds and then put a hand down and started teasing my balls. She pushed her nipple hard into my mouth and said, "Come baby, let me see you come." Less than a minute later, I came, and it went half way up my stomach.

She said, "Wow. I guess you weren't kidding about being turned on. I think maybe we might have found a new favorite beach."

We went back two more times, and she went topless both times.

Sandy, Part 2

After awhile, Sandy and I had gotten ourselves into a routine and slowly drifted apart. We still had fun and still had sex, but the novelty had worn off, and we realized we were just kind of hanging around without purpose. It wasn't bad. it just wasn't good. It had been over two years, and we were both thinking maybe it was time to move on.

She brought it up first.

"Are you happy?"

I replied, "For the most part. Why do you ask?"

"No, I mean with us. It doesn't quite feel the same. I mean, it's not bad, but it just feels like we're married or something."

I laughed. "You mean you feel trapped, and it isn't as exciting as it used to be?"

"Sort of."

"I get it. I kind of feel like that too. Not trapped, but there isn't much to look forward to that's exciting and new. Is that what you're talking about?"

She said, "Yeah, I guess so. It's hard to talk about. I mean, we get along pretty good, but it is still just routine sometimes. It's like, is there more?"

I sat quiet for a minute and said, "Well do you want to break up?"

She replied, "I don't think so. What about you?"

"No, I haven't really thought about it. There is no reason to rush into it. How about we see what happens over the next few weeks and talk some more?"

"Okay."

That was the extent of it. A relationship like that is kind of like a train slowing down, coming into the station. It takes a while. We rolled down the track for another year, and then when we were finally both ready, we gently went our separate ways. Our paths never crossed day-to-day anyway, so it was actually pretty easy. Both of us were okay with it.

The Time-Out

I spent my fortieth birthday in New Orleans. I was single and decided that I was going to take a road trip. I first went west to Memphis and visited Beale Street where Elvis used to play. I headed south to New Orleans and did my best to pick up a one-night stand for my birthday and failed miserably. I didn't know if I was out of my element or league, but I spent the night going from bar to bar, and then somewhere around one a.m., I ended up at a strip club, realizing my birthday was over and I didn't get laid. I downed another couple of beers and went back to the room and went to sleep. I didn't even jerk off.

After an eight-hour drive, I tried again the next night in Atlanta, and the best I could do was get a phone number of a woman from Baltimore who was there on business.

When I got back to DC, I concentrated on building the business and stopped chasing skirts for a while. I wasn't used to rejection, and it didn't feel good. I stayed that way through the winter and then when spring broke and the women started wearing skirts again, I was like a rutting buck. I started frequenting the bars on Capitol Hill and having trysts with some of the girls who worked there. I was being an alpha and scoring solely for the sake of it for the first time in my life. By the time summer rolled around and the city cleared out as Congress went home and people took vacations, I was done with that and forced myself to stop being such an ass. I had always prided myself on getting inside women's heads to make them feel something they had never felt before. The chapter of my life that was me fucking for me wasn't satisfying at all.

Lisa and Carol

Carol was a secretary who worked at an insurance firm next to my work. We had met in a bar one night about twelve years ago and had fooled around many times over the years when neither of us were in a relationship. She referred to herself as a "Catholic school girl gone awry" who loved sex. She was also looking for love, but she was truly a victim of provincial ways, wherein a guy wants to have sex with a loose girl but wants to marry a virgin. Carol could be wild in bed, and guys would wonder how she got that way. I tried to counsel her a little, but it didn't help. We had fun because she knew I wasn't boyfriend material, and I didn't judge her for being so damned horny.

Carol had a friend named Lisa, who had run wild with her when they were in their twenties. They would jump from bar to bar. Lisa was now a born-again Christian and married to another born-again Christian. They had been together for about ten years. Carol and I went to dinner with her and her husband once in their hope of trying to "save us." I took it in stride, but at dinner all I could think of was about the time Carol told me her and Lisa had drunken sex with two brothers in an Ocean City hotel room with two double beds and the lights on. She told me other stories and imagining Lisa wilder than Carol amused me. We made it through dinner without either of us bursting into flames for our sins. Other than Carol telling me they thought I was "savable," I didn't hear too much about them. Which brings me to my story about Lisa.

I was in Safeway one summer evening around five in the afternoon, looking through the fruit near the entrance when I saw a cute woman coming into the store in a see-through yellow summer dress with a white lace bra and panties underneath. The sun was shining right through the dress, and it may as well have been nothing. She was also wearing sunglasses and sandals. When she lifted the sunglasses, I realized it was Lisa and waved to her. She came right over and said hello.

After a little chit chat about how long it had been, and me being the scoundrel I can be, I said, "You really look great. That's quite a change from your church outfits."

"What do you mean?"

"Well, you're in public in a see-through dress. Very cool."

She looked at me in total shock. "You can't see though this."

"Um . . . white lace bra, matching white lace panties . . . I'm not superman. That dress is thin."

"I can't believe you just said that to me. I'm a Christian, and I'm married."

I immediately took it back because I could see she was truly upset.

"I am so sorry. I was just fooling around. I know you're a Christian. I didn't mean anything by it."

"Okay. Well, I need to get my shopping done. I'll see you around."

She walked away quickly, and I went the other direction, thinking that I was probably going to get a phone call from Carol, letting me know that I was going to hell.

About ten minutes later when I was reading the label on a bottle of spaghetti sauce, I heard a voice from behind say, "I would never wear something see-through in public, and I think you owe me an apology for assuming I would."

I turned around and looked at her, staring up at me with a defiant look in her eye. What she said annoyed me a little. I didn't want trouble, and I was genuinely remorseful for opening my mouth, but I had already apologized, and *she* was the one in the see-through dress.

"I said I was sorry."

"You said you were sorry for accusing me of wearing something see-through, but not for assuming that I would even wear something see-through in public. I would never do that."

I was taken aback enough by her self-righteousness, and I couldn't just let it go.

"Okay, I'm sorry that I assumed you had mirrors in your house. How's that?" I instantly regretted my comeback. I was only annoyed, not mad.

"I do have mirrors, and this is not see-through."

I fumbled to make things better but failed miserably.

"Look, I'm sorry you're upset. I really didn't mean anything bad. You're a very pretty woman, and I'm just a guy. For the record, the dress *is* see-through, whether you like it or not. I will take you at your word that it was an accident, but I'm not going to pretend I don't see what I see. You're still wearing it, and it's still see-through."

She looked at me in disbelief for a second and then said, "You're impossible."

I said, "I get that a lot. Listen, I am very sorry I upset you. If I had known you were this sensitive, I would never have said a word about the dress, and I'm very sorry I assumed you would knowingly wear something like that in public."

In my head I was laughing at the ridiculousness of it all. There was a woman, standing in front of me in a very sheer dress, and while deep in the store it wasn't as obvious. Anyone with a prying eye could see everything.

She said, "I guess that is as close to an apology as I'm going to get."

I didn't want to continue, and I don't think she did either. I said, "Are we okay?"

"Yeah, I guess so."

She turned around, found her cart, and wandered off toward the back of the store. I left before she thought of some other way to twist the truth.

I wasn't home two hours when the phone rang. I was sure it was going to be Carol asking me why I tried to have sex with Lisa in the produce section.

"Hello."

"Hi. Is this Dino?"

"Yes."

"This is Lisa. I'm not mad, but I want to talk about what happened at Safeway."

"I said I was sorry."

"I know, and I accept your apology. I just want to ask you to never mention it to Carol. She has a big mouth, and I just want it all over with."

"Want what over with?"

"Just today. All of it. I want to pretend it never happened, okay?"

"Do you mean what I said; or you wearing a see-through dress?"

She was silent for a minute.

"I just don't want Carol knowing."

"Knowing what?"

"Any of it."

"What difference does it make?" I was curious now and was wondering if Lisa knew I was aware of her past.

"I don't know. It's just embarrassing, and I don't want anyone to know any of it."

"You didn't tell Michael then?"

"My husband? No, he wouldn't be happy with what you said at all."

"What would he say about the dress?"

"If the dress were see-through, he wouldn't like it, but it isn't."

"You can keep saying that, but that won't make it true."

"Why do you keep saying that?"

"Because you were wearing a white lace bra and panties that said otherwise. Why do you deny it? I thought Christians never lie."

"We don't, and I'm not."

I was having fun with the conversation now. I was beginning to think she liked the attention and was calling for more.

"So you don't lie?"

"Right."

"So, and I want the truth now because you said you don't lie. Okay?"

"Okay."

"Are you wearing white lace panties and matching bra?"

"I'm not going to answer that."

"Why not?"

"I'm married."

"Okay, then how about this... If I pretend nothing happened today, wouldn't that make me complicit in a lie of omission?"

"It's not a lie of omission unless it is something the other person deserves to know."

"Like your husband?"

"I asked you not tell Carol."

"So, I can tell your husband?"

"God, no."

I said, "I'm very confused. So, let me get this straight. You came into the store wearing a non-see-through dress, and I guessed exactly what color and style of underwear you were wearing, out of the blue, and then apologized for making shit up, and now I have to promise to make sure I don't tell Carol or your husband, but it's not a lie of omission even though your husband should know if other guys are telling his wife that they can see through her dress when they can't?"

"Is this just a joke to you? I'm truly upset."

"Listen, it *is* kind of a joke to me. You can pretend all you want, and I have no interest in telling anyone what I saw, but you were wearing a see-through dress with white lace panties and bra, and you looked very fuckable, and I'm a guy who says what he thinks, and I know what I saw. In fact, when I close my eyes, I can still see it."

She was silent again, this time for much longer. I could feel the vacuum form from the silence.

"Lisa. Listen to me," I said, " I won't ever say a word to Carol or anybody else. It will be our secret. I don't understand why you are denying the truth, but there is something going on and maybe you should talk to someone about it. I think maybe you wore that dress because subconsciously you are not feeling as beautiful as you once did and got more attention than you bargained for, and now you're feel guilty about it. I don't know, I'm not a psychiatrist."

"I do feel guilty."

"What do you feel guilty about?"

"I'm married to a fine man, and I should never disgrace him."

"You're not disgracing him by wearing something a little risqué once in a while."

"I didn't wear anything risqué. Please, stop saying that. It makes me feel worse."

I was really getting turned on, and wanted to know more about what was really going on in her head.

"Okay," I said. "But answer me this: is it wrong for a man to have a wife that other men are a little jealous of?"

"What's that got to do with it?"

"Well, if you were my wife, I would want you to wear see-through dresses all the time. I would want other men to imagine what they are missing that I was lucky enough to have."

"That is wrong on so many levels. Have you ever even read the Bible?"

"Yeah, yeah, 'don't covet another man's wife.' I get it, but it also says a wife is supposed to honor her husband, and if a woman wanted to honor me then she would need to make all of my friends want her, but come home to me."

"So, you would be okay with other men looking at your wife half-naked?"

"Yeah, I would want a wife who enjoyed letting other men get a glimpse of what they were missing, and what I was going to bed with every night, while they lay next to someone not nearly as hot as you, and dream about you."

"That's sick, you know."

"Tell me the truth. The *real* truth. Now that you have had a little time to think about it, aren't you at least a little flattered that I noticed how hot you looked to a point that I had to say something? And don't lie."

"Flattered isn't the word."

"Well, then what is the word?"

"I don't know. You have me all confused."

"Okay. I don't want to confuse you, but will you think about it and call me again, so we can figure it out."

"I don't know."

"Why not? Maybe you can fix me so I can go to heaven... or at least not burn in hell."

"Do you promise not to ever say anything to Carol about today?"

"If you'll promise to call me again."

"And talk about what?"

"I don't know. You can tell me how you really feel about me picturing you naked."

"I can tell you that now. It's wrong."

"That just tells me what you think about it, not how it makes you feel."

"I can't have this conversation."

"Then I can't promise to not tell Carol."

"You already promised."

"Well, I want a new deal. You think about me picturing you naked for a day, and then call me and tell me how it makes you feel, and I won't tell Carol. Deal?"

"That's blackmail."

"Right, and I want honest answers too. I think your head and your heart love your husband, but your body misses being admired, and I want to know how it makes you feel to know there's a guy out there who openly imagines having sex with you."

"I can't do this."

"I'm seeing Carol Saturday."

"I can't do this."

"Okay, well I need to go now. I need a cold shower."

"Why?"

"Because I think you're still wearing that same dress. I'll talk to you when you call. Goodbye. Have a nice night." I hung up before she could respond.

I immediately called Carol and set up a date for Saturday night, so if Lisa called fishing, it would come up in conversation. I was having fun.

I hadn't heard from Lisa for two days. I figured she was done with our little dalliance, and it was over. Then on Saturday morning around nine a.m. the phone rang. It was Lisa.

"I don't want you to go out with Carol today."

"Why not?"

"I don't trust you."

"You didn't live up to your end of the bargain."

She said, "There was no bargain, just an attempt at blackmail."

"You still didn't live up to it."

"Because it's blackmail."

"Why should I give up free sex with Carol because you don't trust me?"

"Because if you said anything to her, she wouldn't keep it a secret."

"So, it's a secret now?"

"No, it's . . . Why do you always twist things? I just want what happened to just never be told to anyone."

"You mean you want to keep what happened just between you and me?"

"Yes."

"That's a secret. Just like your dress was see-through. You really need to get a dictionary."

I was thoroughly enjoying this. I could tell that she was enjoying my flattery, and this was a way for her to communicate in her state of denial. I was sure she was lonely and wore the dress for the attention but bit off more than she could chew.

"You are impossible."

"I just realized something. I was thinking about that dress and it looked brand new. Has your husband ever even seen you in it?"

"What difference does that make?"

"Has he?"

220

"I'm not answering that."

"I didn't think so. That's why you want make sure our secret doesn't come out, isn't it?"

"No, I just… it's just embarrassing, that's all."

"It's not embarrassing for me, and I'm not giving up sex because you don't want anyone to know you think about sex once in a while."

She was quiet for a minute, then she said, "If I go back to the original deal and answer your questions, will you cancel your date with Carol?"

"Will you be honest?"

"If I'm honest, will you cancel the date with Carol?"

"Only if you answer the question in person in the same dress as you wore the other day. We can meet in the Safeway parking lot."

"No."

"Why not? If it's not see-through, then you have no worries."

"Because I will know what you're thinking."

"You already know what I'm thinking. I'm telling you what I'm thinking."

"No. I will answer over the phone or no deal."

"Okay, but just so you know, Carol loves for me to tell her about women I meet that turn me on, so I'm not going to tell her that it was you, but I am going to tell her about seeing a woman in that dress, and how I can't stop thinking about her. Carol loves to play along and will ask me all kinds of questions and even pretend to be you while I fuck her."

"You can't do that."

"I've done it with other girls before. Don't worry though, I won't use your name."

There was a long silence, and I waited, hoping she might take the bait.

"If I meet you in the parking lot for five minutes, will you cancel your date?"

"You'll wear the same dress… the same everything as the other day?"

"Yes."

"And you promise to answer my questions. You're going to be honest and tell me how it makes you really feel to know I think you are incredibly sexy. Not that's it's wrong, but how it makes you feel?"

"Yes, okay."

I said, "Good. We have a deal. I'm going to call Carol and tell her I can't make it, and I will see you at eleven o'clock. That way if you don't show I can call Carol and put the date back on again."

"I'll be there."

I got to the parking lot about ten forty-five and positioned myself in the far corner so that the sun would be behind her to give me a perfect view through the dress. I didn't know what was going to happen, but I was having a lot of fun. If I didn't know her past, I would have felt guilty. Maybe I should have anyway, but I didn't.

She pulled in right at eleven. I saw her and waved her over. She pulled into a space and sat for a minute before she got out. I opened my car door and sat there so she would come to me and stand where I wanted her to stand.

She walked over, looked at her watch, and said, "You have five minutes. The clock is ticking."

"You're going to be honest with me, right?" I said, stepping out of my car.

"That's the deal." She was feigning like she was mad, but I could tell she wasn't. She was nervous, but definitely not mad.

"So, first question, did you think about how it makes you feel to know men find you desirable?"

"That question isn't on the list."

"There is no list . . . You agreed to let me ask questions."

She looked at her watch. "Four minutes, ten seconds."

"The clock stops when you refuse to answer a question."

"No."

"All right. I'll just call Carol back and say my plans changed and I'm available."

"Okay, okay, we can start again. Repeat the question."

"How do you feel knowing I find you desirable?"

"I don't know whether you find me desirable or not, so I don't have an answer. Next question."

"Okay, you were supposed to think about how it made you feel to know that I imagined you naked. How does it make you feel? And you have to tell the truth."

She thought for a second and said, "It makes me feel like there is something wrong with you."

"Did you imagine me seeing you naked like you promised?"

"I did my homework, and that's my answer."

"Did it excite you?"

"No."

"You're tough."

She looked at her watch. "You have two minutes, forty seconds."

"Does it excite you that you are standing in front of me with the sun shining through your dress and I can see your panties and bra?"

"Well, you can't, so the question is moot."

"Stop the clock. That's a bullshit answer."

"The clock is ticking. It was truthful."

"Nope. The clock stops or I call Carol."

"That's not the deal."

"It is now. We both know that half the reason you're here is because you like me wanting you. You just don't want to admit it because of your church stuff. You say you're telling the truth, but you're not even telling the truth to yourself."

She was really nervous now. I didn't know if I had angered her or freaked her out, but I definitely upped the ante.

"I'm here because I don't want you having sex with Carol while thinking about me. That is it. That, and I don't trust you to not tell her about this stupid dress that isn't too thin."

We had forgotten all about the clock. I was enjoying the view, looking at her in the thin yellow dress with her white underthings.

I said, "Okay, now your being honest. So, let's talk about that. I think you are very beautiful. I always have. If you were my wife, I would make you wear dresses like this all the time, and since I can't do that, I don't see any harm in pretending while I am with Carol. I just think you're jealous that she is going to get passion that you earned by looking so good. So, here's a question . . . What do you think about that?"

"I think I'm married, and that you shouldn't be telling me things like that."

I said, "Why not? It's true. Just because you're married doesn't mean you're not hot."

"I'm not hot."

"Oh, you're hot, all right. You've been married, what? Ten years? That's a lifetime. Having sex with you would be like me having sex with a virgin. Everything I would do to you would feel new."

"Why are you talking to me like this?"

"Because I don't want to have sex with Carol and think about you. I want the real thing."

"And you think I'm just going to jump into bed with you?"

"No, but it sure is fun getting inside your head."

"Your five minutes are up. Are you going to live up to your end of the bargain?"

"Do you mean am I going to not have sex with Carol and pretend it's you?"

"Yeah. And never say anything to her about any of this."

"Well, there is one more condition."

"What's that?"

I picked up my digital camera and held it up.

"You cover your face with your arms, and I get a picture of you in that dress."

"No, way."

"That's the condition."

"That's not fair."

"I know, but I really want a picture."

"Why?"

"So, I won't be tempted to call Carol for phone sex and accidentally slip."

"Just take the picture." She lifted her arms up and put her elbows in front of her face, and I snapped three pictures really fast.

"Okay. I'm done."

She said. "So, you're going to keep your promise?"

"Cross my heart and hope to die." I smiled at her. She was a little flustered, and I got the impression she wanted to talk longer.

I said, "Listen, If you ever want to just talk, you can always just call me. I can be a good listener."

She looked surprised at my comment and seemed to have to think for a minute as to what to say.

She finally, said "Thanks, but I don't think my husband would like me talking to someone who has admitted that he wants to have sex with me."

I said, "The lord works in mysterious ways," and then opened my car door. "Think about it. You have the number."

I was hoping for a phone call, but it didn't come. After a few days, I called Carol to say hi and fish. Lisa was right. Carol couldn't keep a secret and she didn't. She told me that Lisa had called, and during the conversation asked her about who she was dating, and "somehow" my name came up, and Lisa tried to convince her that she should just stay away from me so she could find a husband. She told me Lisa said I was probably just using her for sex, and didn't care about her. I told her that it was just God talking, and that Lisa probably just needed to get laid. Carol then proceeded to tell me that Lisa had told her a couple of years ago that her and her husband only have sex every couple of months and that they never have oral sex because "wives don't do that."

I asked her more about when they were younger, and she confirmed what I already knew. Lisa was definitely the wild one of the two. I knew that whatever seed I planted in Carol's head would get back to Lisa. I decided to play around a little bit, and I told Carol that maybe Lisa was right, and that we should not hang out so she could find a good guy, and that when

I was lonely I would just jerk off over women I saw at the grocery store. Carol said that was dumb, and I told her to tell Lisa so she would get off her back. I figured it was a mixed signal for Lisa. I wouldn't be seeing Carol, but telling her I looked at girls at the grocery store just might freak her out.

It did.

Two days later Lisa called. It was a Saturday morning around eight a.m. I said, "Hello," and there was silence on the other end of the line. I said, "Hello" again.

"This is Lisa."

"Hi, Lisa."

"Why did you tell Carol that you looked at girls at the grocery store?"

"So you would call me and I could hear your voice."

"That's not funny. You promised."

"Well, I should have made you promise not to sabotage me with Carol."

"I was just making sure you held up to your end of the bargain."

"I didn't say I wouldn't have sex with her again. I just said I wouldn't think about you while I was doing it. Why do you care whether I have sex with her or not?"

"I just don't want you thinking about me and saying anything."

"You know what I think? I think you're jealous that Carol can have sex whenever she wants by making a phone call. You're lucky you let me take a picture of you in that dress. Do you want to know why?"

"Why?"

"Because when she called and wanted me to come over, I had just gotten done looking at it and jerking off. Otherwise, I would have probably gone over and made her do all kinds of things to me while I shut my eyes and imagined she was you."

"That's disgusting."

"No, it's not, and you don't think so. Carol told me that you guys barely have sex anymore, which means I was right. Your head and your heart love your husband, but your body is dying for attention."

"Just stop. That's out of line."

226

"Maybe, maybe not. But I still think your jealous of Carol. Am I wrong?"

"Yes. You are wrong. Carol needs to have what I have, a loving husband and stability."

"And a see-through dress you can't wear in front of your husband, but instead let a man take a picture of you in it after he tells you he wants to take you to bed."

"That's not fair. You blackmailed me."

"No, if I were going to blackmail you, I would use the picture to make you have sex with me. Your face may be covered, but that's your car in the background and his ring on your finger."

"Oh, my God. You wouldn't!"

"No, of course I wouldn't, but you need to at least be honest. This whole thing is because you are not happy with at least part of your marriage, and whether you admit it or not, you like the attention, and you're jealous of the fact that Carol has more sex than you."

She was silent. We sat there on the phone in silence for a good thirty seconds. I decided to try and make things better.

"Look, there is nothing wrong with you wishing your marriage were better. Even people whose marriage is almost perfect wish for better, and nobody has a perfect marriage. You're just going through a tough time right now. It will get better."

"Will it?"

"Sure. All husbands lose a little libido with age. It'll come back. Do you really only have sex every few months?"

"It's been like that for a while now."

"How long?"

"Almost three years."

"Does he have a physical problem?"

"No."

"A girlfriend?"

"God, no."

"So, what do you think it is?"

"He looks at stuff on the computer and then goes in the shower."

"Porn?"

"Yeah."

"How do you know?"

"Well, he shuts himself in his office and says he is doing counseling with people from the church, and its confidential. If I go in, he closes it down and shoos me away, but a couple of times I heard the sex noises, and started going in to check his history when he was in the shower. Oh, and he locks the bathroom door. He used to never do that."

"What did you find in the history?"

"That's just it. Nothing. It's always cleared."

"Then you don't *know*."

"I wasn't finished. I cracked open the blinds in his office and snuck out on the deck and peered in."

"Porn?"

"Yeah, he won't touch me, but he can watch other girls have sex with anybody and everybody."

"Okay, so this is fixable. You just need to not hide flimsy dresses from him. Once he finds out you like sex, he will be all over you. Why watch when you can have the real thing?"

"I tried that. It doesn't work. He doesn't think 'wives' should be like that. They need to be proper."

"Was it always like that?"

"Not in the beginning. I mean we never got too wild, but we had sex a lot. I really love him, you know; it's just so hard feeling unwanted."

"Which is why you bought that dress and convinced yourself it wasn't too thin."

"I don't know. Maybe. I shouldn't even be telling you this. We should stop."

"It's okay. I won't tell Carol."

"Well, Carol should have never told you anything."

She was calming down a little bit. The confession was good for her. We let the silence hang, and she finally spoke.

"Do you really think I'm pretty?"

"No, I said you were beautiful. I also said you were sexy. But I can toss pretty in there; that shoe fits too."

"I don't feel like any of those things."

"So, my opinion doesn't mean anything to you?"

"You just want to have sex with me."

"Yep, and there are a lot of ugly girls out there I don't want to have sex with."

She said, "There *are* lots of girls, I mean, like you said, you can have sex with Carol any time you want. Why do you want to have sex with me?"

"I told you, you're virginal."

"I'm not a virgin."

"Virginal. I don't want to make you feel like a wife. I want to make you feel like woman."

"I don't think I could go through with it."

I decided to let her off the hook, for the moment anyway. I surely did want to sleep with her though.

I said, "Well, if you're happy everywhere else, then maybe having someone make you feel special might be just what the doctor ordered. But how about if we just talk on the phone once in a while and maybe we can figure out a way to get that part of your marriage back on track. You can call me when he's in his office or the shower."

"If I wanted to, you know, would you really, you know? Would we, you know?"

"Yeah. I would sleep with you in a heartbeat. Now why don't you relax and think about what we talked about, and call me whenever you want."

"Okay. Have a nice day."

I felt guilty, but at the same time I really wanted to make her feel good again. It's easy to convince yourself you're not doing wrong when you're in the middle of something like that. I pulled out the pictures and made myself come, thinking about what the future might bring.

Two nights later, Lisa called again. As soon as I answered the phone, she started talking.

"He's in his office again. I can hear everything through the door."

"Then go into the shower and wait for him."

"I can't do that. We haven't showered together in years."

"Sure, you can. Just do it. He will be all worked up and see you naked, and nature will take its course." She thought for a second.

"What if it doesn't? I would be devastated."

"You have to try."

"No, if he wants to have sex with a bar of soap, instead of his wife, that's his loss."

I thought to myself that that was a change of events I hadn't expected. I wasn't sure how to play my hand from here. I had had second thoughts about fooling around with her, and figured maybe I would just help her get him jump-started in her direction again. The devil on one shoulder was definitely having an argument with the angel on the other side. I decided to split the difference and see where it led.

I said, "Well, if he's going to look at porn, then it's okay for you to listen to me tell you how hot you make me. Right?"

"Nice try."

"I thought so."

"This is serious. I was hurt, now I'm mad, and I feel guilty for all of it. I'm talking to you, telling you things I should never tell anyone, and he's downstairs looking at girls do who knows what when he has me right here to do anything he wants."

"Really? Anything?"

"You know what I mean."

"I know. I'm sorry. I've just been thinking about what you would be like in bed, and when I hear the word 'anything,' it makes me regroup my thoughts."

"You're just like he is."

"Well, not exactly. When I make myself come, I'm going to be thinking about you and looking at your picture, not some internet porn star."

"Is that supposed to make me feel better?"

"Sorry."

"It's okay. I'm just upset."

I let the silence build for a minute.

Then I said, "Do you ever wonder what it would be like to be with 'another man'; and when I say another man, I mean me?"

"I don't want to answer that."

"You just did."

"Maybe."

"Maybe you just answered it. Or maybe you think about us in bed."

"I don't know. Of course, I think about things a little. You won't stop talking about it."

"Cool!"

"It's not cool. I love Michael. Do you think I like thinking about another man?"

"Look, you're human. You have needs. He is the one not living up to his end of the bargain. Are you going to just give up sex?"

"No. I just want him to want me."

"He loves you. He just feels guilty because of all that religious stuff. It messes with his head. It's natural for him to want wild sex, and it's religion that makes him think his wife shouldn't do anything but lay there."

"I don't just lay there!"

"Right, you don't. And he feels guilty for enjoying that because, I'll say it again, all that religious stuff. It's a double-edged sword. If you take it too far, this is what happens. He looks at porn and beats off in the shower while his beautiful wife lies in bed in need of sex."

"So, what do I do now? And don't say get a hotel room with you."

"Is that where you fantasized we would do it?"

"You are impossible."

I repeated, "Is it?"

"I never said I fantasized about us."

"Yes, you did."

"I said 'maybe.' That could mean anything."

"It's okay to imagine what it would be like. You won't go to hell."

"So, you say."

I let things get quiet for a moment, and then in a quiet and unassuming voice I asked her, "Have you really at least wondered what it would be like for us to fool around."

"Of course, I've wondered. You said it a thousand times." She wasn't as defiant now. She needed my verbal attention at least. She felt beat out of her job by a computer and a porn movie.

"Tell me about it."

"No."

"C'mon. Just give me an idea. Was it in a hotel room?"

"I'm not going there. You would probably just get worked up and call Carol anyway."

"First off, I'm already worked up, and second, I promised not to fool around with Carol and think of you, and since you're the only girl on my mind, I can't call her."

"Oh, you have scruples all of a sudden?"

"Absolutely not. I just know that you would be jealous, and you have enough on your plate already."

"Why would I be jealous?"

"Because Carol would be getting what you dearly need, and she would probably call and tell you all about how I went crazier on her than I ever have before."

"Do you expect me to believe that?"

"Yeah. Not only do I think your virginal, I think you have a need to prove how good in bed you can really be. I think it would be a night to remember."

"So, you have me spending the night now?" She was intrigued and couldn't hide it. I would have bet money she was fully aroused, at this point.

"Of course. How else can I give you a massage, make you come a few times with my mouth, have sex with you, take a candlelight bath with you, and have sex again in just a couple of hours?"

"Seems you've thought this through."

"Every night like in *Groundhog Day*."

"Why me?"

"You keep asking the same question, but I'll answer it one more time. You love your husband with all your heart, and your mind, and you want to love him with your body, but he dropped the ball and your body needs attention. I don't want your heart or your mind. I want your body, and I think your body wants me. Am I wrong?"

"Probably not…"

"So, tell me, when you thought of us together, was it fun?"

"If I tell you, you'll think I'm weird."

"I won't. I promise."

"Well, okay, but don't laugh or anything."

"I promise. Now tell me."

"Well, I imagined that you blackmailed me with the picture you took to make me strip in front of you. You made me wear the same outfit and meet you at a hotel, and, well, at first you made me stand there and close my eyes and turn around in a circle while you looked at me with my clothes on. Then you made me lift up the dress and show you my underwear, and then you made me slowly strip while you watched."

"Then what?"

"Then it's time for me to go. I'm too embarrassed to tell you the rest. I shouldn't have told you that much."

"Okay, but just one question."

"What?"

"Did it turn you on to be blackmailed."

"I have to go. I'll call you."

"Goodnight." I hung up the phone and wanted to call Carol bad, but I just handled things the old-fashioned way. It was a good night.

I didn't hear from Lisa for a few days and was beginning to think I had pushed her too far. She finally called on day four and said they had been out-of-town on a retreat with the church. She said she could only talk a minute but said she and Michael had sex in the cabin. I asked how it was, and she said she couldn't help but wonder if he was thinking about the videos. I asked why she thought that, and she said because her mind was somewhere else too. She then said, "I gotta go, I'll call you," and hung up. I was intrigued.

That night around ten, Carol called me and asked me to come over and hang out for a while, which was our unspoken invite for sex. I was suspicious that Lisa had called her fishing, and I was right. That was not why Carol was calling though. She was all turned on because she had a twenty-something floor installer putting a new hardwood floor in her bedroom all day, and although she tried her best, he didn't make a move. She lived in a condo, and she said she put on a bikini and walked around the condo for a good while before she went to the pool. When she got back, she put on gym shorts, but paraded around in the bikini top, pestering him with inane questions. He was either too shy or not quite interested enough to make a move.

I told her he probably just didn't want to get fired in case she was only cock-teasing him and he guessed wrong. Either way, she was all turned on and needed relief. Normally, I would have gone right over and had a great time, but I didn't want to ruin things with Lisa. I did give Carol phone sex, and she was happy enough. During our conversation she said in passing that she had gotten another call from Lisa, and that when she told her she was thinking about calling me for some stress relief, Lisa read her the riot act about casual sex. We had a good laugh about it, and then I changed the subject on the assumption that Lisa would follow up, and I didn't want to give Carol any words to put in Lisa's head.

The next day, Lisa called me just as I came into the house from work. I was planning to call Carol just to do some fishing about whether Lisa had called, but didn't have the chance. I could tell right away that Lisa had either found out that we at least talked or was worried that I had, perhaps, gone over. I decided to just get things out in the open and told her Carol and I had talked.

I said, "Just so you know, I gave up guaranteed sex for you last night."

"Really? With who?"

I knew damn well she was just playing coy, and I played along.

"Carol had a floor guy over who got her hot and bothered and wanted me to come over, but I told her no."

"And that was for my benefit?"

"Yeah, I wanted to prove that I can keep my word. I do have a confession though."

"And what is that?"

"Well, first I never mentioned you or any other girl for that matter, but I did give her some serious phone sex for about an hour. She was really worked up over that guy."

"Well, it's your life. You can do what you want."

I laughed to myself. I could almost see her pouting on the other end of the phone.

I said, "Well, if it makes you feel better, I waited until the phone call was over and used your picture to finish my end of the deal."

"Yeah, right."

"Seriously, I told her I came while she was coming, and I had to go because I had a mess to clean up."

"And you swear you never said a word about me?"

"I swear."

"You shouldn't see her anymore. She needs to find a husband."

"You just don't want me fucking her."

"Right, as long as she's getting what she wants, she won't find a husband."

"And that's the only reason?"

"Yep."

"So, it has nothing to do with me and our conversations over the last couple of weeks?"

"Nope."

"So, now that I have proven that I can talk to her without spilling the beans, how about if I have sex with her one more time, and then tell her to find a husband. One more time won't hurt."

"No, you shouldn't have sex with her one more time, and you shouldn't talk sex with her on the phone either."

"Somebody is jealous . . ."

"I just don't want you, you know, talking to her like you talk . . . you know?"

"Like I talk to you?"

"Yeah, I mean, no. I mean. I just don't like thinking about you telling her stuff you say to me and then tell me the same thing and expect me to believe it."

"I told you I faked it with her and used your picture afterward."

"You still talked to her. I'm sure you told her plenty."

"Well, mostly I listened and asked her what she would have done if he had taken the bait."

"Well, I'm sure you said more than that."

"Just for the record, what you're feeling is jealousy."

"I want to change the subject."

"Okay, but just for the record again, I like that you're jealous."

"I'm not jealous. Let's just drop it. If you want to jerk off with Carol, go ahead. Maybe Michael can call her too."

I realized I had probably pushed too many buttons. I decided to dial it back a little.

"Well, and this is the last time I say, 'for the record.' I promise. I didn't go over her house for actual sex because of you, and even though we did have phone sex, I faked it, and looked at your picture as I to used your words 'jerked off.' So, if you want to be mad at your husband for looking at porn, go ahead, but I'm on the phone right now hoping to get a chance to see you naked, so don't say you're number two in my book."

We sat in silence for a good thirty seconds, and then she said, "I'm sorry,

I'm just feeling guilty."

"What are you feeling guilty about?"

"I'm not sure. I'm just mixed up. Sometimes, I feel guilty; sometimes, I'm mad. And sometimes, I *am* jealous. I'm jealous of those girls who have my husband's attention. I'm jealous that Carol gets sex whenever she wants, and I'm jealous that you have this way of getting into my head, but can just decide to go screw Carol, and there is nothing I can do about it."

"I told you I wouldn't."

"Yeah, well suppose she just shows up at your house and demands sex? Then what?"

"Well, first off, Carol and I have boundaries, and she would never come over unannounced. Second, if I say I'm not going to have sex with her, then I'm not."

"Do you promise?"

"I promise."

"And if you do, you have to tell me."

"I won't have sex with her, and I promise I will tell you if she puts a gun to my head and rapes me."

"Sorry, I'm just being stupid."

"So, what are you wearing today?"

"Well," she laughed, "at least you're consistent."

I laughed back. "That, I am. So... answer the question."

"Why do you want to know?"

"Well, I was picturing you naked, but I figured if I can put clothes on you, then I can concentrate more on what we're saying."

"I'm wearing shorts and a polo shirt?"

"What color shirt."

"White."

"What color shorts?"

"White."

"What color underwear?"

"Guess."

"White?"

"You got it."

"Bikini or thong."

"Bikini. I don't wear thongs."

"Why not?"

"Michael wouldn't approve."

"Michael doesn't know what he's missing."

"And you do?"

"No, but I know more about what he's missing than he does."

"How do you figure?"

"I know you like wearing clothes that make you desirable. I know that you are in dire need of physical affection, and I know that he could probably get anything from you that he gets from the porn girls in the videos he watches, if he only tried."

She said, "Now if we can only get him to figure that out."

"You could try just telling him."

"I tried. I walked around the cabin in a towel for almost an hour before he finally took the hint. I tried to be passionate, but his mind was just somewhere else, and as soon as he was done, he went straight into the shower. He sees me as his wife and nothing more. It's depressing. I feel ugly."

I thought for a moment. "Well we both know you don't really feel ugly. I've been giving you too much of a full-court press for that."

"Well, I feel like he's certainly lost interest."

"Just in sex, not in you."

"I know. He is a good husband. It's just . . . so . . . I don't know. I just wish he would *want* me."

"I want you to meet in the parking lot again. I need more pictures."

"More pictures? What for?"

"So I'm not tempted to visit Carol."

"You already promised that."

"Okay, how about just to keep me happy, so I won't try so hard to get you in the sack."

"If I let you take more, it will get worse not better."

"No… No… It will give me… a way to relieve the tension…"

"How about if I just have Michael recommend some porn sites. They certainly take the wind out of his sails." She laughed a little, which made me happy.

"I'm serious. I really want to see you in that dress again. This time with no underwear."

"No, way."

"But you said it wasn't see-through, so it shouldn't be a problem."

"Well, we both know that I may have been mistaken on that point, and the answer is no."

"Please, I know you want to."

She said, "And why would I 'want to'?"

"Because deep down it makes you feel the way you want to feel. Knowing what it does to me makes you feel good. Even if nothing ever happens, you'll always have that."

She was quiet for a long time.

"I don't know if I have the nerve."

"Sure, you do. You know I'm just going to keep bugging you. Just think about how exciting it will be to have me look at you with nothing underneath your dress. It would be fun."

"I thought you said it would be exciting?"

"It would be both. What do you say?"

"If I get there and chicken, out you can't be mad."

"I promise."

"When?"

"Now, before you chicken out."

"I need to shower."

"Okay, I'll see you in the same spot at seven."

"I can't believe I'm doing this."

"I can. I'll see you at seven. Go shower."

I hung up before she could change her mind. I showered too. I didn't think anything would happen at this point, but I wanted to be clean just in case. I put on gym shorts, a T-shirt, and new sneakers out of the box. I wanted to look more alpha than her husband. I wanted to give her something to think about too.

She was about ten minutes late, and I was beginning to think she had changed her mind. She pulled in and I could tell she was wearing the dress but didn't know whether she had kept her nerve about the underwear. She pulled up next to me so our driver's windows were facing each other.

"I almost didn't come. I was too nervous."

"I figured, but you're here now. That makes me happy."

"If I do this . . . let you take a picture . . . do you promise not to have even phone sex with Carol again?"

"Only if you admit it's because it makes you jealous."

"Okay. It makes me jealous. Promise?"

"I promise."

"Ughhh . . . I can't believe I'm doing this."

We were in the far corner of the lot and the sun was even lower on the horizon. It was going to be a perfect picture. I got out of my car while she parked, and I sat down cross legged with my back to the side of my car, camera in hand. She slowly got out of her car like she was going to jump back in and drive away, but she didn't. She turned to close the door, and I could see her bare ass thorough the dress and it looked delicious. I snapped a quick picture before she turned towards me. I held the camera facing her and just kept taking pictures as she walked towards me. The sun was shining between her legs and I could see her dark pubic hair between her thighs as the fading sunlight shone through. I looked at her breasts and they were medium size with little dark nipples. The small nipples made her breasts look larger. She looked completely fuckable, and I remember thinking her husband must be a fucking moron for not enjoying that body on a regular basis.

"I feel so stupid right now."

"You look incredible."

"You just want sex."

"That's beside the point. Your husband is the only straight guy in this county that wouldn't fuck you right now."

She turned red, but was obviously flattered by the declaration, even if it was crude.

"I don't want to think about him right now."

"I agree. Spin for me."

I realized she wasn't hiding her face like last time. She *wanted* to pose for me. I went with it. She rotated slowly while I kept snapping pictures.

I said, "Now put your hands on your hips and smile." I snapped a couple of pictures and continued. "Now, put them behind your back and look at the clouds." I zoomed in right at her crotch and got a perfect shot of her little triangle of dark hair with the sunlight coming underneath. I took a few more, and she said, "That's enough. In fact, it's more than enough. I can't believe I even let you do this. I feel naked."

"You are naked."

She smiled and walked back to her car and climbed in. I walked over and she pushed her sunglasses up onto her head and said, "Are you happy now?"

"Oh, yeah, but I need one more picture."

"You already have like a dozen."

"Just one more, a special one."

"Special?"

"Yeah, hike up your dress and let me take a picture of…"

"No, way."

"I won't get your face, just a close-up of what I can't have."

"No, way."

"I promised never to have phone sex with Carol again… that should be worth it."

"This wasn't part of the deal."

"I promise to blackmail you with it."

"What does that mean?"

"I don't know. I'm just grasping at straws."

She put her hand down like she was going to pull her dress up, but instead reached further and grabbed the seat handle and slid the seat back.

She said, "I can't believe I'm doing this. If you get my face, I will kill you."

I smiled. I knew when to keep my mouth shut. She slid the seat back about half way and then reclined the seat back to give me a nice angle. She then opened her legs a little and put a hand on the end of the dress.

"I'm nervous," she said, looking up at me.

"It's okay. It'll be fun."

"For you."

"For us."

She said, "Okay, I'm really nervous, so I'm going to trust you. I have to close my eyes, but you promise not to get my face, right?"

"Right."

"I'm going to trust you."

"You can."

"Here goes nothing." She closed her eyes and turned her head away from the camera. She slid her dress all the way up, opened her legs wide, and tilted her hips to thrust her pelvis forward. I just took as many pictures as I could in the few seconds I had. I figured I would view them at home and hopefully get lucky.

I said, "Okay, I'm done."

"Remember . . . anybody sees those, and I will kill you."

"Don't worry. These are for my eyes only."

"And you won't even have phone sex with Carol *ever*?"

"Don't worry. I'll just tell her I have a girlfriend."

"Do you have a girlfriend?"

"I'm working on it . . ." I said, lifting the camera. "In fact, I'm going to go home and do some research tonight."

She smiled broadly this time. She felt sexy, and I could tell how good it made her feel. This was fun.

She said, "I have to go."

"When are you going to call me again?"

"I don't know."

"What's your schedule like?"

"I work at the nursing home twenty hours a week, usually from eleven to three."

"What's Michael's schedule?"

"Why?"

"I just want to know a little more about you."

"He leaves for the church every morning at seven and usually gets home and around three, but sometimes he has counseling sessions in the evening."

"Who does he counsel?"

"Married couples. Ironic, huh?"

"What does he do at the church?"

"He teaches Bible classes and works on their worldwide outreach program. He works with Chinese Christians mostly. There is a big community here."

"So, that means you can give me a wake-up call at seven, huh?"

She had moved her seat and dress back into place but seemed to forget she was sitting there in a see-through dress for the moment. I wasn't going to tell her.

"I wouldn't want to interrupt you."

"Yes, you would."

She smiled and said, "Goodbye" as she started the car. I went home and spent the evening looking at some really interesting pictures. This was getting real, and I was surprised at how easily I had gotten past even thinking what I was doing was wrong. In my head I had convinced myself that if she had a fling with someone else, they might try and split them up and ruin everything, but since I was just in it for the sex, there was no chance of that.

Two days later about five after seven in the morning, the phone rang. I answered, and it was Lisa.

"Is it safe?"

"Is what safe?"

"Well, I thought you might be busy looking at pictures. I wouldn't want to interrupt anything."

"Oh, do you mean, was I looking at your pictures and thinking all kinds of dirty thoughts while I pleasured myself?"

"Something like that."

"Well, I did that last night before I went to sleep, but now that I hear your voice, who knows what might happen."

"So, how many pictures did you take?"

"Twenty-three."

"Wow! I thought it was about ten, and that was too many. Are you happy now?"

"Every part of me is happy, except my wrist."

"Your wrist? Oh, never mind."

I said, "Do you want to know what I think of the pictures?"

"No."

"Liar."

"I think they are probably hideous."

"No, you don't. I want to tell you. Are you ready to listen?"

"I don't know. Should I be?"

"You look beautiful, sexy hot, pretty, gorgeous. All of those things, and the ones with your skirt pulled up are driving me crazy."

"Really? I was scared you would hate them."

"Why?"

"I don't know. You're the only person beside my gynecologist who has seen . . . me . . . in over ten years."

"You have no worries. I'm now more turned on than ever. I can't stop thinking about ways to get you in bed. I do have a question though."

"I'm afraid to hear it, but I know you're going to ask, so go ahead."

"On a scale of one to ten, how turned on were you on the ride home from Safeway, knowing what I had just seen?"

"I don't want to answer."

"Why not?"

"Because it will just embolden you."

"C'mon, embolden me. Give me a number."

"Well, it wasn't ten."

"No? Well, what was it… be honest?"

"More like fifteen."

"Sweet! That makes me happy. You deserve to feel like that. It feels good, doesn't it?"

"Yeah."

"So, I have another question."

"Well, it can't be any more personal than that, so go ahead."

"When you get all turned on like that, do you make yourself come?"

"Well, first off, I haven't been turned on like that in years, and second, that's an embarrassing question that you need to ask me again in the evening after I've had some wine."

"Are you turned on right now?"

"No comment."

"Sweet!"

"I knew answering your first question would embolden you."

"I want to listen to you make yourself come."

"For that we would need a lot of wine."

"Then it's a date. You figure out when Michael's out counseling, drink some wine, and call me. I'll take it from there."

"You sound pretty confident."

"I am. I would bet money that you're lying in bed right now, aren't you?"

"What's that got to do with anything?"

"What are you wearing right now?"

"Pajamas."

"Underwear?"

"Nope."

"Loose fitting or tight?"

"Loose."

"So, you *are* still in bed?"

"Maybe."

She was thoroughly enjoying this. I decided to make the teasing a two-way street.

"Well, here's what I want you to do. I'm going to get up, take a shower, and go to work. I want you to lay there with your eyes closed and imagine what your pictures do to my cock, and how good it would feel to have me come into your room and slide it inside of you. Imagine, that before I did that, I blackmailed you, and made you touch yourself while I watched."

"Stop, you're making me crazy."

"Good. I'm going to go now. Just lay there and relax and let nature takes it course. You can call me tomorrow and tell me all about it. Bye-bye."

"Ummm . . . bye."

I hung up and took a soapy shower, thinking about what was going on about five miles away.

Lisa and I talked almost every morning. She liked listening to me pleasure myself, and I could tell she was doing the same, but was quiet about it. She was slowly getting more vocal every day, and I figured it wouldn't be long before we were both fully honest. We talked about her husband less and less, and it seemed she had just resigned herself to the situation. Sex was the only complaint she had. He was a good guy in all other areas, but she was very lonely and didn't understand why he had chosen the path that he did. She even joked about his "office time," saying that he was doing it like three nights a week, which they didn't even do after the first six months of their marriage.

I kept expanding our fantasies and making them more and more detailed and believable, hoping that the inevitable would occur. After about three weeks, she was openly orgasming with me over the phone, as I talked her over the edge with all the things that I would tell her I would do to her. I figured that I would give things another week or two, and then broach the idea of us consummating the affair, but she beat me to it.

She called me just after seven one morning, but instead of her usual happy-to-hear-my-voice self, she was upset.

"Well, I finally got it."

"Got what?"

"Michael forgot to clear the history on his computer, and I finally got access, and I am pissed."

"What did you find?"

"Well, he was out late last night, counseling to a Chinese woman's group about marriage. Then he gets up at five-thirty this morning, goes into his office, and closes the door. I thought that was weird and crept to the door and listened. He was watching porn. I went back to bed, and he went from there into the shower, and then off to the church. Once he left, I went in, and sure enough he had forgotten to erase the history for once."

"Well, what does he look at?"

"What do you think?"

"I don't know."

"Asian women. And not just Asian women, but Asian women with white men. Asian women doing blow jobs. Asian women threesomes. My husband is turned on by Asian women. How the hell am I supposed to compete with that? No wonder he isn't interested in me anymore."

"Do you think he's fooling around with any of them?"

"I don't know. That was the first thing I thought of too. I don't think so because if he was, he wouldn't need to look at porn and take showers."

"Are you going to confront him?"

"No, if that's what turns him on, then there isn't anything I can do about it, except wait it out. I am going to do a little quiet research to see if there's anything funny going on at the church, but I really don't think so."

"Well, at least now you know. It could be worse."

"How could it be worse?"

"I don't know. Gays. Animals. I was just trying to make you feel better."

She laughed through her tears. "I guess an Asian woman is a little better than a goat, huh?"

"Now, that's the spirit!"

She was quiet for a minute.

"Uh-oh," she blurted.

"What?"

"Michael is going away on a ten-day retreat to Michigan in two weeks."

"So?"

"So, it's a big meeting of Chinese Christian refugees. There are like five hundred of them, staying at this lodge on Lake Erie."

"Are you going?"

"No. In fact, he usually invites me to stuff like that, and I usually say no, but this time he didn't even ask me to go. He just told me when he was going."

"Good."

"Why is that good?"

"Because I have a customer who has a cabin in the Poconos, who said I can use it whenever I want, and I've been saving it for a special occasion."

"And?"

"And we can use it for a weekend and make it a 'special occasion.' What do you think?"

"Wow! Um, maybe. Maybe we will. Let me think about it. I'm going to go do some snooping. I'll call you later."

I didn't know whether she was happy or sad. At least now she knew.

Two weeks later on a Friday evening, I was sitting in a rustic log cabin in the Poconos, overlooking a small lake and waiting for Lisa. Michael was in Michigan, and she told him she was going outlet shopping with Carol and spending Saturday night in a hotel room. She told me she would call and tell Michael she was going to bed early so she could get up early and for him to have a nice evening.

It was almost seven and Lisa was going to be there soon. It was late summer, but the evenings were cool, and I had a fire all ready. I had also moved the giant oak kitchen table into the living room and turned it into a massage table by stacking blankets for padding, and then used a top sheet to make it smooth. I had sensual massage oil and had brought some light jazz CD's for background music. The bedroom overlooked the lake and had its own small balcony. It was very private. The only other house I could see was across the lake, and it appeared unoccupied. If it were ski season it would have been a different scene.

I had stopped at a gourmet store and picked up a light dinner of veal piccata and stocked up on wine, which I was sure Lisa would need to relax. I was looking forward to sex with her. I was sure she was going to take out all of her sexual tension on me, and I was ready for it. In the two months we had been playing cat and mouse, I hadn't had sex with anyone else, and deprived myself of personal pleasure all week so I would have plenty of pent-up tension for her.

She showed up around seven-thirty and was as nervous as a cat. We had discussed the fact that we had never even kissed and were only sexual in each other's imagination. She wore a long, light blue, non-see-through dress. She looked pretty, but not like she was going on a weekend of sex with a new lover.

She walked up the steps of the cabin as I stood on the porch and said, "Wow, this is beautiful."

"Come on in."

She had an overnight bag that looked stuffed and an over-the-shoulder carryall. It was a little surreal for both of us. I wasn't nervous, but she was walking gingerly as if the floor could fall in.

I said, "I have wine."

"Yes. That would be good."

She walked in and looked at the giant stone fireplace, the dining room table set with candles for two, and the massage table in front of the fireplace with the couch moved aside.

"It looks like you went all out. Impressive. Did you bring this?" she asked, pointing to the massage table.

"It's actually the kitchen table covered in blankets. I figured after dinner we would give you a nice massage in front of the fire."

"You mean, if I don't chicken out and run to my car and hightail it back to DC?"

"That's what this is for." I handed her a full glass of wine.

She wandered around and looked at the two bedrooms, set her stuff on the end of the master bedroom bed, and then went out onto the balcony.

"Wow, this place really is very nice." I had the feeling she wanted to add "and romantic," but caught herself.

I walked up behind her and put my arms around her waist.

She put her hands over mine and said, "You promised to be gentle and slow. Is that still okay?"

"Of course." I wrapped my hands over hers, and gently pulled her to me, making sure not to bump my semi-erect cock into her. I said, "This night is all about your needs. I am just here to make tonight special for you."

She leaned her head back into mine and we looked over the lake together.

She said, "That sounds nice. I'm think I'm ready to feel special."

I spun her around and looked her in the eyes. I kissed her, gently at first, slowly coaxing my tongue inside her mouth. She was hungry with passion but trying to rein it in. She wanted things to be special, and she knew the only way to do that was for us to make it happen that way. If we let our instincts take over, we would have already been on the bed and in the heat of intercourse. I eased up on the kiss.

"Let's eat," I said. "I picked up some veal. It's warming in the oven."

"Sounds good."

We ate dinner, making small talk with lots of eye contact, and not talking about the impending evening. We talked about the ride up, the directions, and lots of silly nothings to take up time while she got herself intoxicated enough to relax, but not drunk enough to miss anything. I could tell she was happy that my eyes, and, most likely, my imagination, were wandering in anticipation of seeing her naked. I had professed it enough times that there could be no doubt in her mind what my feelings were.

After we finished eating and were clearing the plates I said, "I want you to go take a hot bath and relax with a little more wine. When you come out, I'm going to give you the massage of a lifetime."

"Umm, sounds good, but no peeking, okay?"

"Got it."

She went into the master bath, where there was a large tub that was surrounded by a ledge that I had placed candles on. I went in behind her with the bottle of wine, turned the hot water on, and lit the candles. I set the wine down on the ledge, turned off the lights, and said, "See you in a while. Take as long as you want," and closed the door behind me.

Forty-five minutes later, she came out wrapped in a giant bath towel. I had lit the fire, and the room was warm. I had also lowered the lights, lit a few candles, and put on some jazz. I was wearing nylon workout pants and a T-shirt. I had the massage oil sitting in a bowl of warm water with towels next to it.

"I'm nervous."

"I know. I'm going to go wash up. You crawl under the sheet. I'll take it from there."

"What if you don't like my body?"

"There is little chance of that."

"Are we really doing this?"

"Yes, we are." I walked over and kissed her quickly on the lips and said, "Now get under that sheet before I lose control and just yank the towel away."

"Okay, I'm going."

When I came out after washing up, she was lying face down on the table with the sheet pulled from her shoulders to the back of her knees. This was going to be fun.

I didn't say anything. I went over and adjusted the music level a little, and then I put my hands on the small of her back and gently rubbed her through the sheet. I pulled the bottle of massage oil out of the warm water and put some on my hands. I lightly slid the sheet down, exposing her shoulder blades and began gently but firmly rubbing her neck and shoulders. She moaned slightly, letting me know the pressure was right. I worked my hands all the way up to the base of her skull and worked the tension out of her neck. She relaxed quickly, and I assumed the wine helped a lot. Her hands were at her sides, and I tucked the sheet between her body and arms, leaving them exposed. I slowly and deliberately rubbed each of them, taking care to massage each finger and the palm of her hand, using plenty of oil.

It was a nice sensual atmosphere between the light of the fire, and the candles in the darkened room. I went around until I was standing right in front of her head. I slid the sheet down to the base of her spine and then began taking long firm stokes up and down both sides of her back. I steadily increased the pressure until she groaned slightly as the tension released.

After a few minutes, I pulled the sheet back up, kissed the top of her head, then went to her feet and began rubbing each one, using two hands, pushing my thumbs into the soles hard. She was purring audibly now, and I knew my manipulations were having the desired effect. I slid the sheet up to the back of her knees and did the same firm manipulations on her calves, going from the heel of each foot all the way to the back of her knees and down again.

After a minute or so, I moved until I was by her side and slid the sheet up to the base of her ass cheeks. She tensed up slightly. I was anticipating what I was about to see for the first time and thought perhaps she was reading my mind. I hoped so. She had thin legs, and from the side I could almost see everything but not quite. I began rubbing the back of her thighs all the way from her knees to the bottom of her ass cheeks and back again. She relaxed and began lifting her hips a little wanting me to go further. I kept my distance to prolong the anticipation. I rubbed her thighs pushing into her ass cheeks as if I were headed further, then I put my hands on her ass through the sheet and pulled the sheet down to her ankles. She moaned in feigned disappointment.

I said, "On your back. I'm going to get some more wine."

I walked away, and I could hear her rolling herself over, staying under the sheet. She knew what I wanted, and she was cooperating fully. I came back with two glasses of wine, making sure hers was only half full so she could half sit up and sip it without it spilling. I held the glass for her while she did a half sit-up, holding the sheet in place and took a nice long gulp.

I said, "So far so good?"

"My God, it feels wonderful."

"You ain't seen nothing yet."

"That's what I'm afraid of."

"Okay, close your eyes."

"Yes, sir."

I began tracing her face with my fingertips. From here on out, the hard-relaxing pressure would be over. We were now in a sensual phase, and we both were anticipating the sexual phase that was sure to follow. The anticipation from us both was obvious by our breathing.

I gently ran my fingers through her hair and massaged her ear lobes. She moaned. I stretched her neck and then leaned down and kissed her forehead. I slid the sheet down to the top of her breasts and rubbed massage oil into her breastbone and shoulders. After a few moments of that, I stopped and put my hands on the sheet, hesitating for a couple of seconds just in case she wasn't ready. She didn't flinch. Reaching over her, I lifted the sheet away from her body and slid it down to her belly button, exposing her fully. Her nipples were stiff and her chest was getting red from excitement. She had small dark nipples and her medium breasts fit her body perfectly. I growled ever so slightly, just enough to let her know how happy I was at what I was seeing for the first time.

I pulled the massage oil out and lubricated my hands well. I put them on her sides near her breasts and went down her sides to her stomach, and came back up to the underside of her breasts. I pulled my hands back to her sides again with the back of my thumbs, grazing the underside of her breasts. I put on more massage oil, put my hands back to her sides, and this time went up and over her breasts. She moaned uncontrollably and shivered. I firmly massaged them, giving them the attention they were craving. I did this for about thirty seconds, and then slowed my hands down and let them rest there.

I slid my hands down her stomach, and grabbed the sheet and pulled it back up covering her breasts. I then went to her feet and began rubbing them a second time similar to the first. After a minute of that I slid the sheet up above her knees and rubbed the front of her legs to just above the knees in a steady up-and-down motion. I moved to her side and ever so slowly began sliding the sheet up to the top of her thighs, exposing more and more flesh to my prying eyes. She was almost holding her breath now, and we were both in a state of anticipation that was excruciatingly wonderful. I slid the sheet up until it was halfway up her pubic mound. I folded it to let her know exactly where it was. Her eyes were closed, and she was being as still as a mouse. I oiled my hands again and began on her left thigh, very gently going from her knee until I was almost between her legs. On the second pass, I let the back of my hand graze her pubic hair, which made her suck in air.

I was hard as stone but was saving my erection for later. I switched sides and did the same thing. She was grinding her hips subconsciously now, and I knew she was ready for more. I moved down until I was back at her feet and put my hands on her ankles. I slid my hands up to her knees and slowly opened her legs while lifting her knees up. She allowed it, and I could hear her breathing quicken as she felt me crawl onto the table. When I placed my mouth on the inside of her knee, she let out a gasp. I licked half way up her thigh and then moved to the inside of the other knee. I took my tongue closer, and then switched sides again right where I had left off. I did this twice more until I could feel her pubic hair graze my face.

I pulled my face away and looked at her. I had been aroused by the pictures, but this was much more exciting, and I was close to coming just from what we had done so far. I put my face gently between her legs and breathed in loudly, moaning in satisfaction at her scent. She gasped loudly and followed it with her own groan of pleasure. I pushed my face into her gently but assuredly, using my lips to suckle her and my tongue to taste her juices. She was completely soaked, and it was intoxicating to be a part of it. I opened her legs wider with my hands and then slid two fingers inside of her as I moved my mouth upwards to find her clit. I sucked it gently at first, but after only a few seconds she pushed herself to my mouth, so I began licking and sucking harder and faster while my fingers lifted her to me from the inside. Her hands found the top of my head and she began thrusting into my face and fingers.

Within a minute, she said, "I'm coming. Oh, my God, I'm coming." Her orgasm was powerful and there was no mistaking the intensity of it. It had been too long, and she was allowing the pleasure to take over. She was pulling my hair to the point that it hurt, but I was too busy to notice the pain. She relaxed her grip on my hair and lay back breathing deeply. I left my face between her legs, gently kissing the areas that I knew weren't overly sensitive. I slid my fingers out of her and rubbed the back of her thighs with the palms of my hands.

I said, "Are you okay?"

"I'm better than okay."

I said, "Can we go into the bedroom? I want you."

"Yes."

I said, "I'll meet you there."

I went to the bathroom and washed up. I drank a glass of water, and when I went into the bedroom, she was lying in bed under the sheet. The lights were off, so I left the bathroom light on and the door cracked. I lay down on the bed next to her and kissed her on the lips.

I said, "I have a question."

"What?"

"Did you bring the dress like I asked?"

"Yes. Why?"

"Because I want you to wear it."

"Now?"

"Yeah, I want the first time we have sex to be like I imagined the first time I saw you in it."

"You want us to have sex *while* I wear the dress?"

"Yep."

"Will it make you happy?"

"Yes. Will you wear it?"

"Yes, I want to. Close your eyes so I can go in the bathroom and put it on."

I said okay and rolled over on my back and put my arm over my eyes. She climbed out from under the sheet and grabbed her overnight bag and ran into the bathroom. I moved my arm and watched her cute little butt the whole time.

I took off my clothes and got under the sheet and waited in anticipation.

A couple of minutes later, she cracked the door and said, "Are you ready?"

"Ready and waiting."

The door opened, and she stepped out into the light from the bathroom. I could see that she was wearing the dress with the same white lace bra and panties that I saw on the first day. She just stood there, not sure what to do. I sat up in bed, and then slid until I was sitting on the edge with the sheet covering my cock.

I said, "Come to me."

She walked over and stood in front of me. I took my hands and put them under her dress and rubbed the front of her thighs.

I said, "This is what I imagined the first night after seeing you in the store."

I reached up and took the waistband of her panties and slid them down to her knees. I lifted the dress with my wrists and I slid my hands up her sides, exposing her to my prying eyes. I took one hand and put two fingers inside of her. She put her hands on my shoulders and moaned. She was all in at this point, and we were both ready for what was coming next. I slid her panties the rest of the way down and she stepped out of them, putting a hand on my shoulder as she did so.

I said, "Do you want to see what you do to me?"

"Yes."

I slid the sheet away and she saw my fully erect cock, ready to burst because of her. She stared at it for a long time, waiting for me to make the next move.

I covered myself up and said, "Lay on the bed on your back."

She lay down with her legs straight out and her hands at her sides. I stood up letting the sheet fall to the floor. I gently slid her over to the middle of the king size bed and got on my knees next to her. I leaned over and kissed her deeply. I then slid her dress up as far as it would go. She lifted her hips and I slid it up until it was above her waist. Once it was there, I pulled it down loosely over her so it covered her pubic mound. I opened her legs and climbed between them. I lifted her knees slightly and began to slowly slide myself inside. She audibly moaned. I realized at that moment that she wanted this as bad as I did. I rested my weight on my elbows and kissed her deeply again. I began to slide in and out slowly. I could feel the dress between our stomachs. It was very sexy.

I said, You look so hot in this dress. This is even sexier than I imagined."

"Oh, God..."

We kissed and synced our thrusts together slowly. We made love like that for a while. Soon enough the passion started building and I began thrusting harder. She lifted her knees and began thrusting back just as hard. We were now fucking. There was no other word for it. She had been a good wife for ten years, and she missed her sexuality, and she was giving it all to me. I could tell she was going to come, and I held out a while longer to make it happen. I fucked her as hard as I could as she got closer and closer to coming. I began to growl to let her know how exciting she was.

I said, "You feel so good. You are so tight." That brought her closer, and I said, "I need you to come so I can come. Come, baby. I want to feel you come."

She put her arms around me and pulled me tightly to her as she screamed in ecstasy, and I held out a few more seconds to make sure she was past it, and then I exploded inside of her. I could feel the pulsing all the way down in the base of my balls as I emptied inside her. I slowly went in and out while she laughed in uncontrollable happiness at what she had just felt. I lifted myself up, resting my weight on my elbows and kissed her deeply. We kissed like that for a while, and then as I softened, I slid myself out and got a towel and pushed it up between her legs. I lay beside her and we kissed some more. She was sleepy from the wine and the sex. I cleaned her up as best as I could, slid her dress down, and then covered her with a sheet. We fell asleep a few minutes later.

The next morning, she came walking into the kitchen to the smell of bacon, wearing the dress with no underwear, the bra still on, and her hair all bunched up from the sex and sleep.

She said, "Hi."

"Did you sleep well?"

"Oh, yeah. I feel drunk."

"Drunk?"

"Sort of. Maybe high. Maybe just happy," and she walked over and put her head in my shoulder. She said, "Did I do okay for a virgin?"

"You did great."

"Well, you know, I'm probably gonna need some practice. Is that okay?"

"Right now?"

"God, no . . . I'm still exhausted from last night. But soon."

"Just say the word."

"Don't worry, I will."

We had a nice breakfast and then went for a walk around the lake. We were almost all the way around when she said, "I feel guilty."

"I know."

"No, I don't feel guilty for . . . this. I feel guilty for letting it get this far. I love Michael, but he abandoned me, and I feel guilty for not feeling guilty, or something. It's so confusing."

I said, "Well, let's just forget about Michael for the weekend."

"Okay."

We went back to the cabin and sat out on the balcony off the bedroom, and watched birds with binoculars and made small talk.

After about an hour she said, "I've never had sex with Michael like that."

"What do you mean?"

"I don't know. I mean it's okay, but he never wanted me the way you want me. I forgot how good it feels to have sex with someone who really wants you."

"Michael wants you. He is just mixed up because of the church stuff."

"He wants to watch Chinese women give blow jobs, and he won't even let me give him one."

"Do you want to?"

"Him? Or you?"

"Well, you know how I feel about it? You have my express permission."

"Okay. I'll remember that."

She said, "I'll be right back," and went inside and came back out with a beach towel and an apple. Naked. She lay back on the chaise lounge and said, "I want some sun."

"I'm glad to see you like the place."

"And the company."

I said, "I'm gonna grab a shower."

"I'll be here."

I put a mouth on her nipple and gently suckled, took a nibble from the apple and said, "That's probably what Eve said to Adam."

She took a big bite out of the apple and said, "Maybe." She was smiling wide.

When I came out of the shower, she was lying in bed under the sheet.

I said, "Taking a nap?"

"No, just lying here, hoping for some company."

I left my towel around my waist and grabbed another one and dried my hair.

"Anybody I know?"

She grabbed a pillow and tossed it at me. "You know, I'm nervous…"

I said, "Oh, you want a pillow fight, huh?" and picked up the pillow and started playfully beating her with it. She sat up, holding the sheet in front of her. I put the pillow behind her head and pulled her to me and kissed her deeply. She relaxed. I laid her back down on the bed. I slid the sheet down and lay next to her. We were still kissing, and I slowly ran my fingers over her upper body. I started at her neck and shoulders, down her arm and up again, down between her breasts to her stomach, and finally across her breasts.

When I pulled away, she breathed in deeply and said, "That feels so good." I put my mouth over a breast and gently suckled as I slid my hand down between her legs, playing with her soft curls. I went a little further and could feel that she was damp. I pulled my hand away long enough to loosen the towel around my waist, and then went back to massaging her. She opened her legs and arched her hip to meet my manipulations, and I pulled away from her breast and whispered in her ear, "Do you want me inside you?"

"Yes."

"Can I come inside you?"

"Yes!"

I kissed her as I moved over on top of her and slowly slid myself in. She purred and put her hands on my hips to control the speed. She wanted me entering her slowly. I arched my hips to give her as much depth as possible and held myself there allowing her to feel herself stretching. She moved her hands to my back, and I began slowly sliding in and out while kissing her. She kissed me back hard and moved her hips in perfect synch with mine. We made love this way for over half an hour. It was gentle but firm. When the timing seemed right, I increased my intensity and the forcefulness of my thrusts.

I said, "Do you like my cock?"

"Yes."

"Am I fucking you?"

"You're fucking me so good."

"You need to be fucked, don't you?"

"Yes, I need it bad. I need to be fucked."

I growled and began thrusting with full force for another thirty seconds until I was past the point of no return.

"I'm coming."

"Yes. Come. Fuck me. I want your come. Fuck me! Oh God… Oh God… You feel so good…"

I came in big spurts. I felt her shiver as I came. I was immediately drained from the pleasure, and collapsed on top of her. We lay there in mutual passion with me still inside of her for a long time. She was lying there smiling at what had just happened. She seemed to thoroughly enjoy making me come so hard. I slowly got up to take my weight off of her. I fumbled for my towel and placed it between her legs.

"I came a lot," I said.

"Good."

"Feel it," and I put her hand into the sticky mess.

I said, "See what you do to me?"

"I still don't know why."

"Because you are a sexy, vibrant woman, and don't you ever think otherwise. Okay?"

"Okay."

I tucked the towel back into place then said, "You take a half hour nap, and then a shower. Then we are going shopping. You have a date tonight."

"I do?"

"We are going to the most famous country club in the Poconos."

"Country club?"

"Well, sort of; it's called the 'Country Club,' but it's actually a big country bar with a dance floor, pool tables, the whole nine yards. We are going to have some fun and then come back and have some more fun."

"Okay. I hope I can hold up my end of the bargain, though. You're wearing me out."

"You'll be fine."

An hour and a half later, we were at an outlet mall, shopping for some proper attire for the country bar. It was only around two when we left the cabin, but I had given her a full glass of wine as she came out of the shower, and a second after she was dressed. She had a nice, relaxed buzz as we shopped. I eased her into it, but finally convinced her to let me buy her a micro-mini jean skirt, which fit her perfectly. We found a white blouse that I knew would look good with a button or two left loose, especially with the push-up bra I was going to convince her to buy. We bought the skirt and blouse, and then went to a lingerie store, where we found her some pink panties and a white push-up bra that she enjoyed modeling for me in front of the sales girl.

We were leaving the mall when I did a quick U-turn and said, "Follow me." We went down a side corridor and into a boot shop and bought her some mid-calf cowboy boots. She was reluctant at first, but I told her I needed her to feel like the hottest girl in the place for me, and I didn't want her to have any excuses not to. She was pleased at the attention. We had a late lunch or early dinner, and then went back to the cabin. I moved the couch over, and we watched a DVD while she nodded in and out from the wine and the sex. By the time the movie was over, she was sound asleep. I covered her with a blanket from the massage table and let her doze until seven when I woke her and told her it was time to get ready to head out.

She yawned and said, "Okay, but no looking until I am ready to come out. Promise?"

I promised, and it made me happy, knowing that she had thought about what was going to happen and was looking forward to it. Almost an hour later, she cracked opened the bathroom door and said, "Are you ready to take a look and see?"

"Absolutely."

"You have to be honest. If it looks silly, you have to tell me. Do you promise?"

"I promise. I promise. Let me see what you look like."

She came out looking like a completely different person. She was in full regalia, her hair tied back, and she had applied the perfect amount of makeup. Her tanned thighs were obvious against the denim skirt, and her breasts were pushing up just enough to let you know she was proud of them. The tan boots coming halfway up her calves were a nice finishing touch.

"I don't want to look slutty."

"You don't have the ability to look slutty."

"Aw, that's sweet, but you promised not to lie. All women have the ability to look slutty."

"You don't look slutty. You look hot. I can't wait to show you off."

"Show me off?"

I thought I had said the wrong thing, but she wasn't upset. In fact, she was flattered.

She said, "I kind of like the sound of that. I've never been 'shown off' before."

The country club was a giant bar in the middle of nowhere. It was a Saturday night, and it was crowded but not packed. We took a tall table with bar stools between the pool tables and dance floor along the back wall. Lisa had to watch herself or everyone was going to get a glimpse of her pink panties in short order. She adjusted her seating so she didn't have to worry while I ordered her a double vodka as my way of taking her mind off of it.

We were far away enough from the dance floor that the music wasn't too loud but had a good view of people dancing. We could also watch the four pool tables with the typical country folks, having a good time with their bets and beers. The girls were dressed for fun, and the guys were mostly in boots and hats, looking like they were angling for a girl to take back home in their truck. All in all, these were good hard-working people out enjoying their weekend—the thing beer commercials are made of.

After two drinks, I asked Lisa if she wanted to go out on the dance floor. She was reluctant, and I didn't push it. Halfway through her third drink, a pool table opened and we grabbed it. I discreetly unbuttoned one button of her blouse to provide a little cleavage, and she just watched and shrugged. She was surprisingly good. After about ten minutes, we had an audience, some watching her play while others checked out her ass or tits every time she leaned over for an across the table shot. She was intoxicated enough that she either didn't notice or didn't care.

I asked her, "Where did you learn to shoot pool?"

"See, Carol doesn't tell you everything. We were waitresses at Manny's in Rockville for two years; we used to play all the time to get guys to tip us."

"Well, you're doing great."

"Thanks."

We played a couple more games and then gave up the table. When we were seated back at our table, I asked her how it felt to be gawked at.

"I didn't notice."

"Liar."

"Okay, I noticed a little. It was fun, but kind of scary. It doesn't make you jealous?"

"Why would I be jealous? I am here with the prettiest girl in the place. It's the other guys who are jealous."

She beamed. Just then the DJ put on "Rainy Night in Georgia." Lisa said that she could dance to it. We went out onto the dance floor and embraced in a slow dance to the music. I was holding her close and whispering in her ear how happy I was that she was there with me. She was drunk now and cooed. I continued, telling her that all the guys were jealous of me because they knew I knew what she looked like naked, and they could only imagine it. I slid my hand down her back and onto her ass as we drew closer. Her eyes were closed but mine weren't as I discreetly looked at how many people were watching us. There were a lot. Surprisingly enough, half were women.

She tucked her head into my neck and said, "Thank you."

I said, "For what?"

"I'll tell you later."

"Okay."

We continued dancing as I kissed her neck slowly, enjoying us being the center of attention. The song ended, and we stepped apart ready to head back to the table when the song "Something to Talk About" came on. She said, "Oh, yeah," and just started dancing in front of me with her arms up high and twirling. I smiled. We danced the entire song while she had her eyes closed, opening them only long enough to get her bearings. When the song was over, we went back to the table to a fresh round of drinks.

She took a big gulp out of hers and said, "That was fun. This is fun. You're fun."

I said, "That makes me happy."

"Me too." And she downed the rest of her drink.

I flagged the waitress to give us our check. I didn't touch my beer. The last thing we would need would be to have to explain what she was doing in my car in a DUI arrest. As we drove back to the cabin, she turned the radio up loud and started singing along with the songs. She was definitely plastered. I hoped she didn't drink so much that she would get sick or hungover or both. I did enjoy seeing her totally relaxed, though, especially in that outfit.

When we got back to the cabin, she went to the bathroom. I went out onto the balcony off the master bedroom. She walked up behind me and put her arms around my waist.

She said, "Now it's my turn to take care of you."

"Sounds like fun."

I turned around to face her and kissed her. She explored my mouth with her tongue, letting me know she was now in charge. I put my hands on her ass and then under the back of her skirt, lifting the short skirt up until I was palming her ass cheeks while we kissed. I slid her panties down as far as my arms could reach, and she put her hands down and wriggled them down until they fell to her ankles. She stepped out of them as we hungrily kissed. We continued kissing while she used both of her hands to unbuckle my belt and unsnap my jeans. She pulled them down hard around my thighs, and then pulled my boxers right behind them.

She grabbed my cock which was hard and stroked it up and down. She stopped kissing me, and dropped to her knees and put me in her mouth. She used her hands to cradle my sack and to hold my cock in the right place for her to pleasure me. I looked down at her and she was looking up at me, wanting me to look her right in the eyes. I watched as she controlled the situation. She knew she was driving me crazy, and I finally had to tilt my head back and look at the sky or I was going to come.

After another minute or so she said, "Let's go to bed."

I helped her stand, and then said, "Not yet."

I pulled her toward me, spun her around, and put her hands on the railing of the balcony. It was dark outside, except for a few stars poking through the clouds. I hiked her skirt up over her ass and went inside her from behind. I grabbed her hips and fucked her hard and she fucked me back. She began pushing back harder and harder against my thrusts. She was groaning in pleasure, and I imagined it had been many years since she had had sex this intense. After a few minutes, she put her hands behind her and pushed me gently away.

She said, "Lay on the bed."

I kicked off my shoes and took my clothes all the way off and lay on my back in bed. I saw that she was still dressed, including the cowboy boots.

I said, "Do you need help with the boots?"

"Nope."

She climbed on top of me and sat on my stomach. I could feel my cock between her ass cheeks and the wetness of her pussy on my stomach. She rocked slowly back and forth, and then said, "Now, it's my turn to fuck you!"

I just smiled. She lifted up onto her knees, put her hand between her legs, found my cock, and guided me inside. She then slowly slid down with her head back. I could feel it going deep inside of her. She unbuttoned her blouse and pulled it open. She began rocking slowly back and forth, sliding me in and out of her. She leaned forward, grabbed my wrists, and put my hands above my head. She held them there with her hands on my wrists and began fucking me hard as she pushed her tits into my face. I began licking her cleavage as best as I could while she fucked me. After a few seconds she let go of one hand and unclasped the bra in the front, exposing herself to me, and then grabbed my wrist again, and pushed her breast to my mouth. I sucked her nipple hard. She pulled back and I switched from one side to the other. She began channeling from the many sex talks we had shared on the phone.

"Who's fucking who now?"

"You're fucking me."

"Do you like it?"

"I love it."

"Does it make you want to come?"

"Yes."

"Don't come. Not yet."

"I'll try not to."

She continued.

"Do you want to come?"

"Yes."

"Is it because I'm fucking you so good?"

"Yes."

"Do you want me to make you come?"

"Make me come."

"Not yet."

"I want to come."

"Uh-uh, not yet."

She slowed down to relieve the pressure, and slowly fucked me while I suckled her nipples.

She slowed to a stop, and then said, "Now it's time for me to have some fun," and slid off of me.

"What are you doing?"

"You'll see."

She went over and got the massage oil and came back and said, "I'm going to watch you come."

She lay down next to me and poured massage oil all over me and began stroking me with oil running everywhere. She tried to spread it around and that just turned me on more. She laid her head on my chest and began stroking me steadily.

I said, "Climb on me, I want to lick you while you do that."

She climbed over on top of me as I guided her into place with my hands on her ass. She was still in the skirt and boots and it was an incredible turn-on. She was stroking me, and I was sucking her pussy, doing everything I could to make her come. I was holding my orgasm back, despite my body fighting me otherwise. I wanted her to come. I wanted to feel it on my face.

I was able to make her come first. I could tell she was getting close because she lost the rhythm on my cock, which bought me more time to make her feel good. When she came, she stopped stroking me all together, and I felt her pussy convulse on my mouth. I could feel her shuddering. She was groaning and even laughing in ecstasy as it rippled through her. As soon as she was through the waves of pleasure, she went back to stroking me. I continued to gently lick her. She climbed off me after about thirty seconds, turned around, and got between my knees.

She said, "I want you to watch me make you come."

She used both of her hands non-stop to bring me to the edge of orgasm. I had pulled the pillow up behind my neck and was watching intently as she took good care of me. She could tell I was getting close, and she took her tongue and started flicking the tip of my cock and whispering, "Give it to me. Give it to me." I couldn't hold out any longer and began coming in multiple spurts as she squeezed harder and faster. I had to put my hand down to stop her because it was too intense. She was smiling from ear to ear at what she had just done. I lay back, exhausted. The next thing I remember was her washing me with a warm wet washcloth. She covered me with a sheet and I immediately fell asleep.

I woke up about four in the morning to see Lisa on the balcony in a chair wrapped in a blanket. I got up and went out and sat beside her.

"How are you doing?"

"Good. What a night, huh?"

"I'll say."

I said, "Can't sleep?"

"No, I got up to get some water, and it was just so nice out."

I asked, "What are you thinking about?"

"I don't know. All of it. You know, tonight when I said, 'thank you'?"

"Yeah."

"That was for saving my marriage."

"How do you figure?"

"Well, the truth is, I love Michael very much, and I do want to spend the rest of my life with him, and I realized he and I just need to get through this."

I just stayed silent as she gathered her thoughts.

She continued after a moment. "Well, I was all ready to have a sexless marriage, but after this weekend, I realize that it could never work. I miss it too much and never would have made it. I'm ready to fight to fix him and get him back in my bed where he belongs."

"What are you going to do?"

"I'm not sure, but I'll figure it out."

"Do you regret this weekend?"

"God, no. I don't want to stop seeing you...yet...I haven't even come up with a plan. Is that okay?"

"Sure. We can have our time until you say the word."

She asked me, "Do you regret this weekend?"

I said, "Only that it's ending in about six hours."

She stood up and said, "Let's get a little sleep so we can get up early."

We slept later than we wanted and ended up having breakfast on the balcony, took a long bath together, and then she packed up to leave around noon. She had me keep the outfit we had bought her. I made her promise to come over to my house and wear it for me. She agreed that would be fun. We kissed at the car for a long time before she headed back. It was a good weekend.

Lisa, Part 2

Our affair lasted nearly six months, and when we parted, Lisa was back with Michael, not just in her heart, but also in their bedroom. We had had sex every few days for weeks. She would wait until he went off to church and then come to my house and spend the morning before she went to work. She made me a couple of hours late many times. She was hungry for passion, and could let herself be completely honest when she was with me. She opened up about her desires and fantasies, and the safety I gave her to be a sexual being was what she said she needed in her life for everything to be perfect.

During those first few weeks, she dressed up for me in all kinds of sexy outfits, let me tie her up and tease her, gave me a blow job with a blindfold on, and even let me spank her over my knee after we watched it happen in a porn video. Once the initial excitement of the affair was over, we often talked and conspired to try and evolve her husband away from the computer and into her bed. We often talked at length about what might work and what might not. We decided that the first step was for her to let him know she knew about the porn and was okay with it. She just didn't know how to broach it, so we talked a lot about all the different ways she could make it happen. I tried to convince her that he was still just a guy, and that if he knew he had a sex kitten in the house, he wouldn't be going outside. Nobody with four aces looks for a new deal.

She was worried she would end up losing the good parts of him. After about four months of us having a great time, including a couple of nights in luxury hotel suites while he was off on his journeys for God, she finally got her nerve up to make this happen.

Lisa decided to play the innocent wife and confess to him that she had accidentally gotten on a porn site and looked at it for a while before turning it off and was feeling guilty. She figured he would tell her that was a bad thing, and to make sure it never happened again. Then he would mentally punish her as he had in the past when she was not up to his opinion of how a Christian wife should behave. I convinced her that she had to risk it.

The morning after she told him, she called me first thing all excited.

"Dino!"

"Hi! Did you do it?"

"I did it. I told him I was trapped on some porn merry-go-round, and would he look at my computer to see if there was a virus."

"What did he say?"

"Nothing. He went through my computer and didn't see anything. I told him I think I erased the memory but was 'computer dumb' and didn't want to have anything on there for anyone to see."

"Then what?"

"Well, I waited until we were in bed and I told him I had a confession to make, that I had gotten to a porn site by accident, but watched for a few minutes before I managed to shut it all down. I told him it was weird because I wasn't as disgusted as I thought I would be."

"What did he say?"

"He said that lots of people look at it nowadays, and I would be surprised by the number of people at church who come to him for advice because their spouses looked at it, and it causes problems in the marriage. I asked if it was weird to have women admit their husbands do that, and he said that I would be surprised at how many women actually watch it."

"What did you say to that?"

"I said that I used to read romance novels in college and thought that was pushing boundaries, and maybe porn is just those on steroids. He told me I was probably right, and then turned out the light and kissed me goodnight and went to sleep."

I said, "That's it?"

"Yeah, isn't that great? He just acted like it was no big deal. He didn't lecture me, or warn me, or anything."

"It's a start."

Over the next few weeks she slowly began seducing him with a new haircut, some newer clothes that were a little less conservative. She bought some woman's magazines with sex tips and such on the cover, and began being more physical towards him by rubbing his shoulders and running her fingers though his hair. When they did have sex, she began being much more active and lifting her knees higher and moaning more than in the past. When her and I had sex, it was all about building up her confidence level. I made her feel sexy and confident, and she tried to parlay that into her own bedroom. It was working slowly but surely. He was still going into his office but sometimes he would come to bed instead of the shower and they would have sex. She had mixed feelings about that, but I reminded her that she needed me to get her own confidence up, and she agreed.

I suggested she start reading *Cosmo* magazine in bed and ask him questions about the articles, and if men really think that way. The conversation was good for the marriage. After a few weeks of this I would turn her on at my house by telling her to pretend I was Michael and she was doing him like he had never been done before. She truly longed to be the sexy wife I described. I got some really great sex out of it as she practiced her fantasies on me, knowing that we wouldn't keep this up forever.

She called me one morning and said, "Michael's back."

"From where?"

"From the abyss."

"What abyss?"

"He's back in my bed, silly. We had great sex last night and he might just be fixed."

"Wow! I want details."

"Well, we were just in a good place all day, and then he went into his office and closed the door. I was on the fence because I felt like we were going to have sex, but then was disappointed that he needed outside stimulation."

"So, what did you do?"

"I knocked on the door and came in as he closed the screen as usual. I went over and sat down next to him and asked if we could look at a porn site together."

"You what?"

"I told him that ever since I saw it, I thought about it and wanted to see what it was all about but didn't want to hide it from him. I asked if we could look at it together so I only saw stuff he was okay with."

"What did he say?"

"He said, 'Okay.' I mean, he asked me if I was sure, and that what was seen couldn't be unseen. Then he found a porn site and we watched people have sex."

"What kind of porn?"

"Not Asian, mostly just couples having sex. I think they were maybe even real couples because they were fixed cameras and not like the stuff you and I have watched."

"And?"

"And we watched for about half an hour, and then he asked if I had seen enough and I said, 'If we can watch it again sometime,' and he said, 'Sure.' "

"Then what?"

"Then I went into the shower and when I came out, he was in bed, and we had really good sex like the old days when we were first married."

"So, I guess that means I'm out of a job, huh?"

"No . . . don't say that . . ."

"No, I get it. That was our deal."

"That was our deal . . . but I still need you to see this through"

"Okay."

Lisa and I spent two more mornings, and then an entire weekend together after that conversation.

We spent a very romantic and sexy, fun-filled two nights at the Borgata Casino in Atlantic City while Michael was in California, helping some Christian delegation prepare for a trip to China. Lisa was drunk both nights and was stocking up sex like a polar bear. The second day we were there, I went to the concierge and he scored a Viagra for me so I could keep it up. The backache side effect was worth it.

When it was time for her to leave, she didn't want to go. We had made an agreement that this was the last hurrah, unless things went south again with her and Michael. I told her that now that he was back in the saddle, she couldn't just run to me anymore than she could expect him to run back to the shower and his Asian porn.

I told her it was only the perfect crime if she got away with it, and that as soon as she walked into her house the perfect crime was complete. Her and I were the only ones that knew about us, and she should live the rest of her life with the man she loved. She started to talk, and I was sure she was going to tell me she loved me. I put my hand over her mouth gently and said, "It's only a perfect crime if we don't say anything else. We can each think whatever we want, but we can't say anything else." I uncovered her mouth and she kissed me deep and held on like she didn't want to let go. She eventually relaxed, and she picked up her bag to leave me alone in the room.

I said, "It's okay for us to miss each other. It's also okay for us to talk once in a while, but just for a while so you can concentrate on Michael."

She said. "So are you going back to Carol?"

I just started laughing. I said, "How long have you had that question in your head?"

"A few weeks."

"Why did you wait until now?"

"I didn't want to know the answer."

"Do you want to know it now?"

"No, but I have to ask."

"Okay. I'll tell you. I promised I would never sleep with Carol again, and I haven't, and I won't. I promise."

"What about some other Carol?"

"Well, it's going to take at least a month to recover from this weekend. Why don't you call me and ask me then?"

"Will you tell the truth?"

"I always have, haven't I?"

"I guess so."

"You know so."

"I know so."

I looked at her and said, "Let's just say that neither of us will ever forget the other, and leave it at that. Okay?"

"Okay."

She suddenly came running to me, throwing one arm around my neck while holding her bag in the other. "I do love you, and I do thank you. You helped me save my marriage."

She then turned and walked toward the elevator as fast as that cute butt I already missed could carry her.

I spent a few months getting over Lisa. She called a few times and said she was having a hard time getting over me too. I was sympathetic but took the high road. Her marriage was back on track, and she just needed to move on. I felt like shit sometimes, both for having the affair, and then other times for not letting her relapse. I really enjoyed having sex with her.

I kind of lost interest in dating for a while. I spent a lot of time reflecting on my inability to have anything magical. I had always blamed it on the foster homes and so many different stepmothers, but the truth was that I just wanted it to happen without me having to put any effort into it. I spent another few long months dating only girls that I knew had flaws so there was no chance of a long-term relationship. A few months turned into a couple of years. I had lots of fun. I had sex on the hood of a BMW, in a hotel pool, on a pool table, and once on a living room floor with her roommate watching. It got me through, but it was really just a safety valve until I figured out a way to grow up.

Maryanne and Angie

The next to last relationship I had before I decided to grow up was with a woman named Maryanne. I met her at a sports bar in Chevy Chase, right across the Maryland line from DC. I was at The Catcher's Mitt with a bunch of friends, watching college football when a medium-height, thin, and reasonably attractive blonde came in and sat at the bar next to our table. She was alone and fidgety. I went to the bar for a refill of my beer and said, "Hi, I'm Dino."

She said, "Hi," and continued looking at the laminated one-page menu.

I had a rule. If I said hello and a woman responded with her name, she was okay with a conversation. If she just said, "hello," without offering me her name, I moved on. There was nothing more pathetic to me than a guy in a bar saying, "C'mon, what's your name?" The bartender was busy, so we were there in this kind of awkward place. I had my rule, but it almost seemed rude to not even mention that I guessed the barkeep was busy.

She spoke first. "Did you say your name is Dino?"

"Yes."

"Dino, would you do me a big favor?"

"I guess that depends on what it is."

"Will you let me sit with you and your friends and pretend that you're my boyfriend for a few minutes?"

"Why?"

"Because I'm supposed to be meeting a guy on a blind date, and he just pulled in, and he isn't anything like his picture."

"How do you know?"

"He is standing right there. Does he look 6 foot, 200 pounds to you?"

There was a guy that was about 5'10" and 250 pounds standing outside, wearing a Green Bay Packers ski cap.

"Are you sure that's him?"

"Yes. He said he would be wearing the cap. Will you help me?"

"Okay, come here. I went over to one of my friends who was wearing a Redskins baseball cap and grabbed it and also his Redskins jacket off the back of his chair.

He said, "What are you doing?"

I said, "I'll tell you in a few minutes. Just trust me, okay?"

I slapped the cap on her head and helped her into the jacket. I rushed us over to a booth and sat her in it, and then went back and grabbed a finished plate of nachos and a couple of empty mugs from our table and went back and slid in next to her.

"Tuck your hair into the cap."

She did as I instructed and said, "Oh my God, he's coming in."

"Relax, I've got this." I reached over the seat and grabbed a paper someone had left on the table and put my arm around her and leaned in as if we were reading it together. I whispered, "What's your name?"

"Maryanne . . . Here he comes."

I pulled out my cell phone and waited until he was within earshot and said loudly as he walked by, "Well, Victoria and I have been here for an hour already. I think we are probably going to just go home and watch the game there. Do you want to come to our place?"

It worked like a charm. He walked right past us and on down the line, then back outside to what I assumed was to wait for her.

I turned to Maryanne and said, "How did I do?"

"Great. Thank you."

"So, how did that happen?"

"Match.com."

"You're too pretty for dating sites."

"So, you say. How do you meet people?"

"I just wait until they get in a bind and need my help. Rescuing an angel in distress always give me a leg up on the competition."

She rolled her eyes. I felt like I was just tossed in the trash bin with the Packers fan.

"Too corny for you, huh?" I said, looking at her.

"No, I'm sorry. You're very nice... and quick on your feet. I should be more grateful."

"It's okay. What are you going to do now?"

"Well, I would call him, but I don't ever exchange numbers until I meet face-to-face."

"He looks like he is going to hang for a while. Do you want to go out the back door and get dinner at Amalfi's across the street? Best pasta in town."

"I shouldn't..."

"Why not? Do you have another date with your computer?"

"Ha ha. Alright. We can go."

I stood up and said, "Give me a minute."

I gave the guys a quick rundown and pointed out the guy. I asked them to call me on my cell phone when he left so we would know it was safe. I went back and she stood up. We made sure he was still outside, and then I took the jacket and cap and gave it back, and we quickly exited through the back door and across the street to a nice Italian dinner. We spent almost three hours talking, mostly about her year-long journey through the computer dating world. She had had a run of bad luck and was convinced that everybody lies, and she couldn't understand why, since the truth would always come to light by at least the second date. She said she was going to write a book titled *The Schmoozers, the Boozers, and a Busload of Losers*.

We ended up in a relationship that lasted too long. She was fun, but Maryanne was also neurotic, which was funny until I realized she was truly out there. She was very sexual, which is to say she was always ready for sex. She liked to be the center of attention in the bedroom, and that was okay with me because I liked getting her off. She was a little selfish, in that

I needed to let her know what I wanted, but I was expected to read her mind to figure out what she wanted.

We did have a good time though. We ended up dating for almost two years, mostly because we were both just rolling with things and time got away from us. I realized near the end that I was just kind of going through the motions for the sex and the occasional drunken party partner. I certainly didn't love her, and the truth is she didn't love me either, but she liked that I liked having sex with her, and that I was also pretty honest. We didn't fight, but when we disagreed, she would try and push me until I shut things down. She would then try and fix it with sex.

She also had a jealous streak that annoyed me, because for all the scoundrel things I had done, I never cheated. If I said I was monogamous I was. The jealousy first came out in a big way because of my next-door neighbor. Angie was in her early thirties, and was what men referred to as a "package," which is to say she was a little short, cute butt, firm breasts, and pretty. What made her a package was that she was approachable, and when men were around, she never made them feel like she was out of their league. All the guys liked her because you could tell a dirty joke around her without her getting offended, and she liked flirting. She was indeed a "package."

She had been my neighbor for years before I started dating Maryanne, and we had become good friends. I had talked her through a few boyfriends when she needed advice and helped her fix a few things around her house, but we never fooled around. Mostly because I was nearly twenty years older, and was only a couple years younger than her father. She knew I wouldn't turn her down, but deep down she was looking for love, and I guess when she was just in it for sex, guys her own age were more on her radar. For some reason, it just didn't bother me. She was a rare exception in that department. Usually, when I was even close to the friend zone, I bailed. I wanted to be the guy other guys were friend-zoned for.

Maryanne's jealous obsession with Angie all started one Friday evening when Maryanne was up in my bedroom waiting for me. We had only been dating about two months at that point, and I was stuck on a giant install, and had to cancel our dinner plans. We decided she would come spend the night and we would spend Saturday together. About an hour before I got home, my cell phone rang and it was Maryanne. She wanted to know if I had "double booked" because there was some girl that just walked into the house and right up into the bedroom looking for me, while wearing shorts and a bikini top. I knew right away who it was.

"That's just Angie. She lives next door. What did she want?" I said.

"Well, from the way she was dressed, I guess she wanted sex."

"Doubtful. Seriously, what did she want?"

"She said she needed you to come over and get her shed door unstuck for her, but it sounded like some made up bullshit to me."

"No, the ground underneath is eroding and it happens once in a while. She's okay."

Maryanne said, "I think I should go."

"Why?"

"Girls just don't walk into guy's bedrooms without knocking. unless they are having sex."

"We are not having sex, and she had to have hollered for me. Didn't you hear her?"

"The TV was on, but I still think I should go."

"Stay. I will be there in an hour. We'll talk. There is NOTHING to worry about."

"I'll think about it. I may leave."

"Stay."

"I'll see you when you get here."

Once I arrived, she was calmed down, but wanted to know everything I knew about Angie, like if I had ever slept with her, or had we ever dated, and on and on. I took the high road and brought her back down to earth. I understood the optics, and wasn't upset at her reaction to what had transpired. We went to bed without having sex, but at about four a.m. I woke up with her on top of me, and we fucked crazy until almost sunup.

After that episode, I realized how insecure she was. She would ask me if I was sexually interested in almost any girl we met. The ride home from parties was often a third-degree on every attractive girl that happened to be there. She tortured herself, asking me questions about who I would do if I had to choose. She would gossip about the other women and try and get me to say anything that was even close to finding them sexy. We would get home and she would be all turned on, and we would have great sex. It was very strange. Other times when she wasn't feeling sexual or wasn't really feeling particularly close to me, she didn't care who was around, even if they might happen to be hitting on me. But Angie was always the exception.

If Maryanne came to my house and Angie was there, she was always polite, but frequently asked why I let her hang around. She tried to get me to say Angie was just hanging around because I was good to her and she didn't have to give me sex to get help. I told her that I liked Angie and said to Maryanne, "I can't believe I am saying this, but not everything is about sex."

Maryanne responded with, "For you? Yes, it is."

The petty jealousy about Angie went on for months. Angie spent her summers outside at her above-ground pool, often sun bathing in the late afternoons after she got off work. I would hang and talk with her sometimes and enjoyed looking at her in her bikini, but it never went past that.

Once Maryanne and I went to a party at Angie's, and Angie got really drunk. Her bathing suit bottoms were stretched from being in the pool and were drifting down exposing her butt crack. I discreetly went over and put my arm around her and reached down and grabbed the back of her suit bottoms and pulled them up, whispering to her that she may want to put on her shorts because they were just going to fall down again. I looked up to see Maryanne walking out and heading back toward my house and to her car to leave. I went after her and saw that she was livid with jealousy. After explaining what I did and why, I convinced her to come into the house so as not to make a scene. She was drunk and went straight to the bedroom, sat on the bed, and said, "I want answers."

I said, "Go for it."

"Have you EVER fucked her?"

"No."

"Have you ever kissed her?"

"Only on the top of her head in front of others when she was upset over something."

"Have you ever seen her naked?"

I was busted. I had seen her naked many times over the years. She often sunbathed naked, and I could see everything from my guest room window. I had also seen her have sex on her chaise lounge with a guy she was dating at the time, and last but not least, I helped her change out of her vomit-covered clothes and get into the shower one night when she came home so drunk she couldn't even get her front door open and banged on my door for help. Nothing happened any of those times, but Maryanne was not in a place to believe that. I punted on the last story and said, "This is about you not her. Why are you so insecure? There is nothing going on between Angie and me."

She stayed quiet for a long time. We just sat there in the dark.

She then said, "Will you give me a massage?"

"Sure," I said, and then went to get the supplies while she stood up and began taking off her clothes.

When I came back into the room, she was lying face down on the bed on a fresh sheet she had gotten out of the closet. The lights were still off and it was very dark, but I could see enough to do what I needed to do.

I didn't say anything. I just put massage oil on my hands and began rubbing her shoulders. She let me do what I wanted, and I worked my way down her back to the base and then up again, reworking her shoulders a little harder now.

She said, "I have one more question."

I was a little apprehensive but kept rubbing like everything was normal.

"Go for it."

"Have you ever given Angie a massage?"

"No."

I was glad it was an easy question.

"Have you ever fantasized about giving her one?"

"You said one more question. That's two."

"Have you?"

"I don't think so," I lied.

I kept massaging her back, and she seemed okay with my answers.

After a minute she said, "I want you to pretend I'm Angie and give me a massage."

"Do you really think that's a good idea?"

"Yes, it will help me get her out of my system."

"Yeah, I don't think that will get her out of your system. I think it will make things worse."

"Please? Indulge me. I promise I won't get upset."

"How far do you want me to go?"

"I want the full treatment."

"Happy ending and all?"

"Everything. I want you to pretend that I am Angie, and show me what you would do to her if she wanted you to, and I gave you permission."

"Why does this feel like a trap?"

"It's not, I swear."

"Okay, but if you begin to get upset then you have to speak up, okay?"

"I promise."

"Okay, here we go."

I went back to massaging her, now in a more sensual and sexual way. She was getting turned on.

She finally said, "Are you imagining I'm Angie?"

"Yes."

"Do you like it?"

"It's kind of fun."

"Show me how you would rub Angie's ass."

I put my hands on the small of her back and moved down to her ass cheeks, and began massaging them firmly.

She lifted her butt up like a cat and said, "Angie wants it harder."

I did as she asked.

"Do you think Angie's ass is firm or soft?"

"Firm."

"Firmer than mine?"

"Probably not."

"Angie needs her pussy rubbed."

I slid my hand between her legs from behind, and put my fingers inside of her. She was saturated with wetness and humping my hand as I slid in and out.

"Do you want to taste Angie's pussy?"

I kept feeling like it was a setup, but figured there was at least a reasonable chance that this was really what she wanted, and decided to give it to her.

"Yes," I said. She rolled over and opened her legs.

I went down on her, and licked her aggressively as she moaned in a way I had never heard before. I put my fingers back inside of her and fingered her as I licked her and found myself hard as stone at the situation. I certainly found Angie attractive; every guy would, but I respected the boundaries that occurred naturally as we got to know each other as neighbors. She was a generation younger than me and showed no interest in anything beyond friendship. So, here I was getting into this twisted fantasy with Maryanne in the flesh, and Angie in both of our minds.

I pulled back and said, "Does Angie want to be fucked?"

"Yes."

I got naked and moved her until she was on the bed sideways. I stood on the floor at the side of the bed with her legs pointing towards the ceiling as I laid my cock on her pubic mound and began teasing her with it.

Maryanne said, "Angie is ready for you to fuck her. Go ahead."

"Are you sure?"

"Yes."

I slid myself inside, and she let out a shriek and began fucking me harder than she had ever fucked me before.

"Is Angie's pussy tight?"

"Yes."

"Fuck it good."

"Okay."

I fucked her hard, I pushed her knees to her chest and thrust almost violently as she laughed in ecstasy. I did this for about three or four minutes and then said, "I'm coming."

"Call me Angie."

"Angie, I'm coming."

"Say it again."

"Angie, I'm coming."

"Yes."

I came really hard, thrusting her whole body back and forth. There was something weird going on and it was a huge turn on for both of us.

She wrapped her legs behind my back keeping me there and she was laughing. She was rocking back and forth in pure bliss and she finally said, "I knew you wanted to fuck Angie. I knew it."

"Then why are you laughing?"

"Because now I know you have never fucked her. You were too turned on just imagining it. If you had ever fucked her, you wouldn't have been so hot."

I didn't know if this was a good thing or a bad thing, and I was too spent to think about it. The next day she never even mentioned it, so I figured her jealousy of Angie was over. I was wrong.

It didn't happen all the time, but often enough Maryanne would knock Angie's behavior if she saw anything she disapproved of. She criticized her choice of men and her drinking. She felt like Angie knew Maryanne was a little jealous of her youth, and purposely chose to wear skimpy clothes to come over and say hi. I told her that Angie's behavior and dress was the same whether Maryanne was around or not. That just made things worse.

I would have found it more annoying, but whenever Angie was around Maryanne was more sexual, I supposed, to stake out her territory. It was a double-edged sword. Unfortunately, for Maryanne I would never ever have allowed one person to dictate my behavior towards someone else that wasn't doing anything wrong. I was a scoundrel with scruples.

Angie wasn't an everyday thing at all, but Maryanne's jealousy was always in the background, including anyone else I might be friendly with. The longer the relationship went on, the deeper her jealousy got. I think in hindsight it was because we peaked early, and she couldn't convince me to go deeper into the relationship with her. It was heading towards an inevitable ending at some point, and she knew it. I think she didn't want to get the blame. In her defense, she didn't know that I would never do that, but her insecurity did cause a lot of unnecessary tension.

About two years into the relationship, I came home after a long Saturday HVAC installation to find Angie and Maryanne drunk in my bedroom, trying on bathing suits. They were both plastered and, evidently, it was all planned by Maryanne. She was supposed to be there waiting for me and had brought over a bunch of her old clothes to give to Angie, inviting her over. They had obviously polished off a lot of wine. When I walked into the bedroom, Angie was in a thong bikini that I knew was Maryanne's. Maryanne was in a long T-shirt that was probably mine, and I couldn't tell, but was pretty sure there was nothing else underneath. As soon as she saw me, she said, "Oops, busted!" and then laughed in a drunken stupor.

Angie said, "Hi, Maryanne is giving me a bunch of her old clothes. She's fun."

I was fine with the situation; except I was sure there would be fallout later.

I said, "Well, I hope you got some good stuff."

"I got lots."

Maryanne gathered up Angie's clothes, rolled them up in a ball, and handed them to her.

"Time for you to go. I need to give my man a shower," Maryanne announced.

Angie said, "I know what that's code for," and laughed as she walked out. "Bye-bye, and thanks for the clothes. I'll see myself out."

She went down the steps, and we heard the front door close.

I said, "So what was that all about?" I wasn't mad, but this was totally out of character.

"Nothing."

"Nothing? You're up to something."

"I just wanted to get to know her better, that's all."

"Did you?"

"Did I what?"

"Get to know her better."

"We didn't have sex, if that's what you mean."

I said, "That's not what I meant."

"Linda told her you're a good fuck and love to eat pussy."

"How drunk are you?"

"We had two bottles of wine. How long ago did you date Linda?"

"Years."

"I told her you still do."

"Still do what?"

"Love to eat pussy."

"Okay, then . . . Well, I'm gonna take a shower; why don't you take a nap?"

"Fuck me first."

"I need a shower."

"I need to fuck."

"I'm sweaty."

"Don't care."

I went over to her with the intention of laying her on the bed and then going to the shower. She lay on her back and reached under the pillow and said, "Look what I stole." She was holding a pair of white cotton underwear that I presumed were Angie's.

"Angie's?" I said.

288

"Yep. I want to wear them while you fuck me."

"Why?"

"It turns me on to think about it."

I realized she was really plastered, and I wasn't sure where this was going.

She continued, "I want to put them on and have you lick me."

"You want me to lick you while you're wearing Angie's panties?"

"Yep."

"Why?"

"Why not?"

"You might regret it later."

"Nope," she said, pushing them into my face. "I know you want to. I know you want to lick her pussy. Now's your chance."

I pulled my head back and said, "I'm going into the shower. When I come out, we'll talk about it."

She said, "Okay."

I went into the shower and thought about the situation. The thought of them drunk and naked, talking about me was a turn on. The thought of her going crazy tomorrow if I give her what she wanted was a turn off. I decided to play it by ear and finished my shower.

When I came out, she was lying there in the bed, wearing nothing but Angie's panties. She was playing with her breasts and said, "I'm all ready. I can't stop thinking about your tongue."

"Take off the panties."

"No that's the turn on. I want you to smell her pussy while you lick me." She was almost pouting.

"Why?"

"Cause I know you want to. I'm trying to give you a present."

"You're not jealous that I might be imagining you're her?"

"I want you to. I want to know what it would feel like to be her and have you lick me."

"You're nuts."

"Indulge me."

I dropped my towel, knelt down between her legs, pushed my face into the panties, and breathed in Angie's scent. Maryanne was right; it was a turn on. She grabbed the back of my head and pushed my face hard against her pussy so that I had to breathe through the panties. I began moving my nose up and down her slit through the cotton, and she loved it. She relaxed her hand, and I slid my head back and pulled the panties aside and began licking her. She was saturated and squirming side to side and laughing that same ecstatic laugh she had when she pretended she was Angie before. I moaned loudly to let her know I was excited and she got turned on even more.

She exclaimed, "Fuck me."

I rose to my knees and tried to pull the panties off, and she stopped me and said, "No, leave them on."

I let go of the waistband and, instead, pulled them aside. She helped me slide my hard cock inside her. I fucked her steady as she watched my face. I decided to close my eyes so she would think I was imagining she was Angie. The truth was I was more turned on by her twisted mind than the thought of Angie, but the whole thing was extremely exciting to be a part of. She was humping me back, meeting me thrust for thrust, and holding onto my hips with both hands. After a few minutes she said, "I want to roll over."

I pulled out and she flipped onto her stomach. I pulled the panties down to her knees and pulled her ass cheeks apart while she lifted her hips as best as she could with her knees together. I slid myself back inside, and I fucked her hard while sitting up behind her with my legs on the outside of hers. She and I got into a good rhythm, and after a minute she said, "I told Angie you watched her fuck by the pool. She thought you were watching, and liked it."

I moaned and fucked her harder. She wanted me to be turned on, and I went with it. After another couple of minutes, I told her I was coming. She fucked me even harder. I came inside her, thrusting deep. She squealed with pleasure with that laugh again. I lay on top of her to catch my breath for a minute or so, and then slowly slid out. I rolled over and reached to the floor for the towel I had dropped, but when I went to put it between her legs, she had already rolled over on her back and pulled the panties up and said, "No need, I want to just wear these for a while."

"Well, you can't give them back now."

"I'll wash them first; it will just be our secret." She closed her eyes and drifted off into a drunken sleep.

She ended up sleeping all the way through to the next morning. She got up before me and cleaned up, never speaking about the day before. I didn't want to bring it up in case she wanted to pin something on me to justify her jealous streak.

We dated another six months or so, and then were pretty much tired of each other. We were bickering a lot about little things, and the sex had waned. It had run its course as most of my relationships had, and I decided we needed to have the "conversation" so we could both move on before we hurt each other. I don't have a need to punish, but she had a sharp tongue sometimes, and I felt like I should make it happen sooner, rather than wait for the wrath that she would surely bring to the table when she had finally had enough. I waited until a Sunday when we were both at peace.

I said, "Can we talk about us?"

"Sure."

"I feel like things have changed and we aren't as close as we once were. Are you feeling it too?"

"Are you breaking up with me?"

"I just think we should just take an assessment of where we are, and talk about it."

"You're breaking up with me!"

"I feel like that's what you want."

"Did I say that? Maybe I'm just frustrated because you don't appreciate me like you used to."

She was getting angry, and I began to worry how things were going to play out.

I said, "I think we've drifted apart. We bicker, and I feel like you don't have much respect for me anymore."

"Well, you can be an asshole sometimes, and sometimes I don't respect you."

"Okay, then, what do you think we should do about it?"

"I think you should stop being an asshole."

"Well, I don't think I am an asshole, and so I'm not sure what I should change."

"Well, if you think that, then fuck you. I'm breaking up with you!"

"Okay."

She sat there silent for a moment, and then said, "Okay? Okay? So, you're not even willing to make an effort?"

I saw where this was going and said, "I think we need a break. How about we stop seeing each other for a while, and talk in a couple of weeks."

"You'll still be an asshole in a couple of weeks. You're never going to change."

"You're probably right. Maybe it's best to end it now."

"Fine, that's what you want anyway. I'll get my stuff and go."

"You don't need to get it now. You don't even need to go. We can talk about it if you want."

"Fuck you."

I stood up and said, "I'm going to cut the grass. I'll stay out of your way."

"Well, while you're out there, see if Angie is in her pool. Maybe you can get her to suck your dick, which we both know is what you *really* want."

I just went outside and started cutting the grass. She grabbed her stuff and left. She sent me a three-page email letting me know what an asshole I was. I felt like a weight was lifted off my shoulders and kicked myself for letting the craziness go on for so long. She was making me jaded.

Maryanne called me every few weeks, trying to make amends, but I kept her at arm's length. I let her talk, and I realized she mostly wanted to make sure I wasn't happy or dating any of her friends. I could tell by the conversations that she was fishing. I gave her what she needed. I realized the relationship was like a soda machine; it needed to be rocked back and forth a few times before it would finally tip over.

After another couple of months, it was finally done. I think she just needed to get in the last word. I was happy to give it to her. I was actually hoping she would go find another guy, even if she did it to prove to me that I was the problem. I knew the truth.

Humble Endings—Julia

A couple of months after the breakup with Maryanne was finally over, the first and only real true love came into my life. I say "only" because I realize now that twenty-five years before, although I did *almost* love Inez, I know now it wasn't meant to be. She needed someone other than me, and we would not have survived. I do realize now though that my feelings at the time were however, at least on the right track.

Julia walked into my life by walking into my business. I came from the back to see a very attractive woman a couple of years younger than me, standing at the counter, talking to my manager. We didn't get many walk-in customers in the HVAC business, and I listened in the background as she asked a few questions. She had been referred to us by a good customer, and I was intrigued by her, but not quite sure why. I liked that her mannerisms were genuine. She was smart and in control, but still feminine. After she left, I kept thinking about her and couldn't figure out why. After two days when she was still on my mind, I called the customer who had referred her to me, and asked about her situation. He said she was single and a great girl. I told him that I was interested in asking her out, but didn't feel right asking out a customer, because it would be unfair for them to feel uncomfortable if they weren't interested. He said she was easygoing, and offered to call her to see if she was open to an invitation. He called back and said she was, so I called, and we set up a date.

I met her in front of the Washington Monument in DC. We spent Sunday afternoon walking around the memorials. An hour into the date,

I realized what it was that intrigued me so much. She was about five-foot-five, 120 pounds, brown shoulder-length hair, and in great shape, but the most important thing was that she had something no other girl I had ever dated had. I realized that I could live to be a hundred years old and never get tired of looking at her. No one would say she wasn't pretty, but there was just *something* about her looks, her smile, the brightness and intelligence in her eyes, her persona. They just checked off all the boxes that I didn't even know existed in my mind. It was actually scary.

We seemed to click, and I felt like she felt it too. Usually, I am reserved and have an agenda for sex just in case things don't work out, so I don't end up empty handed. I had no such agenda with her. I just wanted to hear about her life. I wanted to really know what made her tick. I found myself just being honest. I had always thought I was honest, but realized I had been living a very guarded life. I wanted her to know everything about me so there would be no mistakes, no surprises in a few months that could ruin things. I was brutally honest, and she was genuinely open. After a couple of dates and an obvious strong connection, she came over and spent the night. We fooled around like seniors in high school, but didn't go all the way because she wasn't ready. I was fine with it. I didn't need her that night. I needed her every night thereafter, and waiting was a small investment I had no problems with making.

The next weekend we had sex for the first time, and it was perfect for me, and I felt like it was perfect for her too. I was dominant, and she was receptive in such a traditional way that it just felt right. There were no chandeliers, garter belts, or excessive alcohol involved. Just two people learning about each other, both of us eagerly wanting to please the other, without trying to impress the other. I was confident as a lover, and so was she. It was a solid connection and I was very happy. She still doesn't know to this day, but after she fell asleep, I pulled the sheet down and just looked at her naked body for over an hour, like it was the *Mona Lisa*. I was smitten.

We talked often during the next couple of weeks and things were going well. I felt like I had finally found a relationship like I had only read about in novels, or seen in romantic movies. In my head I was imagining the future with Julia. She was constantly on my mind. Just seeing her made me smile. I felt like I had actually for the first time in my life found true love, and it really felt good.

Then I fucked everything up by trying to do the right thing.

Julia had come over and spent the weekend with me and left mid-morning on a Sunday. We had had a great night, and I went back to sleep after she left. Around two o'clock, there was a knock at the door. It was Maryanne. I answered the door in nylon shorts and a T-shirt. I was surprised to see her at the time, but found out later she had been keeping tabs on me through the wife of one of my employees.

She looked at me and said, "Can we talk?"

"Okay, what's up?"

"Can I come in for a minute?" The "for a minute" made me think she just had a prepared speech and needed closure and then she would be gone. I had no feelings for her whatsoever, and remember thinking this was a good thing. That was my first mistake.

"I miss you."

"No, you don't. You miss me wanting you."

"No, I really miss you."

"Well, I'm sorry, but I'm in a new relationship, and you and I are over."

She reached out and touched my crotch through the nylon shorts and said, "We don't have to be."

I pushed her hand away and said, "No, we are done. I don't want to hurt you, but it's over."

She came towards me and said, "I know about your new girlfriend. Tom's wife told me it's serious."

"It might be; she's really nice."

She moved closer. "Let's fuck, one last time."

"No."

"C'mon Dino, show me what you got. Don't be a wimp. You're not married yet."

"No."

I realized she was now almost right up against me, and I was mad at myself for not noticing. This emboldened her, and she put her hand on me again. I pushed her away again, and she said, "Your dick is saying yes."

"My dick is tired."

"Your dick is hard." She reached for it again, and I pushed her hand away again.

"It's over. I think you should go." I tried to keep it as passive as possible because I didn't want a fight and thought she might go there.

"What's the matter? Are you afraid to fuck me? Don't think you can handle it? Can't keep it up because you've been 'making love' to your new little girlfriend?"

"Stop. Just leave."

She tried a new tactic.

"I'm sorry. I'm just jealous. I know I'm being a bitch." She looked as if she was tearing up.

I made my next mistake, and felt sorry for her.

I said, "I get it. It hurts, but you'll find somebody else and forget all about me. We'll end up friends, and everything will be fine."

She wiped her eyes and said, "I'm so sorry," and lifted her arms up to give me a hug. I allowed it in the hopes it was the last one. As soon as I relented, she fell into my arms and held me tight. After about ten seconds she suddenly dropped to her knees, pulled down my shorts, and put me in her mouth before I could even figure out what was going on. I pulled backwards, but she lurched forward keeping me in her mouth for a few seconds. I pulled away hard, pulled my shorts up, and backed away from her.

I said, "You need to get the fuck out *now*!"

She stumbled to her feet and said, "How are you going to explain to your little girl friend that you had your cock in my mouth just a few hours after she left? Are you going to blame it on me? Look it's still hard."

Between the stress and the confusion, she was right. I did have an erection, but it wasn't desire; it was anger. I wanted to fuck her, and toss her out the door. I wanted to sexually humiliate her. But I didn't.

I slowly and deliberately said, "Just-get-the-fuck-out-and-stay-out."

She laughed and walked away with a sense of satisfaction that cut me to the bone. I was feeling emotions I had never felt before. The only other time I had felt close to this way was when I saw the plane take off for California with Inez in it. I was emotionally distraught. I knew I couldn't let Maryanne have that over me as some sort of emotional blackmail, and I couldn't keep a secret like that from Julia. It wasn't fair to her. I thought about it for two days straight. I couldn't think of anything else. I needed to tell Julia so that I could disarm Maryanne, but telling her would surely hurt her. I was also worried that Maryanne wasn't giving up so easily.

I didn't know what other tricks she had up her sleeve, and I didn't want Julia hurt. Julia and I were only getting started, but I felt the need to protect her as if we had known each other our whole lives. I realized two things. One, I, for the first time in my life, was truly in love. The love other people talked about, but I had never experienced, and second, that I was totally unprepared for the dilemma I was in. I had been in many difficult situations before, but this one had me laid out with no solution that could guarantee a positive outcome. I didn't know if Julia really felt the way I did about us, which if she didn't, would make it nothing to fret over, but if she did, I was going to hurt her, and that was the last thing I wanted.

I was in this paradox I didn't understand and had never been in before. I wanted to protect Julia more than myself, but my hurt was potentially more than I could handle, and doing the right thing felt like I might be falling on my own sword.

I decided I had to tell Julia, and that is where I made my third and worst mistake. I tried to explain what happened, and it came out all wrong, and I couldn't fix it. I had decided the best way to handle it was to tell her what happened as honestly as I could without getting too deep into details, but letting her know I didn't do anything. I told her that I needed to get the other relationship over with, and wanted to slow things between us so I could do that with a clear conscience. What I was trying to do was protect her from what I imagined would be a crazy woman trying to sabotage anything we might have.

Julia did the responsible thing to protect herself and extricated herself from the situation. She took control and ended the relationship, saying we could just be friends. She took care of herself, and I didn't blame her for it. I fucked up. I was devastated, and embarrassingly, even at fifty, too inexperienced to know how to fix it. I felt like Julia had no interest in opening herself up to further hurt, and I had no interest in hurting her further. I tried to do the gallant thing and fall on my sword, but it hurt like hell. I had always been a loner, and had no one to talk to about it. I realized that I had had exactly two real relationships in my entire life, and the first one was over twenty-five years before. I wanted to just open up to Julia and tell her exactly how I felt, but if she rebuffed me, I knew I would be broken forever. I decided to let time pass and see what would happen. I unwound every connection I had with Maryanne, and even let her know through the grapevine that Julia and I didn't work out so she would back off and move on, which she did.

I tried to rekindle things with Julia a couple of times, but she gave me no direct signals that I could have a second chance, and I was afraid to push. It is now two years later and I am out in the dating world again finding imaginary faults with every girl I meet so I never feel hurt like that again.

And that is how this story ends for now. I don't know if the follow-up to this will be more irresponsible antics, or if I will find true love. Hopefully, it will be a true love story with a happy ending. For now, the closest I can seem to get to love is a cold winter night in front of a fireplace in the dark, with a bottle of scotch, imagining the *Mona Lisa* I let slip through my fingers.

The End